Praise for the novels of Anne Frasier

Sleep Tight

"There'll be no sleeping after reading this one! A riveting thriller guaranteed to keep you up all night. Laced with forensic detail and psychological twists. . . . Compelling and real—a great read." —Andrea Kane

"Guaranteed to keep you awake at night, *Sleep Tight* is a fast-paced novel of secrets, lies, and chilling suspense." —Lisa Jackson

"Gripping and intense. . . . Along with a fine plot, Frasier delivers her characters as whole people, each trying to cope in the face of violence and jealousies." —*Minneapolis Star Tribune*

"Enthralling. . . . There's a lot more to this clever intrigue than graphic police procedures. Indeed, one of Frasier's many strengths is her ability to create characters and relationships that are as compelling as the mystery itself. . . . Will linger with the reader long after the killer is caught." —*Publishers Weekly*

continued . . .

Hush

"This is far and away the best serial killer story I have read in a very long time. . . . Strong characters, and a truly twisted bad guy. With *Hush*, Anne Frasier slams into the fast lane and goes to the head of the pack. This one has Guaranteed Winner written all over it." —Jayne Ann Krentz

"A deeply engrossing read, *Hush* delivers a creepy villain, a chilling plot, and two remarkable investigators whose personal struggles are only equaled by their compelling need to stop a madman before he kills again. Warning: Don't read this book if you are home alone."   —Lisa Gardner

"I couldn't put it down . . . engrossing . . . scary. . . . I loved it."   —Linda Howard

"Anne Frasier has crafted a taut and suspenseful thriller driven by a villain guaranteed to give you nightmares . . . [ends] on a chilling note you won't soon forget."
          —Kay Hooper

"A brilliant debut from a very talented author—a guaranteed page-turner that will keep the reader riveted from beginning to end."   —Katherine Sutcliffe

"Well-realized characters and taut, suspenseful plotting. It will definitely keep you awake to finish it. And you'll be glad you did."   —*Minneapolis Star Tribune*

"A wealth of procedural detail, a heart-thumping finale, and two scarred but indelible protagonists make this a first-rate debut."   —*Publishers Weekly*

Other Books by Anne Frasier

Hush

Sleep Tight

PLAY DEAD

Anne Frasier

AN ONYX BOOK

ONYX
Published by New American Library, a division of
Penguin Group (USA) Inc., 375 Hudson Street,
New York, New York 10014, U.S.A.
Penguin Books Ltd, 80 Strand,
London WC2R 0RL, England
Penguin Books Australia Ltd, 250 Camberwell Road,
Camberwell, Victoria 3124, Australia
Penguin Books Canada Ltd, 10 Alcorn Avenue,
Toronto, Ontario, Canada M4V 3B2
Penguin Books (NZ), cnr Rosedale and Airborne Roads,
Albany, Auckland 1310, New Zealand

Penguin Books Ltd, Registered Offices:
80 Strand, London WC2R 0RL, England

First published by Onyx, an imprint of New American Library,
a division of Penguin Group (USA) Inc.

First Printing, June 2004
10   9   8   7   6   5   4   3   2   1

ACKNOWLEDGMENTS

Thanks to my brother, Pat, for introducing me to
the beautiful city of Savannah.

A very special thanks to the amazing members of the
SavannahNOW forums. You taught me that
Southern hospitality exists even in cyberspace.

At night I dream.
I dream that I am more than I am.
That I am strong. That I have a secret life.
And in that life, I do things. Secret things.

Chapter 1

Savannah medical examiner John Casper believed in what some scientists termed the cluster effect. Toss a bunch of anything down—seeds, flower petals, cards—they always grouped together.

Same thing with dead bodies.

They never came one at a time, but in bunches. The latest bunch had been large, leaving doctors and assistants working around the clock to process an unusually high volume that had their cold storage overflowing.

Almost caught up, people had headed home complaining of headaches from lack of sleep and too many hours spent inhaling formalin fumes.

Willy Claxton, the one remaining assistant, hovered nervously in the doorway of the main office, just off the autopsy suites. "Storm's blowing in from the Atlantic," he said. "They been talking about it on the radio."

John pushed his paperwork aside and leaned back, chair creaking. "Why don't you go home?" Even in the isolation of the morgue, his head had the heavy feeling that came with a dramatic drop in barometric pressure. "Before the storm hits."

"What about the last body?"

John glanced through the decedent's file. "Pretty straightforward. Looks like a heart attack."

John stood and stretched. He'd been there for over twelve hours. His joints ached, and his skin had a prickly, tight feel from too little sleep. "Help me get him on the table and you can take off."

Willy wheeled the body from the cold unit, then pushed it into an autopsy suite. The room smelled of disinfectant. He locked the wheels; then the two men heaved the corpse from the gurney to the stainless steel table. John noticed the zipper on the body bag hadn't been pulled tight—there was a gap of about two inches.

"Thanks, man," Willy said, snapping off his gloves and tossing them in the biohazard bin. "I need to get home. My wife's afraid of storms."

John nodded, allowing the man his dignity. Everybody knew Willy grew uneasy when darkness came. A lot of people were like that, even some of the other medical examiners. John found it interesting that modern man still suffered from ancient fears left over from a period in history when humans lived in the open and darkness was a real threat. These days, it wasn't the darkness that would get you—it was the people in that darkness. You didn't work in a morgue without coming away with that lesson well learned. Homicides had doubled this year, and the city was feeling as uneasy as Willy.

After Willy left, John suited up in a gown, mask, goggles, and latex gloves, then put on some tunes. Had to have autopsy tunes.

He unzipped the bag and leaned back, waiting for the stink to hit him.

Nothing.

Sometimes bodies didn't smell. Then again, when you worked around dead people as long as John had, your olfactories shut down. The brain finally decided, Hey, I've smelled that before. Smelled that a lot. No cause for alarm.

He spoke into the Dictaphone. "Decedent's name: Truman Harrison. No middle initial. Body belongs to a fifty-one-year-old African-American male with a history of heart disease."

He photographed the body, then removed and bagged the clothing—not easy without an assistant. He examined the cadaver externally, surprised to find no outward signs of rigor mortis or livor mortis. The guy must not have been dead long before being put on ice. And he chewed the hell out of his fingernails, John noted, lifting a hand to examine it more closely.

Outside, the storm was raging, but the autopsy suite within the heart of the morgue was silent. John had almost forgotten about the weather when the unmistakable sound of a lightning strike penetrated the thick walls, rattling glass containers in nearby cupboards. The room was plunged into darkness. Seconds later, the emergency generators kicked in and the lights flickered on.

Everything under control.

John continued with the autopsy. He placed a rubber block under the cadaver's neck, then positioned the scalpel for the Y incision, beginning at the right shoulder, below the collarbone. One inch into the cut the dead body let out a long sigh.

The scalpel slipped from John's fingers, clattering

to the stainless steel exam table. He stared at the dead man's face, searching for signs of life.

A decaying body rapidly formed gas, and it wasn't unusual for a dead person to appear to exhale. Some bodies even moved as the gas shifted around looking for an escape route.

"Son of a bitch." John let out a nervous laugh.

He retrieved the scalpel and poised his hand to continue with the incision. He was shaking. "Shit. What a fucking baby. Calm down. It was just a little gas, that's all."

Too late, he remembered the Dictaphone. With his slipper-covered foot, he shut it off with the remote switch, then stood there, breathing hard. The downdraft fan was humming.

He tossed the scalpel on the instrument tray, then picked up the dead man's wrist and felt for a pulse.

Nothing.

He felt the carotid artery in the neck.

Nothing.

He pulled out a miniature flashlight and checked the pupils.

No reaction. No reflex. No eye movement.

He turned the head from side to side.

"Some skin discoloration." Due to lack of circulation—a fairly significant sign of death. Lips were purple. Fingers and nails, purple.

He rolled the body from one side to the other, checking the back and buttocks. "No lividity."

He let the body drop to the previous position.

In the adjoining scrub room, he rummaged through the cabinets until he found a stethoscope.

Back in the autopsy suite, feeling foolish and glad

nobody else was around, he turned off the downdraft fan and placed the stethoscope against the dead man's chest.

Was that something? A faint sound? A gentle *lub* . . . *lub*? Or was it his own heart beating frantically in his head?

He pulled the stethoscope from his ears, then began another search, finally finding what he was looking for. A mirror. Round, eight inches in diameter. With a paper towel he rubbed it clean, making sure there were no smudges or fingerprints on the glass. Then he held it to the dead man's mouth and nose.

Primitive but effective.

Keeping an eye on the clock, he waited a full minute before lifting it away.

On the surface of the mirror was a small cloud of condensation—a cloud that gradually vanished as John stared at it in horror and disbelief.

This couldn't be happening.

Not again.

Chapter 2

In the Savannah Historic District, Elise Sandburg pulled orange juice and milk from the dark refrigerator while lightning flashed and thunder rattled the windows of her old Victorian house.

"I was going to make French toast." She closed the refrigerator door with her elbow and placed the cartons on the antique table where a hurricane candle burned in front of her thirteen-year-old daughter.

Audrey stared straight ahead with bleary eyes, her shoulder-length curly auburn hair tangled from sleep.

"Guess we'll have to settle for cold cereal," her mother said. "A substation was hit, which means we might not have any power until tomorrow."

Audrey didn't care. Tomorrow she would be home again. Her *real* home. French toast wouldn't have made everything suddenly wonderful. Why did her mother think that? She wasn't a little kid anymore. French toast wasn't going to make staying at her mom's any better.

She wanted to be home, at her dad's, in her own room, her own bed, near her friends. Not here, where everything was weird even when the electricity was on.

Years ago, Elise—Audrey called her mother Elise, at least in her mind—Elise had started restoring the place, digging into rooms, tearing the walls down to stinky old boards, and stinky, stained wallpaper and holes big enough to crawl through.

Then one day she just stopped.

The floors still creaked, and doors opened by themselves. Her mother—Elise—blamed it on gravity, said the building had settled, and the doors were now hanging wrong, but that didn't make Audrey feel any better when one would swing open behind her.

Elise was coming at her now, with stacked bowls in one hand, a box of cereal in the other, another tucked under her arm. Wearing an old gray Savannah Police Department T-shirt and flannel pajama bottoms. No bra.

Her chin-length hair was straight and dark; her eyes had strange lines going through them.

"This is cozy, isn't it?" Elise asked, sitting down at the table.

Cozy?

Sweet kitty!

Audrey liked to make up phrases. *Sweet kitty* was her newest, and a big hit at school. One day she hoped she'd turn on the TV and hear somebody say one of the cool phrases she'd invented. One day, maybe she'd turn on the TV and David Letterman would shout, "Sweet kitty!"

Audrey poured herself some juice, then reached for a box of cereal.

"I read about a girl who got her name changed,"

Audrey said, cereal spilling on the table. "Said it was easy." She poured milk and picked up a spoon.

"Do you want to change your name?"

Audrey shrugged, trying to look unconcerned even though her heart was racing. "I've been thinking about it."

"Some cultures believe children should be able to name themselves," Elise said. "I always kind of liked that idea except a child might go for years with no name. Or end up with baby's first word, which would most likely be *Mama*, or *Dada*, or a favorite toy or food."

Audrey should have known Elise would actually *like* the idea. Her dad had freaked when she'd mentioned it to him.

"Have anything in mind?" Elise asked around a mouthful of food.

"I kind of like *Bianca*. And *Chelsea*. And *Courtney*."

Elise gave it some thought. "Those are nice names." She nodded.

"What do you think about *Savannah*?" Audrey asked. "Then I could be Savannah from Savannah."

Elise leaned closer, forearms braced on the edge of the table. "Or how about Georgia from Georgia?"

This wasn't going the way it was supposed to. But then, nothing involving Elise ever did. Audrey had been anticipating an argument. Looking forward to an argument. Didn't Elise care what she called herself?

"In school, we looked up our names to find out what they mean, you know." Audrey frowned, confused and annoyed. "Mine means nobility."

Elise put down her spoon. "Not nobility. Noble strength."

"Anyway, who thought of *that* name?" It couldn't have been her dad. No way could it have been her dad.

"I did. But your father agreed it was lovely."

The phone rang.

Elise picked up the portable, remembered the power was off, then hurried down the hallway in the direction of the land phone.

Did Audrey really hate her?

Or did her attitude have to do with age? How much was typical thirteen-year-old behavior?

Thirteen was a horrid age. The only thing worse was fourteen, which Audrey would be in seven months. Elise had smoked her first cigarette at eleven. Thirteen-year-olds were doing drugs. Having sex. Having *babies*.

She hates her name.

What was wrong with the name Audrey? It may not have been something Elise would choose now, but she'd been eighteen when her daughter was born, and the name had seemed pretty damn cool.

The call was from Major Coretta Hoffman, head of Homicide. "I want you and Detective Gould to stop by the morgue before coming in this morning," the major said. "We've had another body come to life."

Another body.

The hair on the back of Elise's neck tingled.

Two "awakenings" in a single month. The first had been an accident, a mistaken call in the emergency room, the unfortunate patient an overdosed prostitute with a record who'd come around in the morgue.

She'd heard about it. Read about it.

It wasn't common knowledge, but occasionally people were pronounced dead when they weren't. Not something people liked to think about, but it happened.

But two times? In a month?

Was there a connection? Or was it simply an extremely strange coincidence?

"I'll be there as soon as I can." Elise hung up and made her way back to the kitchen.

"David Gould?" Audrey asked.

"Major Hoffman."

"Oh." Audrey seemed disappointed. "I like your new partner."

"Hmm," Elise said. Audrey was definitely part of a minority. "What makes him so special in your book?"

"He doesn't treat me like a little kid. And he doesn't ask stupid questions like 'How's school?' Or 'Where'd you get that curly hair?' And he doesn't seem like a cop at all." She thought a moment, then added, "He doesn't really even seem like an adult."

Unfortunately, Elise had to agree.

Elise had planned to spend more time with Audrey this spring and summer. Toward that end, she'd hoped an enthused new partner would be sent her way. One who was eager to dive in and give her the assistance she so desperately needed.

A pipe dream.

Her new partner seemed barely able to get his own paperwork done, let alone help Elise with a backlog of reports, filing, and cold cases.

David Gould. Used to be an FBI agent, but claimed he'd been in the market for a less stressful job. Translation: an *easier* job.

And while she wasn't into gossip like so many others in the police department, she liked to know who was watching her back. All she knew about Gould was that he'd been shipped down from Cleveland, Ohio, where he hadn't been all that long.

And she was beginning to suspect they'd been glad to unload him.

Chapter 3

David Gould had run five miles with another five to go when his pager went off. He didn't check it.

When he'd started out, the streets had been dark and deserted, with fog clinging to rolling lawns and areas of dense vegetation. Now it was light. The storm had moved on to Atlanta, and traffic was getting heavy. Sidewalks were littered with shredded leaves and crushed blossoms. In a couple of areas, he'd spotted some downed trees.

Helluva storm.

He should probably run with a cell phone, but that would have been a pain in the ass. Besides, the purpose of the run was to get away from everything for a while. Time to empty his mind and let himself fall into that semihypnotic state, lulled by the rhythmic pounding of jogging shoes.

His pace was even; the only thing that ever changed was the intensity of the pounding, varying upon the surface he traversed. The soft, hollow thud of earth was interrupted by the more solid connection of asphalt, which in turn gave way to cement and the crunch of gravel.

Gravel was his least favorite because the sound wasn't as clean.

His head was always full of clutter that served no purpose other than to confuse him and complicate his thought processes. Running helped. Running for him was the equivalent of defragmenting his hard drive. By the end of the day, he usually felt pretty level, pretty good about things, but with each morning came a fresh wave of clutter and the desperate need to purge himself.

David moved through Forsyth Park, past the fountain with the spouting mermen and the guy selling salvation. A homeless woman crawled from under a blooming magnolia where she'd nested for the night. Several people he didn't know told him good morning.

They were so damn friendly here. It pissed him off.

So far, David hadn't experienced the Savannah John Berendt had written about. David Gould's Savannah was a darker place, a place that had more to do with life on the streets than with life in a multimillion-dollar mansion. Not that Savannah wasn't one of the most beautiful places he'd ever seen, because it was. The city's beauty and uniqueness were directly related to the twenty-two squares designed by the founder, James Oglethorpe. Two- and three-story historic homes, with their graciously curved front steps that led to tabby sidewalks and brick streets, surrounded the silent and sheltered communal gardens canopied with Spanish moss.

Contrasting with the beauty was a darkness and mystery that saturated the Southern cityscape. A false Utopia that at once compelled and repelled.

When had the darkness started? David wondered.

Before the Civil War? Before Sherman? Or had Sherman's visit marked the beginning?

Whatever the origins, the darkness had left the city with a strange vibe David couldn't quite put his finger on, but it felt a little like an episode of *The Twilight Zone*. He just kept hoping Rod Serling would step from behind a building and explain it all to him. . . .

The sun hadn't been up long, but it was already getting muggy. And buggy.

With spring came unpleasantness. Things like sinus headaches. Mold. Wood rot. Palmetto bugs. Which were actually huge, flying cockroaches. Who was anybody kidding?

And rats.

Jesus, the rats. The city was crawling with them. His partner had assured him it wasn't always like this, that the excessive rain and demolition and construction projects had driven the rodents into some of the most touted eating establishments in the city.

They couldn't be poisoned. They'd die in the walls, and wouldn't that be a stinking mess? A couple of restaurant owners had taken to sitting up all night with .22 rifles, blasting the rodents as they made an appearance.

After businesses closed, people gathered outside the darkened windows of Savannah restaurants to watch the rats come out to play. Watch them scurry across tables, knocking down salt and pepper shakers, their eyes glowing. But then, residents had to get their entertainment somewhere. Local theaters rarely screened decent movies, and the music scene . . . well, there wasn't one, unless you counted the requisite blues and jazz that was more the equivalent of free chicken wings.

Spring and warmer weather also brought murder, with the city already breaking last year's record, not that anybody was bragging. Well. Some people may have been.

At the intersection of Abercorn and Gordon, David paused and checked his pager. E. Sandburg, just as he'd suspected. She'd left a message: "Meet me at the morgue."

Quaint.

He headed home, passing a group of young girls jumping rope, chanting a reminder of where he was:

Lady in a black veil
Babies in the bed
Kissed them on the forehead
Now they're both dead.

Red Xs on their gravestones
Black Xs on their lips
Silver dollars where their eyes should be
Mama put a hex.

His apartment was on the third floor of a building called Mary of the Angels.

Once it had housed children orphaned by a yellow fever epidemic that had ripped through Savannah in 1854. After that, it had been the final home to tuberculosis patients during a time when TB was a death sentence.

"Oh, David. This is horrid," his sister had announced

when she'd visited the area on a business trip. "Was this the only apartment you could find?"

"It was the first apartment."

Now he unlocked the door and stepped inside, his Siamese cat saying hello, circling his legs and meowing.

Isobel had been his wife's cat. She would be his ex-wife if the lawyers ever got their asses in gear and finished the paperwork. Beth had begged him to take care of Isobel while she lived her new life on death row.

Siamese were supposed to be independent, but Isobel was one of the neediest damn cats David had ever seen. Then again, maybe the traumatic events of the past year had been tough on her too. Maybe she needed a shrink. A kitty psychiatrist.

David took a shower and dressed in gray pants and a white shirt. Shoulder holster and gun. He preferred a .40-caliber Smith & Wesson. He liked the weight, liked the accuracy, and liked the way it fit compactly against his body. He finished off with a jacket that matched his pants.

He'd been in Savannah three months and still felt as if he'd stepped into somebody else's life. As he moved through the days, nothing seemed to touch him—nothing felt real. It wasn't just Savannah. Nothing had felt real in a long time.

Antidepressants did that to a person.

Keys.

Badge.

Handcuffs.

And then there were the assholes at Headquarters who'd given him a hard time since his first day in their lovely city. Especially a couple of detectives

David called various names, depending on his mood. Starsky and Hutch. Cagney and Lacey. Crockett and Tubbs. Shari Lewis and Lamb Chop.

They'd started the feud.

What exactly did they have against him?

He was from Ohio.

Translation: the North. The big, bad North, where all the obnoxious, rude Yankees lived.

Apparently the Civil War was still going on; the South just hadn't gotten the memo telling them it was over.

Screw them. He should care, but he didn't.

David knew his detachment wasn't acceptable, knew he should see a local therapist, but he couldn't seem to drum up enough enthusiasm to follow through on the idea. And anyway, he'd been evaluated by FBI psychologists and had been pronounced mentally sound. Why would he want to argue with that? Everybody had problems. Everybody was a little wacko.

Chapter 4

Elise pulled into the morgue parking lot, spotting David Gould's black Honda. He must have been watching for her in his rearview mirror. As soon as she cut the engine of her old yellow SAAB wagon, he stepped out.

A bit under six feet, he was dressed in a loose-fitting suit that made her think of old movies. His hair wasn't short or long, the color somewhere between light and medium brown, a few sun-bleached streaks here and there from hours spent outdoors.

Fellow workers had commented on seeing him running ten miles beyond the city limits. In the dark. In the rain.

Running.

He seemed so perpetually disinterested in everything that it was hard to imagine he could have the ambition to go a mile, let alone ten.

Outwardly, he appeared fairly average, but Elise had occasionally caught something disconcerting in his blue eyes, something that made her uncomfortable and told her David Gould was in no way average.

He had that FBI ability to blend, and if you didn't look at him closely, he seemed like a lot of other men. The kind who wore a suit and worked in an office and exercised four times a week. Had a wife and a couple of kids and cooked out in the backyard on weekends. Went to church on Sundays and could even hide Easter eggs and play Santa Claus upon occasion.

Gould could be that man, but he wasn't.

Elise knew better.

He wasn't making any effort to become a part of the community. A part of anything. He wasn't winning any friends or influencing people within the Homicide Unit. He didn't seem to care whether anyone liked him or not. She got the idea he just wanted to be left alone.

There was a greenness, an immaturity, about him that Elise suspected was something else. She couldn't classify him in her mind. Who he was. What he wanted. Why he was there.

He had a story; she just didn't know what it was. Yet.

Had he been sent there as some kind of reprimand? Was he just biding his time until he could return to wherever he'd been before Cleveland?

Dr. John Casper was waiting for them. Elise had met him a few times and liked him. He was friendly, natural, unpretentious.

The young doctor's curly hair was messier than usual, his white lab coat wrinkled, looking as if he may have slept in it. His face was pale; his eyes had dark circles under them.

Elise introduced him to her partner, and they shook hands.

"Where's the body?" Gould asked, glancing around the dim hallway.

"Paramedics took him to the hospital."

"Then he's still alive," Elise said.

"If you want to call it that."

Dr. Casper told them about the rush of bodies they'd had, about how everyone was working overtime. "But I don't think it would have mattered if it had been slow. I still don't think anyone would have noticed." He motioned to some plastic chairs lined up against a light green wall.

While Elise and her partner settled themselves, Casper pulled a chair around so he sat facing them. The young doctor wiped a shaking hand across his face. "You have bodies do that sometimes."

"Do what?" Elise asked.

"Move. Expel air. It's unsettling as hell, but it happens."

He crossed an ankle over his knee and began fiddling with his tennis shoe, jabbing the plastic end of the lace into an eyelet. "In med school, we used to deliberately pump bodies full of air so that when a student cut into them—" He stopped short, as if suddenly remembering he wasn't speaking to fellow med students. "Sorry." He was sweating profusely. "I'm just so fucking—oh, shit."

"That's okay," Elise assured him. "Something like this has to be extremely upsetting."

Dr. Casper wiped his face with the sleeve of his lab coat. "I haven't slept in almost two days. I always get a little twitchy when I don't sleep."

"Were you performing the autopsy by yourself?" Elise asked.

"It was getting ready to storm, and I told Willy—he's a morgue assistant—I told him to go home." Dr. Casper laughed, as if something had just come to him. "If Willy had been here when it happened, we'd have a cutout in the wall the shape of a running man." He laughed a little more.

"Did you notice anything unusual about the body?" Gould asked, leaning forward. Forearms on his knees, hands clasped, he appeared almost interested.

"Well, it didn't smell, but I had the downdraft turned on. And contrary to popular belief, not all bodies smell."

Elise wasn't falling for that. Coroners spent so much time around stinking bodies that the mild ones no longer registered.

"And there weren't any signs of lividity. That's rare, but not impossible. I've seen it before. If a body's put in storage right away, it can look pretty fresh." Dr. Casper got an odd expression on his face. "Unless those weren't dead either."

Elise didn't have an answer; she was no good at false reassurance, and she could proudly boast that she'd never in her life uttered the phrase *Everything's going to be fine*.

She glanced at Gould. He lifted his eyebrows as if to say, *This is your show. I'm only your sidekick.*

Elise brushed away her impatience to focus on the situation at hand. "We'll need the name of the physician who pronounced him dead and signed the death certificate," she said.

"Already looked it up." Dr. Casper pulled a piece of paper from his shirt pocket and handed it to her. "Dr. James Fritz."

"Know him?"

The young doctor shook his head. "Name's familiar. Never heard anything bad about him, anyway. And we always hear the bad stuff. Apparently the patient had a history of heart disease. Died, or appeared to have died, at home. Wife called 911. No vital signs. At the hospital, he was pronounced dead."

"What about the case three weeks ago?" Gould asked.

Elise was a little surprised he remembered the case of three weeks ago. They hadn't been involved in it. All Elise could recall was that the victim had died shortly after his "awakening."

"Different hospital, different doctor," Casper said. He tugged at his shoestring again. "I became a coroner because I like working with the dead, not the living," he said. "I've never wanted to have anybody's life in my hands."

"Any chance this guy will wake up and tell us what happened to him?" Elise asked.

"My guess is that he's in a vegetative state. He was only taking one shallow breath a minute. The brain needs more oxygen than that."

Gould linked his fingers together. "What about people who've been pulled from frigid water and been clinically dead for hours only to be revived?"

"Ask five doctors their definition of death and you'll get five different answers," Casper told them. "Without the use of expensive equipment, it's sometimes impossible to tell if someone is really dead. The standard for determining death is the irreversible cessation of spontaneous cardiopulmonary functions."

He seemed to be regaining some of his confidence

now that he was able to reference his medical school education. "We now know that the boundaries between life and death aren't so clear. Hundreds of papers have been written on the subject, with no definitive definition of death."

"Let me get this straight," Gould said. "Are you saying there isn't an established criterion for determining death?"

"The Uniform Determination of Death Act, UDDA, has outlined two specific criteria for determining death, dealing with circulatory and respiratory functions and brain death, but there are no cost-effective tests to measure those things," Casper told them. "The standard procedure is to observe the patient for two minutes for signs of breathing or heartbeat. Even with expensive testing using ECGs and contrast dye X rays, there have been cases of cold-water drownings that have proved even the most sophisticated equipment fallible."

Dr. Casper shook his head, amazed by what he was relating, even though he'd obviously studied the subject. "Here's an interesting tidbit for you: There's actually a group pushing for a standard for determining death that would allow for the burial of brain-dead bodies with spontaneous respiration and heartbeat."

"That's disturbing as hell," Gould muttered while Elise stared at the doctor in horror.

"What was that line from *The Wizard of Oz*?" Gould asked, looking up at the ceiling. "Something about not being merely dead?"

Casper thought a moment. " 'She's not only merely dead—she's really most sincerely dead.' "

Both men laughed, instant comrades.

Elise frowned. She didn't know who irritated her more, Casper, for so easily breaking through Gould's shell, or Gould, for instigating the inappropriate behavior. Or was she just jealous because they were having fun and she wasn't?

That possibility also irritated her.

As Gould caught her glare of disapproval, his laugh quickly fizzled to an aw-shucks crooked smile.

Why, the man was quite charming when he pulled himself out of his malaise.

"Actually," Casper said, managing to get control of himself, "the simplest and best way to know if someone is dead is to wait for him to rot."

Gould glanced at Elise, one eyebrow raised. "The medical field has come so far," he said dryly. "What will it be next? Holding three-day wakes so we can be sure our loved ones are actually dead?"

"Might not be a bad idea," Dr. Casper said, only half joking.

Elise thanked him for his time; then she and Gould headed for the hospital where Truman Harrison had been taken. As far as she knew, she'd never talked to a dead man before.

Chapter 5

Someone was crying.

Elise heard the woman as she and Gould approached Truman Harrison's hospital room. That individual sound of sobbing triggered a companion response, and at least two other people joined in.

Ten feet from the open door, Gould stopped. "Christ." He fell back against the wall as if trying to hide from a shooter.

What now?

"I don't know if I can go in there. I don't like hospitals. I don't like dealing with—" He pointed in the direction of the sobbing. "I don't like dealing with that kind of emotion."

Elise knew it wasn't fair, but she suddenly blamed Gould for everything that was wrong in her life at the moment—the main thing being her lack of time for Audrey. Her reaction may have been extreme, but she didn't have the energy or the inclination to hold David Gould's hand.

"Maybe when you were an FBI agent you could keep your distance," she said, unable to mask her annoyance, "but dealing with grieving families is part of a detective's job. It's never easy, but it's something we have to do."

"Did I ever tell you about the time I got my appendix out?" he asked with agitation, obviously stalling.

Why couldn't she have gotten a *real* partner? "This isn't about you," she told him.

"Wait."

Stalling.

"What I have to say makes sense."

She crossed her arms and leaned against the wall. She'd give him one minute.

"When I was twenty years old, I had an emergency appendectomy," he said quickly. "They prepped me, doped me up, and wheeled me into the operating room, where they began administering anesthesia. But instead of knocking me out, the drug made me hyper-aware. My senses were intensified. The nerve endings under my skin were electrically charged." He lifted a hand, fingers spread, as if to demonstrate. "I could feel the hairs growing from my pores." He lowered his voice to a whisper and leaned closer. "I could hear conversations *two rooms away*."

"Are you telling me you were awake through the whole operation?" She needed to trade David Gould in for a new model.

"I could feel and hear everything."

"How horrible." She didn't believe him.

"You don't believe me, do you?"

"Well . . ."

"That's okay. Nobody did. Not the doctors or nurses. Or my parents. My girlfriend. Why should you? But that's not why I chose this moment to tell you a little story about myself. What I'm *saying* is that our buddy Harrison might be able to hear what's going on around him, even though he's in a coma."

In his roundabout way, Gould was finally making sense. Maybe she wouldn't trade him in just yet. "I'll be careful."

"Assume he can hear everything."

"I'll keep that in mind." She looked closely at his ashen face, experiencing a pang of empathy. "You going to be okay?" A partner with a hospital phobia. What other surprises did he have up his sleeve?

He nodded, gave his shoulders a loose shake, and followed her into the room.

A woman in a white suit sat near a sunny window. Two other people, a younger man and woman, hovered nearby. The crying, at least for now, had stopped.

A comatose Mr. Harrison was lying in bed, attached to an IV and a heart monitor that pulsed steadily. The woman in the white suit turned out to be Mr. Harrison's wife, the other two people his children.

Elise introduced herself and Gould. "We're going to be looking into the case, trying to find out how your husband ended up in the morgue . . . prematurely."

"He woke up in the middle of the night," Mrs. Harrison explained. "Said he felt sick. On the way to the bathroom he collapsed. I called 911 and an hour later he was pronounced dead."

She started to cry, fought it, pulled in a trembling breath, then continued. "I hate to think of him being put in that body bag. Hate to think of him in that morgue. On the autopsy table—*when he was alive.* It's a nightmare. That's what it is. A nightmare."

The beeping of the heart monitor suddenly increased. Heads swiveled and everybody turned to stare at the screen as the pulse rate dropped back to its previous level.

"Did he hear me?" Mrs. Harrison asked. "Do you think he heard me? Doctor said he can't hear anything."

Elise and Gould exchanged glances.

Strange.

Yep.

The family gathered around Mr. Harrison's bed, everyone talking at once, trying to elicit a response or an increase in pulse.

Nothing happened.

Elise asked Mrs. Harrison a few more questions, then produced her business card. "Call if you think of anything you may have forgotten to tell us."

Outside the hospital room, a young office assistant was lying in wait. "The administrator would like to talk to you," she said, stepping forward.

She led the detectives to an elevator, down a carpeted hall, to a large meeting room. They were welcomed by the hospital administrator, the head of ER, the hospital's press liaison, and the doctor who had been unfortunate enough to pronounce poor Mr. Harrison dead. Completing the group was a grim-looking bald man with a briefcase, who turned out to be the hospital lawyer.

Elise and Gould sat side by side at the table.

The ER head, Dr. Eklund, pulled out several sheets of paper. "We have some of the lab work back on Mr. Harrison," he said, passing copies to Elise and David.

It was pretty obvious that management wanted to get its side of the story out as quickly as possible.

"Traces of TTX were detected in Truman Harrison's blood."

"TTX?" Elise asked.

"Tetrodotoxin. A toxin that's common to several varieties of marine life. I'm willing to bet we'll discover that Mr. Harrison recently ate at some exotic seafood restaurant."

"Isn't TTX found in the puffer fish?" Gould asked.

"Among other things."

The doctor cleared his throat, his hands clasped on the table. "In Japan, people actually eat puffer fish in order to get high from the poison," he explained. "There have been a number of fatalities from it. Apparently it's also becoming fashionable here. Our comatose Mr. Harrison probably visited a sushi bar where they serve the delicacy."

"Have you questioned his wife?" Gould asked.

"She doesn't know where he ate the day he was poisoned."

Elise recognized a choreographed delivery when she saw one. As if on cue, the lawyer presented them with some official-looking documents. "This," he explained, "is a copy of the Presidential Commission's definition of death. And this is the Uniform Determination of Death Act. If you read both, you'll see that we followed their suggested criteria and that there was no negligence on the part of Mercy Hospital or anyone on our staff."

Covering their asses. That's what they were doing. Elise scooped up the loose sheets of paper and tapped them together. "We aren't here to pass judgment on anyone," she told them, trying to remain calm—at least outwardly. "Our job is to collect information."

"You can understand the hospital's concern," said the administrator, a well-dressed woman of fifty. "The press could turn this into a circus. The hospital's reputation is at stake."

"We don't work for the hospital," Elise said, getting abruptly to her feet. She'd heard enough. "We work for the public, and they have a right to know what happened. If Mr. Harrison ingested a toxin at an eating establishment anywhere in the bistate region, we have to determine the location of that establishment and quickly relay information to the media. Harrison may not be the only poisoning case. You need to make your staff aware of the symptoms. You need to contact specialists and find out how it can be treated. This isn't the time to focus on protecting your reputation. It's time to protect the public."

That said, Elise turned to leave. Gould followed a little more slowly, giving the group a small salute before walking out the door.

The elevator was occupied, so Elise took the stairs.

"Way to go," Gould shouted, hurrying down the steps after her. He caught up as she exited for the parking area. "You really chewed out their corporate asses."

She swung around to face him, at last able to release the anger she'd been holding in check. Too bad Gould was the recipient. Later she would regret her outburst, but right now it felt damn good. "And you didn't think they needed chewing out?"

Gould put both hands in the air. "I was just admiring your ability to get so worked up, that's all."

"Is that because getting worked up is something you can only admire from a distance?"

"What's that supposed to mean?"

She stopped and cast a glance around. "Where's my car?"

"I drove." Gould pointed to his black Honda. "You left yours at the morgue."

He unlocked his car with the automatic opener and they both slid inside.

"It just doesn't seem like you care about anything other than to be occasionally amused by it," Elise said. There. It was finally out. She'd told him what she'd been thinking for the past three months. "You aren't engaged."

He reversed the little car, then quickly exited the lot. "I can do my job without being *engaged*."

"A good cop has to care about people."

"You get hurt that way. You burn out that way."

"Is that why you wanted to avoid Mr. Harrison's room?" she asked. "Because you go out of your way to keep an emotional distance?"

"I told you. I don't like hospitals."

"Well, that's too damn bad! Neither do I! Do you think you can run from everything unpleasant?"

"I try."

Why couldn't they just have a normal conversation? Why did he have to make everything so hard?

"So." He stopped at a red light. "You're telling me I should do something about my attitude."

"Some adjustment wouldn't hurt and might even make your life easier." And hers.

"Hmm."

Remarkably, he seemed to give her words consideration.

"You might have a point."

This had been so easy. "Please give it some thought." Why hadn't she brought up his attitude before? Communication. That was what it was all about.

"Just say no," he said.

"Say no?" For a total of thirty seconds, their conversation had made sense. "Say no to what?"

"Some things I need to deal with, that's all."

"Such as . . . ?" She wanted to keep the moment of frankness and camaraderie going.

"Nothing I want to talk about." *Slam.*

Oh, forget it. If she was from Venus, Gould was from a planet in a galaxy that hadn't yet been discovered. "I need food," she announced with a conscious effort to change the subject.

She was only thirty-one, but lately she'd noticed her brain didn't function as well on an empty stomach. "Swing by a drive-through on the way back to Police Headquarters," she told him.

The light turned green and he shot through the intersection. "Sounds good to me."

They ordered hamburgers, fries, and soft drinks.

Elise normally preferred healthy meals, but the frustration of the moment made her abandon her good intentions.

Once they had their food, Gould headed for the Savannah Police Department and parked in the lot across the street. On the way to Elise's office, they passed a group of coworkers, two of them homicide detectives Gould had been fighting with since his first day on the job. Elise had worked with both. Mid-thirties. Married, with kids.

"Cagney." Gould gave them a nod. "Lacey."

Their real names: Detectives Mason and Avery.

"Heard you got assigned the zombie case," Mason said, addressing Elise. He glanced at his partner, and pretty soon they were both hunched over, laughing into their fists like a couple of schoolboys.

"Appropriate, wouldn't you say?" Avery asked once he'd come up for air.

Gould shot Elise a curious look.

Apparently he was the one person in Savannah who didn't know everything about her—which was at least one bonus brought about by Gould's lack of social skills. Normally new recruits had Elise's history spelled out to them within days.

Avery's question was proof that no matter how hard you tried, you couldn't outrun your past. But Elise was always hoping people would at least lose interest.

That hadn't happened.

Everyone in the police force knew Elise had been abandoned in a cemetery as an infant. They knew that soon after her rescue a rumor began to circulate, claiming she was the cursed, illegitimate daughter of Jackson Sweet, a powerful white root doctor who'd died about the time Elise was born.

Nobody wanted a cursed infant, but eventually she was adopted into a rigid Christian family, where she was treated with a rather odd and aloof kindness. She spent her early childhood as an outsider, someone without a true identity, but the mystery and supposition surrounding her heritage gave her foundation and definition.

During those isolated years of early childhood, she read everything she could on root doctoring. By the time Elise was Audrey's age, she was learning simple spells and herbal remedies while studying under a hag who was looking for someone she could "pass the mantle" to.

But those days were long over.

She'd spent her entire professional career trying to put her past behind her in order to build credibility among her peers. But in Savannah, a place that seemed impervious to the outside world, you *were* your past.

Shrugging off Gould's silent question and ignoring Avery's taunt, Elise headed upstairs.

The office she and Gould shared was located on the third floor of Savannah Police Department Headquarters, with a window overlooking Colonial Park Cemetery. The city was proud of the historic police building, but even the addition constructed years ago wasn't enough to keep the PD from bursting at the seams.

Elise was afraid that once they were alone Gould would grill her about Mason's and Avery's comments. Anybody else would have been full of questions.

Instead, he planted himself in front of his computer, sandwich wrapper rustling, while Elise got on the phone and tried to contact Truman Harrison's coworkers in the Savannah Street Maintenance Department.

Behind her, she heard the rapid clicking of keys. "Not a homicide case," Gould muttered. "Don't know why Hoffman gave it to us."

Elise ended her conversation with the maintenance department secretary. "As soon as we find the restaurant where Truman Harrison ate, we can turn this over to the Department of Public Health. If his wife decides to sue the hospital, it will be a lawyer's game. Six years later, when it finally goes to court," she said, without trying to hide the annoyance she felt when it came to the legal system, "we'll be expected to recall every minute detail as if it happened yesterday."

"What I don't get is why it didn't kill Harrison."

"Maybe he ingested it before. Maybe he's built up a tolerance to it. Some poisons are like that."

"Here it is," Gould announced, fingers pausing on the keyboard, eyes focused on the screen, the hint of excitement in his voice getting Elise's attention.

" 'TTX is one of nature's strangest molecules and one of the deadliest poisons on earth,' " he read. " 'Gram for gram, it is ten thousand times more lethal than cyanide. A few short minutes after exposure, it paralyzes its victims, leaving the brain *fully aware of what is happening*.' "

He fell silent while continuing to read to himself. A few minutes later he let out a loud, derisive snort. "Guess Lacey wasn't so far off after all. It says here that tetrodotoxin is one of the ingredients used to make zombies."

Elise thought about that for a moment. "Makes sense."

He swiveled around to face her, hands braced behind his head. "I suppose you're going to tell me you believe in zombies."

"Zombies exist."

He dropped his hands, physically portraying his frustration. "Are you insane? Is everybody in this town insane?"

"You've seen too many B movies. Have you heard of *The Serpent and the Rainbow* by Wade Davis?"

"I think I caught a few minutes of it on Showtime before switching channels."

"That could have skewed your perspective. In the book, Davis postulates that zombies are very real, but never actually die. He suggests they are dosed with a powder that can be absorbed through the skin, leaving the victim in a state that mimics death. After the burial, the voodoo priest returns in the middle of the night and digs up the corpse, which isn't really a corpse but a somewhat lobotomized, oxygen-deprived individual, whom he then sells as slave labor in some town far from the victim's home."

"Who says it's hard to get good help nowadays?" Gould turned back to his computer and finished off his sandwich while continuing to search. "Here's an interesting tidbit," he said. "Some people think the mysterious deaths surrounding the curse of King Tut were due to a poison similar to TTX. They suggest the poison was sprinkled in places where grave robbers could come in contact with it. If they had a cut finger or hand, it would enter the bloodstream."

"Transdermal delivery," Elise said. "Just like Wade Davis' zombies."

"Apparently."

She swung toward him. "Did you know that mandrake was used in the time of Christ as an anesthetic, but also to simulate death?"

He nodded. "I've heard that."

"Some historians even say it was hidden in the vinegar given to Jesus."

"Hence, the resurrection?"

"It's a theory. Not a popular one, but a theory."

"But then, who cares about being popular?"

An interesting comment, considering the source. "It's human nature to want to be liked," Elise told him. "To seek the approval of our peers."

"That kind of mind-set is a weakness, especially for a detective, who should be focusing on the truth."

There was no middle ground with him. If he was looking for an argument, she refused to participate.

He unscrewed the cap from a bottle of water and took a swallow. "This little history lesson has been very enlightening, but I don't think it has anything to do with us or Truman Harrison."

"Let's hope not."

He sized her up. "That didn't sound convincing or heartfelt."

He was right, Elise realized with a gnawing deep in her stomach, afraid that the case wouldn't be resolved as easily as she'd hoped. Just hours in, it already seemed to be plunging her into the murky waters she'd spent the last thirteen years trying to leave behind.

Chapter 6

He was beginning to smell like the poisoned rats that died inside the walls. That's how I knew he was dead.

I've always hated that smell.

I love death, but hate the smell of it. How can that be? And how terribly unfair. To be so drawn to something, yet so repulsed by it at the same time.

He'd been a good boy. Sweet and unresponsive, just the way I liked them.

Soft skin.

Soft hair.

But now he smelled like a dead fucking rat.

Walking backward, I grasped the corners of the blanket and dragged the wrapped body down the grassy incline. It was hard to get a good grip because the leather gloves kept slipping. I had to repeatedly reposition my fingers and hands.

Darkness had fallen over Savannah hours ago, and everyone was safe in bed. Even the crickets were asleep.

I paused and straightened to pull in a deep breath, my face turned away from the stench.

Night air.

A heavy, mysterious mixture of salt marsh, vegetation, and rich earth.

I bent and resumed my task.

The narrow, worn path led directly to the boat dock. The terrain became steeper, making my job easier. At one point, Jordan almost got away from me.

The johnboat with its metal hull was moored under the dock, half of it visible from where I stood. It was the easiest thing to shove the body over the edge.

It dropped into the boat with a heavy thud. I untied the thick rope and joined the dead man, taking a position near the back.

I grabbed the oars.

They made a hollow sound as they knocked against the boat before dipping into the smooth, black water.

I'm a good rower. I can row with very little noise. Just a few soft splashes that could be frogs.

Above me, a sliver of moon watched from the sky.

I remembered that moon. That moon had been my friend before.

Death is a seductive, erotic thing.

The night air was heavy. In the darkness, in the marshy swamplands, I could see balls of undulating, drifting light, floating among the trees and low-growing vegetation.

Some people think the eerie glow is caused by slip-skin hags, the kind of evil night creatures that leave their shed skin on the bedpost and take on a cloak of invisibility. But I know the light for what it is.

Trapped phosphorus, caused by rotting tree stumps.

No magic. Just science.

Now that I was away from the shore and houses, I

rested the oars in their holders and started the outboard. I was strong, but not a fucking rowing champ.

The motor was quiet. Soothing almost.

I was in no hurry. I let the motor push the boat through the inky water. Trees bent over the waterway, and occasionally Spanish moss brushed my cheek.

Death is a seductive, erotic thing.

I was hyperaware of my dead friend in the blanket. I would like to look at him one more time in the moonlight, but I was getting small whiffs of his stench, even though he was wrapped and immobile.

Better to leave him alone.

The journey took less than an hour.

The johnboat had a flat bow that could slide right up to the water's edge and over the ground, giving me a level surface to work.

I tied off to a tree, then dragged the body from the boat.

I could have just attached cement blocks to his feet and dumped him somewhere deep where fish would nibble until there was nothing left but bone.

That would have been the best thing to do. But for some reason, I couldn't make myself do it. I don't know why. Maybe it seemed too easy. Or maybe it was because dead bodies belong in the ground.

Didn't need a flashlight.

I could make out the darker shapes of trees. And on the ground, bushes and small shrubs. Gravestones.

A cemetery.

A good place for Jordan.

There wasn't much of a slope, which was why I'd chosen this particular resting place. I dragged Jordan up the incline, across a flat, grassy area, into a stand of dense trees. Then I returned to the boat for a shovel.

The ground was harder than I'd thought it would be. I dug for a long time, then sat down on a log and had a smoke.

Should have just dumped him in the river. Why hadn't I just dumped him in the river?

I knew the answer.

I get these ideas in my head, and I can't get rid of them. They won't go away. They *never* go away until I see them through. Doesn't matter what they are. It can be as simple as something telling me to go touch a particular railing. Or brush my teeth. Wash my hands.

When I got in that mode, I had to do it. No questions.

Just do it.

That's how it was with the cemetery. Bury Jordan in a cemetery. Seemed like a good idea. But the fucking ground. And the fucking shovel. It was dull. Like trying to dig with a board.

I took a couple more quick puffs, dropped the filterless cigarette, and ground it out with the toe of my boot. Even though the place was littered with butts, I picked it up and stuck it in my pocket.

Leave no clues. No solid ones, anyway.

Back to work.

I dragged the body into the shallow trench. I tossed dirt until the entire thing was covered with at least a good six inches. Then, with my gloved hands, I raked leaves over that.

I carried the crappy shovel back to the boat, then pulled out a backpack. At the burial site, I removed some items and arranged them nicely on the grave.

A silver dollar.
A bottle of whiskey.
Things a dead guy would need.

Then I pulled a small flannel bag from my pocket, opened the drawstring, and reached inside.

Chapter 7

"Watch the road," Eric Kaufman warned.

Amy jerked her mom's van off the shoulder and back between the white lines. The windshield wipers were going full blast, but they couldn't keep up with the condensation. "It's so foggy." She put the headlights on high and they both recoiled from the glare. She switched back to low beam.

"There," Eric said, pointing.

Amy exited the two-lane to a gravel road with dense vegetation on both sides. Five minutes later they arrived at their spot—an old plantation cemetery on the edge of Savannah, overgrown and forgotten.

Eric dug into a paper bag and pulled out two beers. He popped one open and handed it to Amy before opening another for himself.

He took a long swallow, then contemplated a tombstone that was barely distinguishable in the yellow glow of the van's parking lights. "Do you ever think about what it's like to be dead?"

"Don't say that!"

"Everybody dies," he told her.

Eric knew it was mean, but he couldn't help himself. He liked to tease. "It could be a car wreck. Or a virus. Cancer. Maybe a hockey puck to the chest. I knew a kid that happened to. Hit in the chest with a puck doing over ninety miles an hour. Killed him. Stopped his heart." He snapped his fingers.

"Quit!"

She sounded like his little sister.

"People are walking cartoons, ignoring the iron beam when they bend to tie a shoe," Eric said. "Sometimes I feel like I should hook a loudspeaker to my car and drive down the street shouting warnings. 'Watch out, little kid. Don't ride that bike in the street. Watch out, old lady with the big purse. You may as well be wearing a sign that says beat me up and rob me.' "

Eric didn't know what was wrong with him. He had been in a weird mood all day. A weird mood ever since high school graduation. He didn't want to grow up. He didn't want to have to make big decisions. He didn't want to have to go to college, get a job, wear a suit.

"When I was in Girl Scouts, we had part of the highway we kept clean," Amy announced as she finished off her beer and stuck the empty in the sack. "You shoulda seen the stuff people threw out. I hated them for being such pigs. You wouldn't believe all the rubbers we found."

"You picked up rubbers?" Eric asked, horrified. The image of Girl Scouts in their little green hats, sashes, and uniforms picking up rubbers—even if they wore gloves or used a stick—was disturbing.

There were a lot of things in the world innocent kids shouldn't have to see. "That's disgusting!"

"Some were pretty fresh."

"Stop it. Now *you're* scaring *me*. I've heard enough, so just stop it, okay?"

"Oh, it's fine for you to talk about dying and I can't talk about filthy rubbers?"

"I just hope to hell you wore gloves." He finished off his beer. "I don't want to talk anymore." Maybe rolling around naked with Amy would make him feel better.

While a CD played, they climbed in back and began making out. Eric was surprised at how fast he forgot about everything. They started breathing hard and the windows fogged over.

"I gotta pee," Amy announced in the darkness.

"Go ahead." He sat up and reached into the sack for another beer.

"Aren't you coming with me?"

He popped the top. "Nobody else here. Just go behind the van."

She always wanted him to go with her and stand guard to make sure somebody didn't surprise her in the middle of a peeing session. One time she'd squatted in front of a bunch of cars and somebody turned on his headlights.

Amy was completely uninhibited when it came to her body, but she still hadn't liked getting caught with her butt hanging out. Wasn't cool, and everybody she knew was concerned with being cool.

"Somebody might pull up," she said.

Eric put his beer in the holder. "Okay, I'll come." He hadn't meant to sound so annoyed.

"Forget it. I'll go by myself." She started to step from the van, then paused. "Did you hear that?"

"What?"

"Some weird sound."

She turned down the stereo until they were surrounded by nothing but the trilling of cicadas.

"I don't hear anything," Eric said.

"It was probably a cat. Or my imagination. You know how I am."

Amy had a history of seeing and hearing things that weren't there. Like the time she swore she'd seen the guy from Tora! Tora! Torrance! in the school cafeteria, claiming he'd ordered a veggie burger and fries. Or the time she'd gotten to shake hands with the president of the United States, and thought he'd said, "Like to fuck you." Everybody else heard, "Good luck to you," because she'd been about to compete in a state swimming competition.

Amy ducked from the van, slamming the door behind her. Eric waited a few seconds, listening to her crashing through the brush before deciding to grab the keys from the ignition and go after her.

He followed the sound of snapping twigs, making his way around broken tombstones ensnarled by vines and roots and deep grass.

"Amy?"

He could hear her moving to his right.

He took a few steps that direction, just beyond the haze cast by the parking lights, unzipped his pants, and peed. He was rezipping when his ears picked up a muffled sound that seemed to come from inside his own head. He froze, ears straining, the hairs on his neck standing up.

"Amy?"

Another noise. This one directly below him.

Something pattered across the toe of his sneaker.

What the hell? Was Amy hiding, tossing dirt at him?

Something touched his ankle.

It felt suspiciously like a hand.

"Ha-ha. Very funny."

She was trying to get him back for not immediately volunteering to baby-sit while she peed.

Branches snapped and he looked toward a faint circle of light to see Amy walking toward him. "Did you say something?" she asked.

Eric's jaw dropped and terror rapid-rushed through his body, weakening his muscles, making it impossible to breathe or move.

It seemed years later that he was finally able to bend his neck to look down.

A clawed hand was reaching out of the ground, its fingers wrapped around his shoe.

Jordan Kemp had been buried alive. Swaddled in a heavy wool blanket, he was dragged through heavy brush.

He couldn't move, couldn't speak. Trapped in his own body.

He'd been deposited in a low area like a ditch. He could smell the damp earth, the wet leaves.

Was he dead?

He'd heard the sound of a shovel striking the ground, slicing through soil. Heard heavy breathing. A clump of earth hit him in the face. That was followed by another and another.

Then silence.

Dead silence.

Inside his head, he cried and screamed.

Nobody heard.

Nobody came.

His mind drifted. Sometimes it shut off completely.

Then a sound came to him. Like somebody moving around.

He didn't want to die like this. Didn't want his mother to find out he'd become a prostitute. He could see it in the papers.

Body of male prostitute found in shallow grave.

They would think he got what he deserved. *He* would think he got what he deserved.

Once more he tried to move, tried to make a sound. Air left his lungs and rushed past his lips. He let out a faint whimper.

He tried again.

Louder. Had to be louder.

He moved a finger. Just a twitch. Then another.

Like being reborn.

Sensation gradually seeped into his body. He slowly became aware of his arms, his legs. Of the weight of the soil against his chest.

He heard a muffled snapping, a crackling, not far from his head. Was someone taking a piss? Because that's sure as hell what it sounded like.

Wasn't that a zipper?

If he could only cry out, only see—

His hand.

It was the only thing he could move. He struggled to lift it until it broke through the loose soil. Until he felt something.

A shoe.

An ankle.

A person!

He heard a shout, followed by the sound of running feet. Not moving toward him, but away.

No! he cried out in his mind. *Don't go!*

He fought the heaviness, rocking left and right, trying to make more room.

Air.

Needed air.

The muscles in his neck tightened. In one swift movement, he strained upward, his head breaking through the soil. Like a swimmer, he surfaced and gasped, sucking dirt into his mouth, his lungs.

He gagged. He coughed. Sitting up, he pulled his arms free, then his legs.

Naked.

Cold.

He grabbed the blanket and wound it around himself. His body began to tremble, to come alive.

Music.

He heard music.

Somehow he shoved himself upright, then stiffly shuffled in the direction of the sound.

Couldn't feel his feet.

Couldn't see.

He fell down. He got back up.

Follow the music.

The music would save him.

His legs shook. He felt dizzy and sick. Even though he was free of the grave, an overwhelming sensation of impending doom washed over him.

He was going to die. He *was* dying. Right now. His body was shutting down, giving up.

Follow the music.

Hurry. Follow the music.

He stumbled into a cleared area. He stood there swaying, trying to see where the sound was coming from, but everything was out of focus.

The music stopped.

Not much time left. You'd better haul ass.

He ran.

Or at least he thought he was running. Prancing along, stumbling, trying to hurry before he fell again. Because if that happened, he wouldn't be able to get back up. That would be it. Last call for alcohol. Checkout time.

Straight. Go straight.

He zeroed in on the vehicle and flew toward it, the dark wool blanket fluttering like wings.

With one quick, forward motion he slammed into the van, smacking his forehead, his palms spread flat against the window.

A girl screamed.

He tried to cling to the glass. His legs buckled and he hugged the van as he melted to the ground.

Help me, he said, but no words came out. *Help me!*

He was pretty sure he'd died and come back to life. And now he was dying again.

How many times could a person die? he wondered. Were people like cats? Confused, he began to crawl, to drag himself back into the woods until he blacked out.

The death he'd been expecting was very near.

Chapter 8

Officer Eve Salazar was thinking that the night had been fairly quiet when the police scanner flashed and the dispatcher spit out a suspicious-person code. The location, an abandoned cemetery where kids liked to hang out, was close. Her partner, Officer Reilley, flipped on the siren and swung the car around in the middle of the deserted street, tires squealing.

Kids thought cops liked busting parties, but Eve hated it. It made her feel like such a hypocrite.

Two miles later, Reilley executed a sharp right turn, leaving the blacktop behind. He barely slowed as the car bounced roughly over a narrow, rutted lane, the road eventually opening to a clearing.

Directly in front of them was a blue van.

Reilley jerked the patrol car to a stop while Eve scanned the area with the searchlight.

Silence, fog, and broken gravestones.

"This place is creepy," she said.

"Didn't you ever come to a cemetery to make out?" Reilley asked, stepping from the squad car. Eve ignored his question, called in their position, then followed, panning the clearing with her flashlight, the fog creating a glare.

"What's that?" she asked, freezing the light.

She shifted the beam up and down; the movement made the shadows jump.

"Let's check the van."

Eve shone her light through the passenger window into the front seat. Empty. She knocked on the glass. "Police. Anybody in there?"

She heard scrambling; then the door burst open and a girl of about seventeen tumbled out.

"Oh, my God! Am I glad to see you. I always hated cops, but I love you." She threw herself at Eve, hugging her tightly. "I love you!"

A blond-haired boy fell out behind her.

Both kids began babbling at once, trying to tell them what had happened.

"Somebody grabbed me," the boy said, his chest rising and falling, his words rapid-fire. "We ran back to the van and called the cops."

As the story progressed, it became more ridiculous. Eve began to think the kids were victims of a practical joke. She looked up to see Reilley standing with a hand pressed to his mouth, trying not to laugh.

So much better than finding somebody dead, Eve thought. Give her a practical joke any day.

"Then this guy in a black cape—" the boy said, gesturing wildly. "He comes swooping out of the woods and slams into the van. Just throws himself at the van. Attacks it. Isn't that right, Amy? He attacked it, didn't he?"

"Yeah. He came outta nowhere. He was flying."

"And I couldn't find the van keys." The boy reached

in his pocket, pulled out a set of keys, and stared at them. "They weren't there before."

Reilley turned his back to them.

Don't laugh, Eve prayed. If she as much as heard a smirk coming from him, she'd lose it. The kids were scared to death. They didn't need adults laughing in their faces.

"Where did he hit?" Eve asked, moving toward the van.

"On the passenger side. Near the door."

Eve ran the flashlight beam over the indicated area. "It's dented," she said with surprise.

Reilley turned back around to join them. "Is that blood?" He pointed to a dark smear.

Eve leaned close. "Maybe. Or makeup."

"Makeup?" the girl asked. "What do you mean, makeup?"

Reilley let out an exasperated sigh. "Somebody's playing a trick on you." He was growing tired of the situation.

"This was no joke," the boy insisted. "If you think it's a joke, why don't you find the guy? He ran off that way. Into those trees."

The kid was cocky. Reilley wasn't used to being challenged like that. Before he had a chance to jump all over him, Eve nodded. "Good idea." She began moving in the direction he'd pointed, her flashlight trained on the path before her. She heard Reilley following behind.

Poor kids.

She stopped abruptly, panning her light across the ground. Reilley ran into her, grabbing her by the waist. "You never answered me about making out in a place like this," he said, his breath against her neck. His hand moved up to her breast.

They'd been dating for two months, but she disapproved of sexual contact on the job. She knocked his hand away. "Look, Romeo."

"Reilley. Name's Reilley."

Directly in front of her, in the glow cast by her flashlight, was a dark heap.

Something left by the merry pranksters? Eve wondered. A blanket arranged to suggest the shape of a person? Or was there actually someone under it?

The air was wet. She could feel the dampness on her face.

Without hesitation, Reilley stepped around her and approached the heap. Eve remained where she was and reached for her gun, releasing the snap on the leather case. "Careful," she warned.

One of these days he was going to jump into a situation too quickly and wouldn't live to tell about it.

Reilley touched the shape with one booted foot. He gave it a nudge. Eve could see it was heavy and solid. "A body?" she asked.

In all of her years as a cop, she'd never gotten sick, but now a surge of nausea swept through her.

To her shame, she believed in ghosts. She'd seen ghosts, and she didn't like them. Not a damn bit.

This is a spooky place.

Her heart began to hammer, and she felt twelve years old again, sneaking into an abandoned house that was supposed to be haunted. She'd come face-to-face with the ghost of a young woman who'd killed herself after being forced to marry a man old enough to be her grandfather.

Eve wanted to call for assistance, but she didn't have any reason for such action other than an irrational fear of the unknown.

Reilley crouched near the pile. Eve pulled her gun, but didn't release the safety.

Reilley tugged at one corner of the mud-caked blanket to finally expose a bloody, smudged face.

The stench of death hit her.

No ghost.

"Whew," Reilley said, recoiling.

A moment later, he forced himself to lean forward again. He examined the body in silence, then finally let out a frustrated sigh and rocked back, sitting on the heels of his boots, one arm dangling over a bent knee.

"Dead?" Eve asked, even though her nose had already supplied her with the answer to that question.

"Yep. Better call Homicide."

"Don't touch anything."

"I know, I know."

She radioed the dispatcher with her shoulder mike.

"How old, do you think?" she asked once she'd finished the transmission.

"Just a kid. Not over nineteen or twenty."

Reilley's voice was sad as he continued to consider the body in front of him. It was times like these, when he allowed her to see his sensitive side, that Eve could almost imagine loving the guy. Almost.

"Jesus!" Reilley dropped his flashlight and scrambled backward, landing on his ass.

"What?"

"His eyes. Weren't they closed a minute ago?"

She trained her light on the muddy face. Eyes that had been closed were now wide open.

Something woke him.

Jordan Kemp felt cool air against his skin. Even though his eyes were closed, he could sense a light shining in his face. Was that the tunnel everybody always talked about? Would there be dead relatives waiting for him on the other side? Relatives he'd always hated?

He wanted to explain that the prostitution thing had started out as something temporary. Quick money so he could get his life on track. But once he'd started living that kind of lifestyle, he couldn't go back because he was already tainted. And truthfully, he hadn't wanted to go back, because prostitution had become his reality.

But he didn't want to go to hell for it. If he'd known Death was going to come knocking so soon, he would have been good.

"Yep," interrupted the voice of a man. "Better call Homicide." That was followed by, "Just a kid." The guy sounded sad.

Not dead. Couldn't they see he wasn't dead? Not yet.

Hafta tell 'em. Hafta let 'em know.

People always said he was bullheaded. That he could levitate if he ever set his mind to it. He didn't make himself levitate, but after a bout of skull-exploding concentration he managed to open his eyes.

That's when all hell broke loose.

"Radio the paramedics," the man shouted.

Too late, Jordan would have said if speech had been possible.

Too fucking late.

The passenger-side tire dipped into a rut, and the steering wheel was wrenched from Elise's hands as she maneuvered her car along the overgrown road leading to the abandoned cemetery. Beside her, Gould let out a curse as his head smacked the window.

"Sorry," Elise said.

Inside the wrought-iron cemetery gates, Elise pulled to a stop. Through silhouetted live oaks and draperies of dangling Spanish moss, people moved in front of headlights, creating beams of diffusion. A low-lying fog shifted and swirled like a staged special effect while police cars parked erratically and an ambulance waited, light flashing, doors open. Yellow crime scene tape wrapped around trees and cemetery statuary.

She and Gould were met by one of the first officers on the scene. "Paramedics pronounced the victim dead," Officer Eve Salazar told them, hand resting on her belt. "They worked for ten minutes, but weren't able to revive him."

"Where's the body?" Elise asked.

"Waiting for the ME." She jerked her thumb behind her. "Due to the circumstances, the crime scene's been compromised."

"What about the kids? We're going to need to get their statements."

"Taken down to the police station. They were pretty upset, and we thought it would be better for them to wait there."

Elise nodded. She wouldn't have wanted Audrey to

remain at the scene any longer than absolutely necessary.

What had at first appeared to be a practical joke had turned into a homicide, with two innocent kids inadvertently stumbling across a body that was still alive.

Not an unusual scenario. Sometimes victims of crime were dumped because they were thought to be dead. And it wasn't all that strange for kids to come across bodies, since the same kind of seclusion appealed to both teenagers and killers.

Elise and Gould followed a path that had already been tagged with yellow markers as Officer Salazar led them to the body. A small group stood around it, the area illuminated by high-powered lights run by small generators. Elise recognized Abe Chilton, head crime scene investigator.

"Smells like he's been dead a few days rather than a few minutes," Elise said, hand to her nose. She turned to Salazar's partner. "Are you sure the victim was alive when you found him?"

"He opened his eyes," Officer Reilley insisted.

"Could that have been a postmortem muscular response?" Gould wondered aloud.

"The guy was alive," Reilley insisted.

"What about the site where the teenager was grabbed?" Elise asked.

They doubled back, then veered off to follow another path lined with markers.

"This is the place." The glow of Salazar's flashlight revealed a shallow grave. "Kid said a hand came out of the ground."

An indentation revealed where the body had been.

Nearby stood an unopened bottle of whiskey. Beside it, a silver dollar.

"Gifts for the dead," Elise commented. "Or in this case, the undead."

"A killer who leaves presents?" Gould asked.

"So the victim doesn't come back and haunt him."

"Nice." Gould trained his flashlight away from the disturbed earth. "Drag marks."

"It starts at the water's edge," Officer Salazar told them. "Musta come by boat."

"Any evidence?" Gould asked.

"So far, a couple of footprints." Salazar shrugged. "Maybe a man's nine or ten."

"There's some weird shit going on in this city," Reilley said. "Some really weird shit."

Gould nodded. "Weird shit happens."

Abe Chilton and some of his team appeared out of the darkness. "I want you to see this." Chilton raised his flashlight, pointing the beam at a nearby tree. Nailed to the trunk five feet from the ground was a small twisted figure.

"Mandrake root," Elise said. The human-shaped root was said to scream when pulled from the ground.

"Nightshade?" Gould asked.

"One and the same."

While Chilton kept his flashlight beam directed on the tree trunk, Elise continued to visually examine the small figure. It was wrapped in brown paper, probably torn from a grocery sack.

Root work. "This might reveal our victim's identity," Elise said.

Somebody handed her a pair of latex gloves. She

snapped them on, then stepped closer. Others stepped back.

Elise removed the root from the rusty nail, then unrolled the paper to reveal a name written over and over in black ink.

Seven times seven. The root worker knew his or her stuff.

"Jordan Kemp," Elise said. "Somebody call that in."

Two minutes later, they had a report. "Jordan Harold Kemp," Officer Salazar reported. "White male. Age twenty-one."

"Any record?" Elise asked.

"Arrested twice for prostitution."

"Should have a print on file, then."

Officer Salazar shot a worried look from Elise to the root she cradled in her palm. "I don't like the looks of that," she said nervously.

"It won't hurt you," Elise assured her. "It has nothing to do with you."

People often got curses, spells, and root work confused. "See this?" Elise pointed to a leaf that had been glued to the body of the root. "It's acacia. Ancient Egyptians made funeral wreaths out of acacia leaves."

"So it's a tribute," Gould said.

It was amazing how quickly Elise's years of study came rushing back. As if the knowledge had always been there. As if she hadn't spent over a decade trying to forget everything she'd ever learned.

"A single herb can be used for a lot of different things, in a lot of different ways," Elise said. "It all depends on how it's handled and what it's with."

"And acacia with nightshade . . . or mandrake root . . . ?" Gould prodded.

With a rotting corpse just yards away and an ancient spell in the palm of her hand, Elise suddenly felt bathed in certainty. "That particular combination," she explained, "is used to resurrect the dead."

Chapter 9

Audrey gripped the metal bat and dug her cleats into the loose soil. Behind her, the catcher kept up a stream of chatter that was supposed to make her miss the ball.

It was the bottom of the eighth inning, and the catcher had been taunting everybody throughout the game. Audrey's coach didn't let them use negative chatter, so it was really hard to take when the team they were playing could say anything they wanted.

Not fair!

"Aren't those your mommies on the bleachers?" the catcher teased in a baby voice. "Your two mommies?"

Audrey glanced over to where Elise and her stepmother, Vivian, sat with Audrey's baby brothers. Each woman held a baby. The twins were wearing the matching blue hats Audrey had gotten at the mall.

Audrey loved her little brothers. They got a kick out of her too. She could act goofy and make them laugh in stereo until tears streamed down their fat little cheeks.

Audrey kept her eye on the pitcher and moved out

of the batter's box. She took a few practice swings, then stepped back up to the plate.

In the outfield, the opposing team chanted, "Batter, batter, batter . . ."

"Swing."

Audrey swung.

"Strike!"

Once you missed a ball, the pitcher liked to keep the balls coming, one after the other, so you didn't have time to pull yourself together. Right now she was standing sideways, concentrating on her next release.

"Choke up on that bat," Audrey's coach instructed.

The catcher kept up her taunts in a high-pitched singsong. From the outfield came, "Batter, batter, batter . . ."

"Swing!"

The bat connected solidly.

Audrey didn't wait to see where the ball was heading. She dropped the bat and ran for first, her cleats digging into the ground.

The ball moved with rocket speed—a line drive between third base and shortstop, about a foot above the ground. The outfielder made a dive and missed.

Elise didn't know much about softball, but she knew a good hit when she saw one. She started to jump to her feet, then remembered the baby. She clung to Tyler with one arm, while cupping her free hand and shouting as Audrey rounded first, then second.

Home run? Was it going to be a home run?

Two outfielders scrambled for the ball, one of them

finally sending it infield to the pitcher just as Audrey tagged third.

Stop! Stay there! Elise thought.

Audrey didn't hesitate. Didn't even think about playing it safe. She flew for home. The pitcher shot the ball to the catcher.

Beside Elise, Vivian shouted, "Slide! Slide!"

Audrey slid. Riding into home on her hip and thigh, crashing into the plate just as the ball smacked the catcher's mitt, enveloping the players in a cloud of dust.

Had the catcher fumbled?

Had she dropped the ball?

Elise stared at the umpire, her heart in her throat.

After what seemed the longest pause in softball history, he shouted and gestured wildly. "Safe!"

The winning run.

Game over.

Elise cheered madly. Beside her, Vivian joined in.

The noise frightened the twins; they began to bawl, their little mouths wide, faces red.

Elise bounced her knee. "Don't cry, sweetie."

That didn't help, because Tyler was afraid of her.

"Have you ever seen anybody slide like that?" Elise asked over his head.

"Not a girl."

Both women laughed.

The ball teams lined up for the traditional high-five and "Good game" pass.

On the bleachers, people gathered up their belongings and climbed down until it was just Elise, Vivian, and the crying babies.

"She hates me," Elise said, watching her daughter move through the line of girls.

Vivian dug into her blue diaper bag and produced two teething crackers, which she handed to the boys. Like a flipped switch, they both quit sobbing and took the treat. "Who?"

"Audrey."

Vivian twisted around to stare at Elise. "What are you talking about?"

"She doesn't want to visit anymore. Not that she ever wanted to visit much anyway."

"It's not you," Vivian reassured her. "She's at that age when friends are so important. She wants to be near them."

"She's slipping away."

So many songs had been written about how quickly kids grew up, and how parents had to be there or miss out. Those songs may have been clichés, but they were true.

It had all started gradually.

When Audrey was a baby and Thomas had remarried, it seemed logical for Audrey to spend her days with Vivian rather than a baby-sitter. And when Elise was working odd hours—which was most of the time—Audrey stayed with Thomas and Vivian. They loved her every bit as much as Elise did, which made it easier for Elise to sleep at night and do a good job during the day, knowing Audrey was safe and loved and well cared for.

When it came time for Audrey to begin school, it seemed practical for Audrey to go to school near Thomas and Vivian. Schools were better and less dangerous in the suburbs, and if Elise was working late, she didn't need to worry about Audrey.

Even before the twins came along, Thomas, Audrey,

and Vivian had been a real family with a traditional life. And they had a *schedule*. A routine to their days that rarely varied. That was important. Something a child needed.

Sometimes Elise felt tainted. Tainted by her past. Tainted by her job.

Vivian was solid. Stable.

People thought it strange that she and Elise were friends, but to Elise it had always seemed natural. There had never been any hostility in the divorce, only a realization that she and Thomas couldn't have been more wrong for each other.

Audrey looked in their direction and waved.

Elise and Vivian waved back.

The mob broke apart and Audrey ran toward the bleachers in her red-and-white uniform with matching striped socks. Along one side, from waist to ankle, was dirt-stained evidence of her slide.

She put down her ball glove and held out her hands to Tyler. He began squealing in delight, arms outstretched.

"Got him?" Elise asked.

Audrey kept her eyes locked on her little brother. "Yep," she said with a beautiful smile. She tucked Tyler firmly against her. He immediately grabbed her hair with a gummy, cookie-encrusted fist.

"Oh, my God!" Audrey said. "He is *so gross*! He's getting my hair full of gross stuff!"

Elise watched as her daughter and Vivian looked at each other and began laughing hysterically.

The family life Audrey had with Thomas and Vivian was good. She was happy. But for Elise, the price of that happiness may have been the loss of her daughter.

Chapter 10

"As your psychiatrist, I have to ask—are you thinking of harming yourself?"

"Of course not."

"Are you thinking of harming anyone else?"

With the phone to his ear, David Gould stared at the cat for a long time. Beth's cat.

"David?" his psychiatrist asked in her calm voice. "David? Are you still there?"

"No. I mean yes—I'm here. And no, I'm not thinking of harming anyone else."

Getting off drugs cold turkey—no matter that they were pharmaceutical—had seemed like a good idea on Friday, not long after Elise had brought up his lack of engagement. Today was Sunday. Well, actually Monday, since it was long past midnight, and David was crawling out of his skin.

Stopping the antidepressants was doing a strange number on his head.

In all the time he'd been taking them, he hadn't experienced a single high or low. He hadn't experienced anger, or joy, or sorrow. He wasn't even sure he could

say he existed. But now . . . now all that was changing. Now he was AWAKE, with capital letters. Awake
after almost two years of being dead.

*But you wanted to be dead. Didn't you even ask the
cops to kill you? To put you out of your misery? To
stop the pain?*

Agony rushed up his throat, threatening to choke him.

He couldn't deal with the memories now. One thing
at a time.

Control. Control. Control.

It was an FBI agent's mantra. It was *his* mantra.

This was like a rebirth. A baptism.

Emotions he'd forgotten existed pulsed through
him. Pain. Anger. Sorrow.

Wonderful emotions. Overwhelming emotions. Too
many at once. Too intense. Let some of it in, but not all
of it. Slam that door. He couldn't handle it all. Not yet.

"Is there anyone in Savannah you can call?" Dr.
Fisher asked.

He hadn't switched psychiatrists when he'd moved
to Savannah because he hadn't wanted the people he
worked with to know he was seeing a shrink—something that had turned into an issue in Ohio. As soon as
coworkers had become aware of his problem, things
changed and they began to second-guess him. Not a
safe situation for anyone involved. When he realized
what was going on, he decided to start over somewhere new. A clean slate.

"Your partner, perhaps?"

His partner? "Out of the question."

What would he say to Elise? Hey, I'm flipping out
and wondered if you could come over and hold my
hand?

"You've been working with her for three months. Surely it wouldn't be out of line to give her a call."

Three months. Yeah, normally you would kind of know somebody by then. "I've been a little . . . disconnected."

David was sitting on the floor of the combination living room/kitchen, back to the wall, phone balanced on one thigh.

He noticed that his leg was jiggling.

He made it stop.

The room was dark—the only light he'd turned on was the one above the stove. "Believe me, calling my partner is out of the question."

What was that smell? Like wood that had been soaked in urine for twenty years. And sick, fevered bodies.

Yellow fever.

It's my apartment. My fucking apartment.

No wonder his sister had been so appalled.

Sorry, Sis.

His apartment smelled like a nursing home and he hadn't even known it.

His leg was jiggling again.

"Are you still on your meds? Both the Paxil and Valium?"

"I may have missed a few doses."

"You can't do that."

"Actually . . . I'm thinking of quitting them both completely."

"David, that's not a good idea. You've been through a very traumatic event."

"It's been almost two years."

"That's not much time when dealing with something of this magnitude."

Why had he called her? He knew what the problem
was. And he knew how *she'd* fix it. But he was tired
of being a lobotomized idiot. If the idea behind the
cocktail she'd prescribed was to feel nothing, then it
had certainly done the trick.

Then she said the *C* word. And the *T* word.

"It's not good to quit cold turkey. There have been
some serious problems with patients who weren't
stepped down gradually."

Yep. David had heard about them. Not only heard, but
seen. Some people went nuts. They even killed. Antidepressants were being found in the bloodstreams of
murderers. Was it because they were the ones who
needed help, or did the drugs finally establish an unreal-
ity that allowed them to move past the thought, the fantasy stage, to take a step they would normally not have
taken?

He'd been prepared for some violent mood swings.
Maybe even a few crying jags he could blame on
some old movie, but not the sweating and shaking and
stomach cramps.

Not the crawling out of my fucking skin.

Not the desperate need to move, to do something,
anything.

Jiggle, jiggle, jiggle.

Chewing on his knuckle.

This is like trying to kick heroin.

Not that he personally knew what that was like, but
he'd seen *Trainspotting*, and he was expecting a baby to
start making its way across the ceiling at any moment.

"I can't sleep. I haven't slept in three days."

He couldn't wind down.

He'd already run ten miles. Should he run ten more?

"Have you been drinking? Your voice sounds slurred. You aren't supposed to drink when you're taking either of your medications."

Too late. Desperation had come knocking. "Everybody knows that, Doc."

From his position on the floor, David looked up at the kitchen counter at all of the empty beer bottles. He didn't have a lot of experience with overindulgence. He'd planned to drink only one or two beers. Just to take the edge off. After six, the edge was still there, and he was feeling like a drunk on speed.

Jiggle, jiggle.

"You've probably built up a resistance to the Valium. I'd tell you to double your dosage if I could be sure you haven't been drinking," she said.

He tasted blood and realized he'd gnawed through the skin on his knuckle. He sprang up off the floor and grabbed the bottle of tranquilizers from the counter.

Had he taken one? Or two?

He squinted at the pills inside, as if they might be able to tell him something. And how long ago? Minutes? Hours? Couldn't remember.

"David, if things get worse, go to the hospital. Do you hear me? Or call your partner. I have an idea. Why don't I call her for you? Would you like me to do that?"

"No!" Jesus! "I have a reputation to maintain." Jesus.

His laptop was in sleep mode next to the beer bottles. He touched a key and it came to life. He opened the drop-down menu and scrolled to a bookmarked Savannah Web site, spotting something he hadn't noticed before.

Savannah Legal Escort Service.

Hmm.

The picture got fuzzy.

His head suddenly felt heavy as hell.

He let the cursor hover over a small photo of a dark-haired woman, clicked to enlarge it.

The antidepressants had made him almost asexual. He'd hardly thought about sex in almost two years. Now he was feeling horny. Maybe sex would make him sleep. Used to work. Years ago.

Bracing the receiver between his shoulder and ear, he typed his address into the form on the computer screen and ordered a girl.

Just like that. With a few keystrokes.

"Isn't the Internet amazing?" he asked around a thickening tongue, fighting the impulse to drop to the floor, thinking he'd better wait until he was off the phone.

"Oh, yes," Dr. Fisher agreed. "I never dreamed we'd be able to do the things we can do with it."

David stared at the blurry face on the screen. "Me either."

Flora Martinez drove through the deserted Savannah streets, the directions she'd printed from the Internet on the seat beside her. The wipers beat quickly, but with each sweep heavy dew reappeared.

Normally she didn't take cold calls. It was dangerous, and you never knew what kind of freak or freaks you might run into. But business had been slow, and she had a lot of bills to pay, so she'd had her photo put up on the escort service's Web site.

Escort service.

They'd been taught to always call it that, no matter what. A couple of girls had actually come across some naive gentlemen who'd thought it *was* an escort service.

Rent a date.

They'd just wanted to rent an attractive girl to decorate an arm at the company party. Sad and funny. A lot of things were sad and funny.

She located the address.

Mary of the Angels.

Shit.

She pulled to the curb, dug her cell phone from her purse, and called Enrique. "You know the job I just got? You won't believe where it is." She craned her neck to look up at the four-story stone building. "Mary of the Angels."

Enrique inhaled loudly. "No way."

"I'm looking at it right now."

"Don't go in. Only a crazy person would live there."

Anybody who'd been in Savannah long enough had heard of the place. There was supposed to be a tunnel that ran from the old Candler Hospital to a nearby cemetery. Years ago, the tunnels had been used to transport yellow fever victims straight from their bed to the ground so people wouldn't freak out over the high number of deaths.

The bodies were supposedly piled in the tunnels until they could be buried under cover of darkness. She'd heard that sometimes the piles moved, either from rats rummaging through the carcasses or because someone had been pronounced dead a little prematurely.

The building was haunted. That's what people said.

Flora believed it, because she believed in ghosts

and if any place was haunted, it would be Mary of the Angels.

"Maybe he's new in town," she said into her cell phone. "Maybe nobody told him about it."

"Don't go, Flora," Enrique begged. "Come home."

She smiled. It was sweet of Enrique to worry about her.

"I'm going to check it out. If anything seems weird, I'll leave."

"Keep your phone handy."

She told him good-bye, and tucked the phone back in her purse, leaving it open for easy access.

David was the customer's name. She'd written it in her schedule book under the date.

She found his apartment number taped to the intercom system. Nearby, the heavy scent of tangled wisteria begged her to stay outside.

She pushed the button and the door buzzed. She entered and took the stairs to the correct floor.

She didn't have to knock. He was waiting for her, door ajar.

Dressed in faded jeans. Barefoot. Shirt unbuttoned, tails untucked. His hair was sticking up in every direction, as if he'd been raking his hands through it again and again.

"Don't let the cat out," he said thickly, stepping back as she entered.

She closed the door behind her, listening for any sound beyond the living room and kitchen. "Anyone else here?"

The place smelled like a litter box. But at least the guy had a cat. A guy with a cat was harmless, right?

He frowned, as if he didn't get the question or its purpose. He shook his head.

"I like to ask," she explained, dropping her purse on the counter. "If there's more than one person, I don't stay. You know what I mean?"

"That you're a one-guy woman?"

"That's right. One at a time." More than one could get ugly. More than one could get dangerous.

"You're in luck," he said. "Because I'm a one-woman man."

He was making a joke.

"You're cute," she said suspiciously.

Most of her clients were gross. They were often fat and bald, and they sweated profusely with the kind of nervous perspiration that smelled so bad. They were usually businessmen with wives and kids. She rarely got cute ones. When she did, they always wanted her to do something she didn't want to do, and she usually ended up running.

"So what's wrong with you?" she asked. Should she get the hell out of there? "What kind of weird shit you into?"

"I'm antisocial."

She laughed. A real laugh. "That's why you called me?"

"I'm not going to go to a bar and pretend to be interested in a girl just so I can have sex. I have no interest in socializing. That's all. Too much work." He waved a hand. "Too much trouble. This way there is no pretense. Nobody gets hurt."

He was okay. Just wasted. Really wasted. Barely able to stand, wasted. "Did you see our price list?" she asked.

Some of her associates played fantasy games with the customers. Flora never pretended it was anything more than what it was. A business transaction. Payment for goods received.

"We take cash or credit. No checks. Pay is by the hour. If we go as much as one minute over sixty, you pay for another full hour. Those are the rules."

"I might want you to stay all night."

"Night's almost over."

He glanced at a window, as if the news surprised him. "Until I have to leave for work, then."

She shrugged in signature prostitute lingo, then followed with the cliché, "As long as you're paying. And just so you'll know, that payment is for my visit. Sort of a consultation. The sex is free." All legal that way. Or kind of legal.

"Want something to drink?" he asked.

"How about a glass of water?"

With slow, deliberate movements, he filled a glass and handed it to her.

"I like your place," she told him.

Now it was his turn to laugh. "You're kidding, right?"

"It's creepy, and I like creepy things." She took a swallow of water and strolled around the room. "I'll bet a lot of people died in this building."

She put down the glass and pulled her white, gauzy top over her head, dropping it on the floor. "Bedroom this way?" she asked, heading down the short hall and peeking into the only other room in the apartment. It was dark, with a rectangle of light from the living room spilling on the floor. "You haven't lived here long, have you?"

"Three months."

"You need something on your walls." There was nothing but a bed with rumpled white sheets, and a dresser. "Posters or something."

He came up behind her. "What's this?" He touched a small, circular, raised area on her lower spine that was exposed by low-slung black pants.

"A mojo."

"Mojo?"

"It protects me from evil."

"Evil . . . is everywhere."

"That's why I need a mojo."

"A little scar . . . won't protect you."

"It might."

"You talk too much," he said.

"Oh, that's right." She turned in his arms. "You don't want any socialization."

She smiled at him. He smiled back.

He was so damn cute! He took her fucking breath away.

They stripped.

He had an athletic body.

Not a spare ounce of flesh.

Swimmer? Runner?

All sinewy muscles just below a smooth layer of skin.

She produced a condom.

He wasn't too drunk to put it on.

He cupped her waist with his hands. He tasted her breasts.

She dug her fingers into his damp arms, and lifted herself closer.

He smelled like beer and soap.

He was intense. Alive. Electric.

"Lie back on the bed," he said softly, gently, as if he cared about her.

She tumbled backward, and suddenly imagined that she wasn't a whore, and that they'd met somewhere else. At the office. No, jogging through Forsyth Park. They saw each other every day. They always smiled and said hello. One day he asked if she'd care to join him for sweet tea in a little nearby café. A week later, dinner.

"I'll bet somebody died in this room," she whispered against his jaw. "Maybe in this very bed."

"You're weird."

"Thank you."

"I'm dying right now."

They fell in love.

After the jogging and the café and the dinner, they fell in love.

She was a nurse.

No, an art student at SCAD. He was—

He slipped inside her.

She had a moment to marvel at the sensation. Because she was a young art student. Not a virgin, but not very knowledgeable when it came to men and sex.

"You're shaking," she said. His body was trembling.

"I haven't had sex in a long time."

"How long?"

"I don't know."

"A couple of weeks?" she guessed.

"Years. It's been years."

Years. "Oh, sweetie." His confession made her feel special, made her feel in some way . . . brand-new.

She wrapped her arms around him, sheltering him, lifting herself to meet his strokes. She was a young art student; he was her dark, mysterious lover.

Chapter 11

Gould was late.

Elise sat at her desk in Police Headquarters, reading a clipping about the first misdiagnosed death that had also ended up at the morgue. Name, Samuel Winslow. The subject had lived only a few hours after being found. In the article, the EMT said the body was lifeless and that he'd detected a strong odor, like decomposing flesh.

> "Eyes were fixed," he said. "The skin on the arms was purple due to lack of blood circulation. I checked for a pulse in the carotid artery, but couldn't detect anything. The subject presented all the signs of death, and any medical professional in my position would have made the same presumptive diagnosis," the EMT said in his defense.

Her phone rang. It turned out to be Seth West, a coworker of Truman Harrison's—one of the last people on her interview list.

"Truman and I ate fast food the day he died—or the day we thought he died," Mr. West told her. "He had a hamburger, fries, and a soda."

"Any fish?" Elise asked. "Or seafood of any kind?"

"Nope."

After a few brief follow-up questions, Elise thanked him and disconnected.

No seafood. But that didn't mean he hadn't eaten any that day. He just hadn't eaten any in front of Seth West.

A sound in the hallway got her attention. David Gould came tumbling into the room, slamming the door behind him. Without looking left or right, he dived for his swivel chair and collapsed. "Oh, fuck." He spun around, crossed his arms on the desk, and dropped his head on them.

His hair was sticking up and bent. He reeked of alcohol.

He'd dressed himself, but not very well. His shirt-tail hung from below his jacket, and Elise had noticed several buttons undone as he'd flown past.

Wow.

She'd wanted him to loosen up, but this wasn't what she'd had in mind.

"I spent last night at a softball game," she said, directing her words at the back of his head. "How did you spend your evening?"

"Something very similar," he mumbled, rolling his forehead back and forth against his arm.

"I'm sure."

"My head. My fucking head."

"You smell like you took a bath in beer."

He pulled open his jacket and took a whiff. "I don't smell anything."

"Take my word for it. You stink."

"All right, then."

She pulled a bottle of water from her bag, opened it, and placed it on the desk in front of him. "Why didn't you stay home? And now that you're here, why don't you go back?"

"I'll be okay." He straightened, eyed the bottle of water, then reached for it with a trembling hand.

Now that he was upright, she could see he hadn't shaved. And Gould was one of those guys who needed to shave twice a day.

"Go home," she cautioned. "Before somebody sees you."

He lifted the water to his mouth, quickly draining the entire bottle. "I said I'll be okay." He stood and buttoned his shirt, tucked in the tails. Then he tried to smooth down his hair. "There." He tugged at his jacket. "Fresh as a daisy."

"Only if a daisy smelled like Jack Daniel's and was in need of a shave."

"Are you making fun of me?"

His collar was twisted. She stood and adjusted it. "I'm only trying to tell you that you aren't exactly a favorite around here, and Major Hoffman might just be looking for a reason to send you on your way. Do you have an electric razor with you?"

He ran a hand across his jaw. It sounded like sandpaper. "A guy shouldn't be penalized because he doesn't kiss ass."

He seemed a little hurt to find he was regarded with a lack of favor within the department.

"I can't be telling you something you don't already know," she said, sitting back down and opening desk drawers until she found a bottle of Tylenol. She held it within his line of vision.

He shook his head.

She dropped the Tylenol and shut the drawer. Sighing, she decided that as long as he wanted to act like he could be productive, she might as well discuss the case. "I've talked with Harrison's coworkers and all of them say they never saw him eat fish the day he collapsed."

She grabbed a pen and leaned back in her chair. "So, what I've been wondering is if there's a connection between the body that showed up in the cemetery last night, Truman Harrison, and Samuel Winslow, the misdiagnosed death of three weeks ago."

Gould perched himself on the corner of his desk. He wasn't wearing socks. "Maybe," he said. "Maybe not. It could all just be coincidence. A weird cluster of events."

Elise got on the phone and ordered a crime scene team to inspect and collect possible evidence at Mr. Harrison's home and workplace. His locker. Vehicles. Wherever he spent time.

As soon as she hung up, her phone rang.

John Casper.

"You know the guy who came in last night? Jordan Kemp?" he asked. "I've found something you might be interested in. Can you stop by?"

"Be there in thirty minutes." She disconnected. "Feel up to formaldehyde fumes and corpses?" she asked Gould. The morgue could be tough even on a good day.

"Formaldehyde and corpses?" He gave her a weak smile. "Two of my favorite things."

The morgue was located in a new building on the outskirts of town, next to the crime lab. Not handy for police detectives, but they'd needed the ground and space.

Elise and Gould followed Casper to the walk-in cooler, past several sheet-covered forms, to the body of Jordan Kemp.

"I wanted you to see this." Casper uncovered the body, which had been left facedown.

Elise leaned closer. On the lower spine, just above the tailbone, was a raised circle slightly bigger than a silver dollar.

"Teflon body art," Casper explained. "I was thinking it might be a gang symbol."

"It's not a gang symbol," Elise said, straightening. "Have you ever heard of Black Tupelo?"

"Isn't that a bar?"

"Among other things. A bar. Massage parlor. Plus a front for prostitution. It's located downtown, near the river."

"And what does this have to do with body art?" Casper asked.

"Black Tupelo belongs to a Gullah woman named Strata Luna."

"I've definitely heard of her," Casper said.

"This is the trunk of the tupelo tree," Elise explained, pointing. "And these three lines are branches. It's a very simple, effective design actually."

"You mean to tell me she *brands* her prostitutes?" Casper asked in a horrified voice. "Like cattle?"

"It's a mojo," Gould said.

"Mojo?" Elise frowned up at him. How did he know about mojoes?

He was staring at the emblem, looking queasy again.

"Who told you that?" she asked.

He shrugged. "Just something I heard somewhere."

"I don't know about a mojo, but it's definitely a *logo*."

Casper pulled up the sheet, covering the body. "That's not all. There's something else you need to know. We got the lab work back and you're never going to guess what we found."

Elise was afraid she could, but allowed Casper his moment.

"TTX," Casper said.

That news was still settling when Elise's phone rang.

It was Major Hoffman. "Truman Harrison is dead," she said. "For real this time."

Chapter 12

Enrique and Flora watched as Strata Luna nailed a small cross made of wooden Popsicle sticks to the trunk of a tree. On the double headstone that marked her daughters' graves, she poured the loose incense she used to communicate with the dead. After a brief sizzle and flame, the pungent odor of saltpeter and herbs filled the gathering darkness.

It was late. After closing time. The caretaker of Bonaventure Cemetery had unlocked the gate so Strata Luna could visit the graves in private.

Enrique nudged Flora with his elbow. "Come on," he whispered.

They turned and walked away from the woman cloaked in black.

In all the times Enrique had been coming to the cemetery with Strata Luna, he'd never witnessed anything weird—and didn't want to. The dead could stay dead as far as he was concerned. He once thought he'd seen someone return from the grave—and his heart had nearly popped through his chest. But then he discovered the person had never really been dead in the first place.

He hated the dead. But the undead . . . ?

Whole different story.

Strata Luna was practically a mother to Flora. To Enrique, quite a bit more . . .

He suspected Flora knew he sometimes joined Strata Luna in her bed. Not that the woman in black cared much for him. He doubted she'd ever really cared for any man except the root doctor, Jackson Sweet. No, Enrique was just performing a service.

He wasn't complaining.

Strata Luna thought he was somebody she could teach and mold. Thought she had him under her control, but she was mistaken. Nobody controlled Enrique Xavier.

There were things about him she didn't know. Things Flora didn't know. He had a life outside Black Tupelo and Strata Luna. A secret life.

"I'm cold," Flora whispered. "Mosquitoes are biting me."

Enrique rubbed her bare arm, causing friction. "You're the one who wanted to come," he reminded her.

Unlike Enrique, Flora was drawn to death. She liked to explore cemeteries, and she'd been on every single Savannah ghost tour more than once.

"Don't give me that shit, Enrique. You wanted me here."

He laughed—a little nervously.

It was true. He didn't like roaming around in the cemetery by himself while Strata Luna practiced her communion with the dead.

Flora tugged on his shirt. "Let's go see Gracie."

Darkness had fallen like a shroud, and her face was

hardly more than a blur. He pivoted and walked in the opposite direction. "No way, man. I ain't gonna go see Gracie."

"Come on," she pleaded in a voice that always weakened him. "I want to see her."

Gracie was famous. She'd died over a hundred years ago, when she was six. There was a life-size statue of her somewhere. To the left? Right? He always got all turned around in Bonaventure.

A lot of people claimed to have seen little Gracie wandering around the cemetery, which was one of the reasons Enrique had asked Flora to come along. If he ran into Gracie, he didn't want to be alone.

"Don't talk about her," he whispered. "She'll hear and you'll draw her to us." And with Strata Luna over there, holding the door between this world and the next wide open, no telling who might show up.

Flora scampered away. "Gracie!" she called. "Oh, Gracie!"

Enrique ran and grabbed her, putting a hand over her mouth.

They'd known each other for years, and were like brother and sister. "*Shut up!*" he hissed against her cheek. Her hair smelled like flowers.

Flora pried his hand away. "Shhh. Listen," she said, laughter still in her voice. "Did you hear that?"

"What?"

"Something moving."

Enrique straightened in the thick darkness, his eyes and ears straining. Up high, against the sky, he could make out dark curtains of dangling Spanish moss. Lighter objects near the ground were tombstones and cemetery statues.

He hoped none were Gracie.

Damn Flora.

He heard a sound in the distance that made the hair on his scalp stand up and his heart begin to hammer.

Was that a little kid? Talking? Laughing?

That's what it had sounded like. A little kid.

Oh, man.

What was he doing here?

"Don't you two have any respect for the dead?" came Strata Luna's angry voice out of the darkness, no footsteps to announce her arrival. "Fighting and laughing and carrying on. You should be ashamed."

Guilty, they both fell as silent and sober as chastised children.

"Let's go back to the car," Strata Luna said. "And hope you haven't caused my calling-up-the-dead spell to go bad and curse us all."

Chapter 13

The morning after the visit to the morgue, Elise sat across from Major Hoffman's desk while Gould perched in a nearby chair.

"I could use more manpower," Elise said. She didn't want her request to imply that Gould wasn't holding up his end, but there were times she felt as if she were trying to solve the case on her own.

"Jordan Kemp's death could still be drug-related and self-induced," Hoffman said in her soft, Southern voice. "And so far, no connection has been made to Harrison. Until we have that connection, it's going to be hard to justify pulling people off other cases—but I'll see what I can do. At least temporarily."

"Thanks." Elise wasn't surprised. Dead prostitutes weren't a priority. Not the major's fault. It was just the way things worked.

"What about the other body that woke up in the morgue?" Major Hoffman used a spoon to scrape the last remnants of yogurt from a plastic container. Her nails were long and red; her makeup was flawless. "Samuel Winslow?"

Major Hoffman was a black woman in a position predominantly held by men. For years, the city government had ignored Savannah's crime problem. When Hoffman came along as head of Criminal Investigation, she immediately put foot patrols in downtown parks and tourist areas, creating a visual presence. She was also working on creative ways to address the racial tension within the city.

"The body was cremated, and there were no indepth tests run after the initial autopsy," Elise said. "The lab work showed he was a heavy drug user, with large quantities of heroin in his bloodstream, along with a trace amount of morphine. At the time, it seemed to be a pretty straightforward misdiagnosed drug overdose."

"Understandable given the circumstances."

"One other thing." Elise pulled a Polaroid photo from her bag and slid it across the desk. "This artwork was on the body of Jordan Kemp."

Major Hoffman examined the photo, then passed it back. "Black Tupelo."

"Right."

"Did the first prostitute have this kind of marking?"

"No. And no sign that it may have been removed."

"I've scheduled a press conference for an hour from now. Is this Black Tupelo information something we want released yet? What do you think, Detective Gould? You've been awfully quiet."

He shifted in his chair. "At this point, I think we should keep it to ourselves until we have more to go on."

"I agree. What else do you have on your agenda?"

"We're paying a surprise visit to Black Tupelo," Elise said.

"Good luck if you're hoping to speak to Strata Luna. She has little tolerance for the police."

Elise had never met Strata Luna, but like everyone else in Savannah, she was intrigued by her. "I'm hoping to persuade her." She never gave much thought to her own past, but this was a time it might come in handy.

"I'm guessing it will take a court order," Major Hoffman said.

"Which wouldn't make her any more willing to help us."

"Do it your way. In any event, it won't hurt to approach her softly," the major said. "I would also suggest you investigate a rumor I heard of a zombie with a Black Tupelo logo."

"You're going to have to fill me in," Gould said as Elise executed a left turn. "Who exactly is Strata Luna?"

They were in a police car, heading for the riverfront and Black Tupelo.

"You've probably driven by her house. A mansion set back off the street in the Victorian District. It used to be a morgue."

"Morgue?" He groaned. "Why am I not surprised?"

"Strata Luna rarely goes anywhere but Black Tupelo. And when she does leave her house, it's in the backseat of a car with her face hidden by a veil."

"Why the veil? Is she homely? Or just eccentric?"

"I'm guessing she's in a state of perpetual mourning. She lost two children. Or maybe she's playing into the folklore that surrounds her."

"And that would be . . . ?"

"Strata Luna's mother was a Gullah priestess, and Strata Luna grew up in a world of powerful women who could wield a strange control over men. Her mother died of a consumptive curse put upon her by a jealous neighbor. Strata Luna and her two younger sisters participated in the secret ritual of sanctified communion where they tasted of their mother's heart, and burned and inhaled her soul."

"Oh, for chrissake."

"I'm just relating the myth. You're to decide if it's truth or fiction. Anyway, the girls were unskilled, but they possessed their mother's beauty and charisma. They began selling their bodies to men who didn't quibble about the exorbitant price. By the time Strata Luna was in her twenties, her sisters had married and Strata Luna was running her own prostitution business. She didn't believe in borrowing money, but she eventually saved enough to purchase a warehouse near the river."

"Black Tupelo."

"She refuses to have her photo taken. It's said that in cases where the photographer uses high-speed film, a dark image can be seen just beyond her shoulder. Some claim it's the devil, but others say it's the soul of her mother looking for her heart, her spirit trapped between two worlds."

Gould shook his head. "What bullshit."

"Shut up, listen, and learn. As I said, Strata Luna had two children, both girls. Both died tragically. The first child drowned in a garden fountain on her mother's property when she was maybe eight or nine."

"Jesus," he said, suddenly sounding truly upset by her story.

"The second committed suicide about four years ago. Found hanged in a shanty on St. Helena Island. She was an adult by that time. Around twenty-seven or twenty-eight, if I remember correctly. After her death, Strata Luna began to constantly dress in mourning attire."

A block from the Savannah River, in an area surrounded by brick warehouses, Elise pulled to a curb. She shut off the engine and paused with her hand on the door. "One of the big stories is that Strata Luna's mother taught her the secret art of zombie making, and it's rumored that her prostitutes are all zombies she's created."

Gould laughed.

They stepped from the car.

"You laugh now," Elise said. "But if you live around here long enough, something will eventually happen to at least make you wonder . . . and make you respect the power the mind can have over the body."

"I'm not trying to diminish what you're saying. I've witnessed mass hysteria, but you can't expect me to accept everything you've just told me as fact."

She smiled a little grimly. "Of course not."

They traversed a cobblestone alley until they reached a narrow metal door that looked like a back service entrance. In the center of the door was a discreet Black Tupelo logo.

"Been seeing that a little too often lately," Gould mumbled under his breath.

"I have the feeling we're going to be seeing it a lot more."

There was no handle. Only a keyhole, a doorbell, and a tiny window covered with heavy screen.

Gould rang the doorbell.

"Attempts have been made to close this place down, but it's hard to get somebody on a prostitution charge," Elise said. "You basically have to catch them in the act." She also suspected that a lot of officers didn't want to mess with Strata Luna—they were afraid of what she might do to them and their families.

As in a tiny confessional, an inner door on the window slid open. "Yeah?" came a male voice.

Elise and Gould pulled out their badges and held them high while Elise made introductions.

"You wanna come in?" the voice said. It was Hispanic. Young. Bouncy. "Sure, you can come in. Have a drink. Listen to the jukebox."

The door swung open.

Elise stepped inside, going from full sunlight to a darkness that left her disoriented while her pupils adjusted. Gould bumped up against her from behind.

The place smelled like fermented beer and cigarette smoke. A jukebox in the corner played blues.

"Come in. Have a seat. Look." The young man made a sweep of his arm to the wall behind the bar. "Our liquor license. It's up-to-date. That's what we do here. Sell liquor. And food. Like to see a menu? It's a little early, but I can fire up the grill."

Elise was thinking something to eat might be a good idea. Give them a chance to talk to the young man.

"No, thanks," Gould said.

Her eyes were adjusting to the dark.

Wooden booths lined the wall opposite the bar. In

the far booth sat two women, talking, drinking, smoking.

"Maybe something to drink," Elise said. "Nothing with alcohol. We're on duty."

"Sweet tea? We've got the best sweet tea in the city."

Elise slid onto a barstool. "That sounds great."

"I'll have the same." Gould took the stool beside hers.

"Flora!" the young man shouted to one of the women in the back. "Sweet teas . . . for the *detectives*."

While waiting for their tea, Elise pulled out five-by-sevens of the two male prostitutes, the photos enlarged mug shots she'd found on file. "Have you seen either of these men?"

The young man picked up the photos and carried them to the light above the cash register. A few seconds later he returned. "No." His voice was neutral.

"Sure?"

"Positive. Are they in trouble?" the young man asked.

"They're both dead."

"Both?" he asked, appearing surprised for the first time.

"Both."

"Shit. That's too bad." He frowned and shook his head. "Way too bad."

The tea arrived. A lovely olive-skinned woman with long, dark, auburn-tinged hair served Elise's drink. The woman was placing the second drink in front of Gould when her hand froze.

An attraction to Gould?

A split second later, she was moving again, setting the glass on the wooden bar.

Elise was never one to pass up an opportunity. "Have you seen either of these men?" She slid the photos across the bar.

The woman gave them a cursory glance, then shook her head. "No. Never." She had a slightly Hispanic accent. "Is that all you need?" The question was for both of them, but the woman was staring at Gould.

"Where's your rest room?" he asked, sounding a little panicky.

The bartender pointed and Gould disappeared.

"I'm Enrique," the young man told Elise. "Enrique Xavier. If you need anything, just call me."

Elise fiddled with her napkin. "Enrique, I wondered if it would be possible to talk to Strata Luna."

"Strata Luna don't talk to nobody."

"I've heard that, but in light of these two possible homicides . . . I thought she might be able to help us."

He shook his head. "No way, man."

"Why don't you ask her?"

"She'll say no."

"I'll take that chance."

He shrugged, picked up a nearby phone, and punched in a number.

"There's a lady here. A detective," he said into the receiver.

Elise handed him her card.

He grabbed it. "Detective Sandburg. Wants to know if she can talk. Just for a few minutes." He lit a cigarette, picking tobacco off his tongue. "Yeah, that's what I told her. Sorry to bother you."

Elise leaned in Enrique's direction. It was time to play the conjurer card. "Tell her I'm Jackson Sweet's daughter."

Enrique hesitated, then passed on the information. Elise watched his expression change and knew she'd won. Five minutes later, the arrangements had been made.

Where was Gould? Why hadn't he returned from the rest room?

Bent over the sink, David tossed the wet paper towel into the trash. Eyes closed, he backed up until he hit the solid brick wall. His heart hammered like a son of a bitch. There was a weird humming in his head.

Jesus.

The girl from the other night. He couldn't remember much, but he was sure it was her.

Jesus.

What had he done? What was he doing? This was so fucked-up. He used to be professional. He used to be a good agent. What—

"What the hell is going on?" came an angry whispered demand.

He opened his eyes to see the girl, Flora, standing three feet away.

"You're a *detective*? A fucking *detective*? Is this some kind of setup?"

"Listen. My being here today is just a weird coincidence. And the other night—I've never done anything like that before. I'm not sure how it happened."

She jammed a finger into his chest and glared at him. "There is no such thing as a coincidence. And you're a cop!"

"I don't even know if I want to be in law enforcement anymore." God. He was admitting things to this woman he hadn't even admitted to himself.

"Oh, I get it," Flora said. "You're going through a midlife crisis."

"No, just your everyday crisis."

"Do you know how common it is for men to turn to prostitutes when they've hit the bottom of a downward spiral? For them to seek the company of strangers? To want to be held in the arms of a woman they don't even know? What do you think that's all about?"

"If Freud were here, I'm sure he could clear things right up."

A knock sounded on the door. "Gould?" came Elise's voice. "You okay in there?"

Flora let out a smirk and opened her mouth to reply.

In one swift motion, David pulled her against him, a hand pressed to her face.

"Fine," he shouted. "Be right out."

Elise's footsteps faded. He released the girl. Her lipstick was smeared. She wasn't mad anymore. "You weren't setting me up?" she asked with a coy smile.

Shit. Was she was going to try to blackmail him? He could see the headlines now: YANKEE COP AND BLACK TUPELO HOOKER. "This is just between you and me. Nobody else." He wiped a finger across the lipstick smear, trying to fix it, realized what he was doing, and stopped.

"How about if I come by your apartment tonight?" Her smile was bigger now.

"Don't trouble yourself."

"Not in a professional way. I think you need a friend."

"I have a cat."

She laughed. "Like I said the other night, you're funny."

"Mr. Funny Man—that's me."

"Strata Luna has agreed to meet with me," Elise told David.

"How in the hell did you swing that?"

She slid from the barstool. "Mutual connection."

They stepped outside. David paused in the sunlight, the full impact of her words sinking in. "You said *me*, not *us*."

"She'll only meet with me if I come by myself. That was her stipulation."

"Depending on the location, we should be able to make it look like you're by yourself."

"Strata Luna isn't a threat. I'm going alone. It won't be a problem."

Not a good idea. Not a good idea at all. "You're talking about a woman who ate her mother's heart."

"Folklore."

"Folklore you presented as fact. Will you at least tell me where this meeting is going to take place?"

"Can't."

He stared at her for a long moment. Straight shimmering hair. Like a sleek black cat. "I thought you were smarter than that," he said.

The door swung open behind them. Flora.

"You might want these." She held out their unfinished drinks, which she'd poured into transparent take-out containers.

While she smiled wickedly up at him, David accepted his cup, topped off, complete with straw and lid.

"Did you see the way she looked at you when she

served us our tea?" Elise asked once Flora was back inside. "She's smitten."

"Smitten? Don't you have to be over ninety to use that word?" *Wow. Elise has the weirdest eyes. . . .*

He'd noticed them before. Who wouldn't? But out in the intense sunlight, he could see metallic flecks and lines in about a million colors.

In her lady-of-the-manor Southern best, she said, "Are you making fun of me?"

There were occasions when Elise had very little accent. At other times, like now, she could sound as Southern as a Georgia peach. The accent seemed to be a tool she pulled out from time to time for effect.

His mother and sister would adore her. Which was why they must never meet. They would feel it was their matchmaking duty to push them together, since they considered it their duty to find him a mate. They would also want to tell Elise about David's past. He didn't want anybody to know. If no one knew, it might make it less real.

"She said she was Jackson Sweet's daughter," Strata Luna said.

Flora and Strata Luna stood in the third-story window of Black Tupelo, watching the two detectives as they walked down the cobblestone alley.

"Jackson Sweet?" Flora asked. "The conjurer?"

"Jackson was more than that."

The older woman smelled of secrets, of pungent herbs and rich, loamy soil. The scent saturated her hair. Her clothes. It seeped from her pores.

Flora wasn't interested in Jackson Sweet or the female detective.

She watched until the pair rounded the corner. "He's the guy I was telling you about."

"You like him." A statement.

"I do."

"But he's a policeman."

"So?"

"Police don't fall for people like us, silly child."

Flora continued to stare in the direction David Gould had gone. "He could love me," she said softly. "Jesus fell in love with a prostitute."

"Jesus this, and Jesus that," Strata Luna chided. "Everybody's always talkin' about Jesus. A strong woman don't need no man other than for opening jars and having sex."

"Haven't you ever been in love?"

"I'm not even sure what love is, hon. Man-woman love, anyway."

"What about Enrique?"

The older woman laughed her deep, rich laugh. "Enrique is a sweet, gorgeous child, but he ain't my equal, honey."

Strata Luna picked up a brush from the dresser, the slight movement causing her black gown to rustle. She pulled the brush through Flora's hair. Flora sighed and closed her eyes.

"There was this one man . . . ," Strata Luna began with a secret smile in her voice. "But I was too much woman for him." She clicked her tongue and shook her head. "Too much woman."

"Someone I know?" Flora felt herself relaxing.

"Before your time."

The room was cool, but Flora could feel the muggy heat of Savannah radiating through the window glass near her face as the rhythmic movement of the brush continued to soothe her.

"If you're serious about this man," Strata Luna said, "I can help."

"I'm serious."

"Then we'll gather ingredients for a spell. How'd that be?" Strata Luna put down the brush and raked her nails along Flora's scalp. "A love-me-or-die spell."

Chapter 14

"What'll it be next?" Gould asked as the light turned green and Elise eased the unmarked police car through the intersection. "A flight to Roswell, New Mexico, to check out the aliens?"

Elise was getting tired of having to constantly defend and explain local culture to her partner. "You have to be more open-minded if you're going to live around here."

"I just think we could focus in a more . . . *practical* direction." Gould fiddled with the radio, getting nothing but static. "Damn," he said, shutting it off. "Why do we always end up with the car with no tunes? And today of all days?"

"Because somebody else always beats us to the only car with a decent radio. And anyway, I don't think the police department considers music a priority."

Before heading out of town, she stopped at Parker's Market, a combination gas station and deli, where they picked up sandwiches.

"I'll drive," Gould offered as they returned to the car.

"That's okay," Elise said. "I know the road."

He shrugged. "Suit yourself."

"So what's the deal with this village we're going to?" Gould asked once they were on their way. "Want my pickle?"

She shook her head. "Chips?"

He accepted the offer.

"There's a rumor about a young man living there who's said to have shown up at his home eight months after his burial," she told him.

"Ah. A rumor. I love rumors," he said in a voice that went along with the rolling of eyes.

"Never discredit rumors."

"Not around here, right?"

Was he being a smart-ass? With Gould, it was often impossible to tell.

"The village we're visiting considers itself a sovereign state," she explained. "It's self-supporting. They have a king. They even have a Web site. And lucky for us, they welcome tourists."

They finished eating.

Gould balled up the wrappers and stuck everything into a brown paper bag. When the conversation lulled, he tried the radio again, apparently hoping for better reception now that they were out of the city. It was worse. He sighed, shut it off, and leaned back in the seat to enjoy the view.

After several turns and dead ends, they finally came to a sign that read: YOU ARE NOW LEAVING THE U.S. AND ENTERING THE YORUBA KINGDOM, BUILT BY THE PRIESTS OF THE ORISKA VOODOO CULT.

Gould stared at the sign. "This is just weird as

hell," he said with a combination of hushed awe and annoyance.

They passed a shack that marked the entrance to the village. Barefoot, dark-skinned children ran across dirt-packed streets. Old men sat in chairs under the shade of corrugated steel porch roofs, watching the day go by.

People were friendly, and it didn't take Elise and Gould long to get directions to the shanty they were interested in. Like all of the others, it looked unable to withstand a stiff breeze.

The sound of the car announced their arrival, and a man and a woman came out to greet them.

"For six days, he was in a cold morgue," the black islander told them from under the brim of his tattered, sweat-stained straw hat. "Then we buried him. Eight months later, he comes shuffling home. Like that—"

He pointed to a young man of about seventeen sitting outside his parents' house. His feet were bare and dust-covered, his hair was matted, and his shoulder bones protruded sharply under the thin fabric of his T-shirt.

"He can't even feed or wash hisself," the mother said, not with sorrow but acceptance. "And our friends—they don't come round here no more. Because of Angel. Say he's cursed. Say he's evil."

"Do you mind if we talk to him?" Gould asked.

"Won't do no good. Can't talk. I don't think he even knows who we are. He just came back here from habit. . . . See how he holds his head like that? All bent?"

"Zombie posture," Elise said.

The mother nodded. "Can't lift it no further. Not

even to eat. But he's a good boy. If I tell him to go in the house, he goes in the house. If I tell him to go to bed, he goes to bed. He's a good boy. Nobody would ever have reason to hurt him."

"Any idea who could have done this to him? And why?" Elise asked.

A look of fear passed between the man and wife. She and Gould were outsiders, and Angel's parents were afraid of angering whoever had done such a terrible thing to their son. If they had an idea, they weren't eager to divulge it.

The detectives attempted a brief conversation with the emaciated young man, but nothing they said brought about any kind of response. He was a shell with nothing inside.

"They seem especially adamant about their son being a good boy," Gould said to Elise while the parents stood out of earshot.

"Are you thinking that perhaps he hadn't been such a good boy before?"

"Exactly."

"Vodun society has its own methods of dealing with criminals," Elise said. "Turning someone into a mindless puppet is an effective way to harness them."

"No jails. No expense to anyone but the family."

"What could he have done that was bad enough to deserve such a life sentence?"

Gould reached inside his jacket. "Maybe we can find out."

He approached the couple again. "Does your son happen to have one of these anywhere on his body?" he asked, presenting the parents with the body art photo.

The parents looked at each other, then back to Gould. "You must go now." It was obvious that they recognized the emblem. And that they were afraid.

"Does your son have this mark on him?" Gould persisted.

"Go!" The old man got to his feet and pointed toward their car. Elise began moving away. Gould followed.

"It's possible that Angel was a prostitute at Black Tupelo," Gould said as he and Elise made their way through loose sand to the car.

"The parents were too effusive about their son's innocence," Elise agreed. "If that's the case, then we have three prostitutes."

"Two of them dead, one a vegetable."

"One may have died of an unconnected heroin overdose."

"It's also possible Angel is being punished by his own society. Could also be an unconnected coincidence."

At the car, Elise paused with her hand on the door handle and looked at Gould. "And then we have Mr. Harrison. Where does he fit in?"

"He doesn't. I'm not saying there isn't a connection. I'm just saying he doesn't fit."

"The victimology is all over the place."

"Which takes us back to the possibility of unrelated crimes," Gould said.

"Could Harrison have been an accident?" Elise added. "Did he get poison meant for someone else?"

"For the moment, let's say they are connected. Then we have to ask ourselves what the killer was trying to accomplish by stepping outside his MO. It could be one of several things: The perpetrator could be doing it for attention. He could also be doing it to confuse us. Or he could be escalating."

Inside the car, Gould removed the plastic lid from his drink. "Here's another angle." He shook the cup, ice rattling. "Remember how Jeffrey Dahmer drilled holes in the skulls of his victims while they were still alive?"

"Oh, yeah." How could Elise have forgotten such a horror? But now that Gould had brought it up, memories of what she'd read about the case came back. "Then he shot them full of battery acid. Yikes."

"In an attempt to create zombies," Gould said around a mouthful of ice.

Of course. "Is that what's going on? Is somebody trying to create mindless playthings? Is this all about absolute control?"

Elise's phone rang.

John Casper.

"I checked out every prostitute we've had through the morgue in the past two years," he told her. "Guess how many came up?"

"I'd think the norm would be around one or two a year," Elise said.

"We've had twelve in two years."

"Wow."

Gould perked up, listening intently to Elise's side of the conversation.

The figure Casper had given her was hard to absorb. And even more astounding was that no one had noticed. "Causes of death?" Elise asked.

"All drug related. And we're talking street drugs like heroin. Cocaine."

"At least that's what it says on the death certificate. Which is why nobody looked into the deaths," Elise guessed.

"Exactly," Casper said.

She adjusted the air conditioner while the car idled. "What about exhuming some of the bodies?"

"That's where we run into a problem. Most of them were cremated."

"Makes sense," Elise said. "It's the cheapest way to go."

"Especially when the state's picking up the tab," Casper added. "A lot of these kids were probably runaways, with no family, no money."

"Perfect targets no one would miss. I'm wondering how long this would have gone unnoticed if Harrison hadn't been poisoned," Elise said. "But what about the bodies that weren't cremated?"

She heard keys clicking. "Three of them were shipped back to their families in different parts of the country. Another one went to Charleston." Some more clicking. "Here it is. One guy, named Gary Turello, is buried in Savannah's Laurel Grove Cemetery. We have all of his identifiable scars and tattoos on file. Just give me a second while I look it up. . . ."

More clicking followed by silence.

"Let me guess," Elise said. "Black Tupelo."

"Yep." That one syllable held tremendous satisfaction.

She looked at Gould, whose eyebrows were raised in question. She nodded.

"If we get him exhumed, what are our chances of finding tetrodotoxin at this point?" Elise asked.

"You can encounter a lot of problems when trying

to analyze samples obtained from embalmed bodies,"
Casper said. "It makes a difference how much embalming fluid the funeral director used. And whether
or not the casket leaked. I've seen organs that had to
have the water literally wrung out of them."

"Thanks for that nice visual."

"You're welcome. Turello was buried a year and a
half ago, but I'd say it's definitely worth a shot."

"Is there any way to rush this through the approval
process?" Elise asked.

"I'll put in a call to the state medical examiner at
the Georgia Bureau of Investigation in Decatur," Casper
told her. "She's the one who'll have to sign off on it,
but considering the gravity of the situation, that
shouldn't be a problem."

"How long will it take?"

"I'm guessing one or two days. Sometimes we run
into people who don't want their loved one disturbed.
That's understandable. If that happens, then we have
to petition the court for disinterment, which could
take a whole lot longer."

"Let's just hope the family complies," Elise said.
She thanked him and disconnected.

In her room above Black Tupelo, Flora assembled
all of the items Strata Luna had told her she would
need for a love-drawing spell: High John the Con-
queror root and goofer dust, along with a piece of
brown paper torn from a bag. Waterproof red and
black pens, a new spool of red thread, a small red
flannel bag, and a sharp knife.

From the other side of the wall, in the room adjacent to hers, came sounds of sex.

Hushed voices. Laughter. The frantic squeaking of a mattress.

Flora should be working too, but she had more important things to do.

On the brown paper, she wrote the name *David Gould* seven times in black ink. She rotated the paper a quarter of a turn and printed *LOVE ME OR DIE* over his name seven times in red ink.

She immersed the name paper in a bowl of her own urine, then wrapped and shaped the soaked paper around the root. That was followed by the goofer dust and red thread.

She wound it round and round until the paper was entirely covered, then tied it off with several large knots, leaving a length of thread for hanging.

Strata Luna had told her the secret was to store the root in the red flannel and keep it wet with urine.

With her finger wedged between two knots, Flora swung the covered root back and forth.

"David Gould, love me or die. David Gould, love me or die."

Chapter 15

Strata Luna had agreed to meet Elise at four in the afternoon in a small cemetery near a church on St. Helena Island, a place that was steeped in Gullah heritage. It was also where Jackson Sweet was supposed to have been born.

Elise followed a crude map that had shown up at her home in a manila envelope sealed with the Black Tupelo design. The church ended up being a two-story clapboard structure blasted gray by wind and sand.

A long black car with Georgia plates was parked not far from the building, its front bumper a few inches from a fence tangled with heavy vine. Elise swung her car around and backed up, keeping a good fifty feet between the two vehicles. She looked over her left shoulder to see her buddy Enrique behind the wheel. He smiled and pointed in the direction of the church, drew an imaginary circle, then walked his fingers in the air.

She nodded, shut off the car, and stepped out, feeling beneath her jacket for the outline of her SIG Sauer. She checked her pocket to make sure her cell phone was handy.

The sand was loose under her feet as she made her way around the church.

Had she herself been born on just such an island? she wondered. Maybe even this island?

It was tough not knowing where she'd come from, tougher yet when Audrey asked questions about her past that Elise couldn't answer. Unlike Thomas and Vivian, who had a history they could share.

Windows in the church were broken. The front door hung by a hinge. Sweet grass grew from the foundation, and live oaks, with their black curtains of moss, cast long shadows. A strong ocean wind blew without pause.

The place was creepy even during the day.

Elise spotted a single set of footprints and followed them.

On the east side of the gray structure was a small cemetery, the ancient, moss-covered tombstones dwarfed by dense, spreading trees.

Under a canopy of leaves, the wind stopped and the protected area turned to twilight. As Elise walked, the sand gave way to packed earth and a soft layer of small brown leaves. Parallel ruts lined the ground, created years ago when coffins were transported by horse and buggy.

Elise followed the faint road, turning when it turned, slowing when she spotted a shadowy figure in the distance.

She approached cautiously, until she was near enough to make out a woman sitting on a cement bench near a large headstone.

Strata Luna.

The woman wore a long black dress and a wide-brimmed hat. For a moment Elise felt as if she'd stepped back in time.

With gloved hands, Strata Luna gracefully lifted the hat's veil away. "Hello, Elise."

Her face was regal, with high cheekbones and large eyes beneath thick, black eyebrows. Full red lips against ebony skin.

No one knew her age. Elise had done the math, and knew she had to be at least fifty. She looked much younger.

Regardless of the myth surrounding Strata Luna, the compelling aura she carried hadn't been understated. It was said that in her youth, men froze in the streets when she walked by, unable to move until she'd passed. Elise believed it.

"So, you're the daughter of Jackson Sweet."

Strata Luna's voice was as mysterious and hypnotic as the rest of her. Deep, slow, metered, and melodic.

"It's a rumor. Folklore."

"Have you had the opportunity to test yourself? Has anyone passed the mantle to you?"

"I dabbled a little."

Elise stepped closer and sat down on the opposite end of the long bench, leaving several feet between herself and Strata Luna.

"Dabbled? That's not a serious word."

"It was years ago. I was a kid."

"But you gave it up for a life of practicality."

"Something like that."

"Come closer."

Elise remained where she was.

"You don't trust me."

"Trust and foolishness go hand in hand."

The older woman laughed, then reached into a deep pocket of her black cotton dress. She pulled out a small bundle of white fabric tied with a long, looped string. "I have something for you. A *wanga*."

A charm.

Piece of candy, little girl?

Strata Luna stood and approached. She was a tall woman, large but not overweight. Smiling, she slipped the *wanga* over Elise's head.

It smelled like herbs.

"It's a good root," the woman said. "It will protect you." She reached out and touched Elise's hair. "Your hair is like his. Dark. Straight. And your eyes. Let me see. . . ." With a graceful motion, she placed her gloved fingers beneath Elise's chin and tilted her face toward her.

Then, as if stung, she dropped her hand away.

"Those eyes . . . ," she said with discomfort. "They're very strange."

Elise was used to such responses, yet had expected more control from Strata Luna. "You undoubtedly know I was left on a grave because of them," Elise said, trying to make light of her past the way she always did.

"Almost every color in there." Still staring, Strata Luna suddenly seemed shaky and old. "And every color makes black." She turned away and sat down, as if unable to look at Elise any longer. Silence grew around them until Elise was afraid the woman wouldn't speak again.

"You knew Jackson Sweet?" Elise finally asked.

Strata Luna pulled in a deep breath and straightened her shoulders. "Honey, we used to drink together," she said, her voice now light and almost flippant, a woman of rapid mood swings. "And we used to fight together. Said I was too pushy for him." She glanced at Elise. "You're his daughter." She nodded. "No doubt 'bout that."

A shock went through her. Elise had never believed the stories. Not really. Not in her heart. Growing up, she'd only wanted to believe them. But now . . . with Strata Luna seeming so certain . . .

"Do you have any children?" Strata Luna asked.

"A daughter."

"Daughters . . . ," Strata Luna said distantly, in a remembering kind of voice.

Elise produced the photos she'd shown to Enrique. "Have you ever seen either of these men?"

Strata Luna stared at them a moment. "I think this one used to work for me." She tapped the face of Jordan Kemp. "I don't recall his name. I'm not sure about the other one." She passed the photos back. "I have a lot of people I support. Some of them stay. Some of them go. I don't always remember names."

"Jordan Kemp and Samuel Winslow." Elise pulled out another photo, this one of the body art.

Strata Luna examined it closely and smiled. "This work was done by Genevieve Roy. See how delicate the lines of the implants are? Not many people are so adept."

"Does it have a purpose?" Elise asked.

"It's a mojo," Strata Luna explained. "People who work for me often get it. I don't insist, but most of them want it. It gives them protection they wouldn't otherwise have."

"Apparently it's not providing enough," Elise said dryly.

"That's because the design has been stolen from me. People who have nothing to do with Black Tupelo are getting it."

"Status," Elise said. She could see that kind of evolution.

Strata Luna waved her hand. "Now it means nothin'. You have more questions? I must go soon. Enrique is waiting."

"We've had some unexplainable poisonings in Savannah. Victims killed with tetrodotoxin," Elise said, pressing forward, realizing this could be her last chance to talk with Strata Luna—at least in an unofficial, casual environment. "It's rumored that you drug your . . . employees to keep them complacent," Elise said bluntly. "And that you use a secret recipe with one of the ingredients being tetrodotoxin."

Strata Luna straightened, her thick brows drawing together in tempestuous irritation. "Are you accusing me of murder?"

"The male prostitute had your insignia on him and tetrodotoxin in his bloodstream. It's only logical that we would question you."

"Escort service. It can be an unpleasant occupation. Sometimes new recruits—and even seasoned workers—have a hard time dealing with the unpleasantness. Sometimes they need a little help to get them through the night. It can be one of many drugs. I help them, but never against their will. And I would never use poison from the puffer fish for that purpose. You're talking zombies and voodoo."

"Maybe someone is eking out his own brand of justice," Elise suggested.

Strata Luna shrugged as if the turn in the conversation was boring her. "You police are always lookin' for a reason, a motive," she said. "Why are you so unwilling to accept the truth?"

"What's the truth?" Elise asked.

"That evil doesn't need a reason to exist."

"I can't think like that. For me, everything has an answer."

The woman shook her head. "You'll change your mind someday."

Elise herself had seen a lot of evil in her job as a homicide detective, but she had the feeling Strata Luna had her beat.

Interview over, she got to her feet and handed the woman a business card. "Thanks for agreeing to meet with me. If you think of anything important, please give me a call."

Strata Luna stood. "I want to show you something. Come. Follow me."

Elise followed her deeper into the cemetery until they came to a small cluster of broken, moss-covered tombstones. The older woman stopped, not in front of the stones, but before a dip in the ground. Scattered around the indentation were a telephone, a mirror, a comb, some change, and a full bottle of whiskey.

"This is why I wanted you to come here today," Strata Luna said. "This is your father's grave. The grave of Jackson Sweet."

The air left Elise's lungs.

She stared at the indentation in the ground. In the distance, hidden in a dark place, hundreds of frogs spilled their secrets, the wall of sound hypnotically rising and falling.

"There can be no marker left on the grave of a conjure man," Strata Luna explained, her voice coming from a million miles away. "Otherwise people dig up his bones for mojoes and spells. They wouldn't leave him in peace. But some of us know where Jackson is buried. And now you know. See the hole?" She pointed. "Root doctors come and dig here."

"Goofer dust," Elise said.

"And now we must both leave something. You cannot visit the grave of a conjurer without leaving a personal item."

Strata Luna pulled off her black gloves and placed them near the indentation.

At first Elise couldn't think of anything to offer. Cell phone? Of course not. She dug through her pockets. Notebooks. ID. Gun.

Her fingers came in contact with a pen. Just a regular, everyday ink pen. Maybe he needed to do a little writing.

She placed it on one of Strata Luna's gloves.

"I have one more thing for you," the woman said.

"I can't accept anything else."

"This ain't really from me." She pulled out a small leather case and handed it to Elise.

"Go on. Open it. It's something that belonged to your father. Something you should have."

The leather was cracked and black and extremely old; the small hinges were rusty.

Elise opened it. Inside was a pair of wire-rimmed glasses with dark blue lenses.

Conjurer's glass. Blue lenses that kept out evil spirits and allowed the wearer to see things others couldn't.

"Put them on. I want to see them on you."

She seemed so sure that Jackson Sweet was her father.

"You're alike," Strata Luna stated.

"How?"

"Your father was a cop."

"Jackson Sweet? No, he wasn't." Elise would have known if Jackson Sweet had been a policeman.

"Not by your rules, but by a root doctor's. He punished bad people and rewarded the good ones. That's better than the idiots with badges we have in Savannah."

A self-proclaimed man of the law? A man who scared the shit out of people, forcing them to mend their ways or face the wrath of a white root doctor? Was that why Elise had become a cop? Was it in her blood? Because she was the daughter of Jackson Sweet?

Intrigued, she removed the glasses from the case. The wire was thin and fragile. She carefully unfolded the antique frames and slipped them on.

Shadows turned bottomless black. The sky turned gray. Sunlight that fell through branches and leaves created a dappling of crescent moons on the ground.

Dizzying.

Disorienting.

Caused by the weird, distorted lenses? Or something else?

At that moment, Elise believed what Strata Luna was telling her. She suddenly had a past, a history.

She'd been abandoned. She'd been thrown away, left to die. But if she came from a world of conjurers and spells, then her life could never have been what other people thought of as normal. Who wanted normal anyway? Instead, she'd met the world in a weird, sensational way.

He would have wanted her. Jackson Sweet had been on his deathbed when Elise was born. Otherwise he would have rescued her, kept her, raised her. She suddenly felt very sure of that.

What about Audrey? Should she tell her? What would she think? How would she react to the news that her grandfather was Jackson Sweet?

Standing in the center of the strange, colorless world was Strata Luna, beaming at her. "Look here, look here, Jackson Sweet," she said. The words were tossed to someone invisible, standing just beyond her shoulder. "You ain't never gonna believe what ol' Strata Luna brought you today."

The two women stood there in the dark, listening to the frogs. Finally Elise told Strata Luna good-bye. She removed the glasses and walked in the direction of the church and the cars.

Strata Luna watched her go, a feeling of loneliness suddenly engulfing her.

Loneliness and fear.

She thought about unwelcome evil and was reminded of another time, a time she tried not to think about—the night her youngest daughter drowned. . . .

Strata Luna had run from the house, a sheer white nightgown billowing around her. Down the flagstone steps, past the hedges and roses and weeping magnolias, her bare feet already whispering that it was too late.

The night sky was a cobalt blue; the trees were black silhouettes standing silent and unmoving. What she saw caused her heart to stop beating for several minutes.

Something floating in the water.

Fabric.

A nightgown.

Ebony hair.

The most beautiful, shiny, ebony hair a child could possibly possess.

No! God, no!

The night sky reflected on the water, a child's hand reaching for the moon and stars. Strata Luna tumbled into the pool, the surface shattering like glass.

She grabbed the body of her daughter. The water tugged, fighting to hold the child, to keep her. Strata Luna finally pulled her free and turned her over.

Dead, dead, dead.

Some people claimed she'd killed the angel herself, with her own hands, holding her under the water until her lungs filled with water. Sometimes Strata Luna thought it was true, since she hadn't been able to foresee her death.

But evil was a part of life.

It was the shadow that followed her.

The shadow she feared had returned.

Chapter 16

David Gould was scheduled for an early flight out of Savannah that would get him to Suffolk County, Virginia, in an hour. From there his lawyer would pick him up and they would drive to meet with his wife and her attorney in order to get the divorce papers signed and finalized. If all went smoothly, he would be back to Savannah by early evening.

It was still dark when he boarded the small commuter jet, carrying nothing but a briefcase with copies of the divorce papers plus some notes on the TTX case. He tried to tell himself that once the papers were signed everything would be over. He wouldn't have to think about Beth again.

Right.

The flight departed ten minutes ahead of schedule.

As David leaned his forehead against the window and watched the airport shrink below him, he tried to empty his mind, a trick he'd learned from a man who taught transcendental meditation. It didn't work this time. Come to think of it, he wasn't sure it had ever worked, because he now understood something he hadn't understood at the time: He could really fool the shit out of himself.

A guy had to be careful about creating his own reality. Because you could get lost in it, so lost that it was hard to get back to the real world.

He had two excuses for his early infatuation with Beth: youth and hormones. Those things together could slant a person's perspective more than heavy drugs.

David Gould and Beth Anderson had been high school sweethearts. That in itself should have been a warning, because at age sixteen most people aren't who they're going to become. Often, they aren't even close.

But you think you are. At sixteen, you think you know everything, and when sex is part of the equation it's hard as hell for a guy to think straight.

Now that he was an adult, David could see his relationship with Beth for what it had been—a purely physical attraction, as shallow as that was.

The shallowness was something he would never have admitted at the time. On the outside, Beth was the perfect woman, with the attributes a male looked for in a potential mate.

It had been biological, all about the continuation of the species, with no logic involved. She had the requisite full lips. She had the correct waist-to-hip ratio. Dark hair. Blue eyes. Great skin, full breasts. And so healthy. Vibrant. His mate radar was saying she would be a good mother who would produce healthy, beautiful children.

And she did.

A boy. A beautiful baby boy.

It was a tedious, unremarkable story, almost embarrassing in its plot. He was in his second year of college, and she was a high school senior when she became pregnant.

Had she sensed that he was drifting away? Had she known he was beginning to notice other girls on campus? Had she suspected he was beginning to think of her as too young, too immature? Had she noticed how he'd changed? How their interests were no longer the same?

Had she become pregnant on purpose?

These were all questions he'd asked himself over the years, but at the time of her announcement there was no question, only the answer to what they must do, what they had always planned to do anyway, which was get married.

Two days after she graduated from high school, they were married and she immediately joined him at George Mason University in Fairfax, Virginia. And when the baby came, a beautiful boy with blond hair and blue eyes, David was happy. Blindly happy.

Warning signs had been there, but he'd missed them. Beth attended to Christian's needs, but didn't cuddle with him or laugh with him. She seemed to resent her own child, blaming him for an unsatisfying marriage.

David got his degree in criminal psychology and joined the FBI. Beth had been proud of that, and by the time he made it through training, they began to talk of having another child.

His beautiful boy . . .

Reading him a bedtime story by lamplight.

Tucking him in, trusting little arms wrapping around

your neck, fine hair that smelled like newness and innocence.

As an FBI agent, his schedule became erratic. He worked long hours. Beth was bored. Deeply depressed. She didn't get along with the other FBI wives, so she had no one to confide in.

An FBI agent's marriage could go either way. Sometimes the job made for a strong relationship at home, and sometimes it was a recipe for failure. David's fell into the failure category.

"You never make me laugh anymore," she once complained.

"I can. I will."

But it was too late.

Beth had an affair.

And one affair just seemed to call for another.

David had been willing to stay together for his son, afraid he might lose Christian, but she'd insisted upon a divorce. Because of his job, she was granted custody, just as he'd feared. Christian could visit every other weekend, plus rotating holidays.

The plane landed, jolting David back to the present.

He was met by his lawyer, Ira Cummings, a serious and sad man. A good man.

Ira drove like he did everything else, with rapid efficiency. Within forty-five minutes of David's plane landing, they were pulling into the parking lot of Sussex I Prison, a maximum-security, high-level prison that housed Virginia's death row population.

They were expected, so it was a matter of signing in; then a guard led them through a series of computerized sliding metal doors with locks until they reached the meeting room. The guard took her place near the door, while cameras watched from every corner.

The long rectangular table was bolted to the floor, and the chairs were attached by chains. A man in a suit sat at one end; a woman faced the door. It took a moment for David to recognize the woman as Beth.

She was fat.

Not yet obese, but she'd probably put on forty pounds. Dressed in an orange jumpsuit, she sat staring at the surface of the table, her hair hanging limply on either side of her face.

He and his lawyer took seats across from her.

She slowly raised her head until she was staring into his eyes, hatred and a smug cockiness radiating from her, a smirk on her lips.

She'd won. Even though she was in prison, she'd won.

You bitch. You evil, evil bitch.

She must have read his mind, because her smile got a little bigger.

It had been his weekend to get Christian. She didn't like David to come to her apartment, so they usually met someplace neutral like McDonald's. That way Christian could get a Happy Meal. That way it could seem like a friendly little outing.

She was late. Not unusual. For her to be on time would have been a bigger surprise.

David ordered a soda and waited, staring out the window into the parking lot while kids played and shrieked behind him in the indoor playground. Fifteen minutes later, he called her apartment. No answer.

Must be on her way.

He waited another fifteen. And another.

He tossed his cup, got in the car, and headed for her place.

Traffic was heavy, and it took him almost half an hour. When he arrived, her car wasn't in the lot.

He knocked on the door. Nobody answered.

He tried the knob.

Unlocked.

The door swung open as if the place had been expecting him.

His heart began to thud in his chest.

"Beth?"

He listened for an answer. When he didn't get one, he followed with his son's name.

The apartment was silent except for the hum of the refrigerator.

His gaze shot around the kitchen and living room; then he was running up the carpeted steps.

Drip, drip, drip.

Coming from the bathroom.

Drip, drip, drip.

A leaking faucet.

He moved down the narrow, carpeted hallway, following the sound.

The bathroom door was ajar. He slowly pushed it open. Slowly stepped inside.

Lying facedown in a tub of water, blond hair spread around his head, was his son.

"No! God, no!"

David pulled him from the tub, turning the child in his arms, water gushing around him. He attempted CPR, but it was too late.

Christian's skin was blue. His lips were almost black. He'd been dead a long time.

David let out a cry of anguish and hugged the dead child to him, out of his mind with grief.

A sound made him look up.

Beth stood in the doorway, her eyes red and swollen from tears, clutching the cat, Isobel.

"Wh-what happened? What happened?" David asked, unconsciously rocking his dead child, unable to comprehend.

"He told me if I got rid of the kid, he'd marry me."

She stroked the cat, cuddled the cat, tilting her head toward it.

"Wh-what? Wh-what are you talking about?"

"Franklin. He said if I got rid of Christian, he'd marry me. So I did. Then I called him to come and get me, but he refused. He hung up on me."

"Y-you did this? Y-you murdered our child?"

The tone of his voice frightened the cat. It squirmed and jumped from Beth's arms, disappearing from the room.

"I had no choice," Beth said.

He had no memory of the next few seconds. Rage was like that.

He didn't know exactly how he got from the floor to her, but suddenly he had her by the throat, pressing his thumbs into her trachea, shutting off the murdering bitch's air.

He would have killed her if the police hadn't come. Her boyfriend had called them, saying he thought his girlfriend may have murdered her child. One more minute and David would have been in prison too.

Killing her would have been worth prison.

"I'm not sure I'm going to sign those," Beth said from her chair across the table.

The lawyers looked at each other.

Her lawyer cleared his throat. "Come on, Beth. Sign."

David wouldn't have even had to come, but he'd thought doing it in person would give him the closure that had been eluding him for so long.

She signed. Paper after paper. When she was done, she tossed the pen down. It slid across the table and hit the floor. Her lawyer had to retrieve it, examining it with concern.

David signed, and they were done.

"You creep! It's all your fault," Beth shouted, her face contorted with rage and hatred. "All your fault! Look what you've done to me! I could have been somebody! I could have been a model. An actress."

She stuck out her chin, displaying a plump and ravaged face. "Look at me now! LOOK AT ME!"

He turned and walked from the room, his shoulders sagging with an incredible weight, while she continued to scream after him.

Chapter 17

Somebody was knocking on his apartment door.

David had gotten home from Virginia a few hours earlier. As soon as his feet touched the ground, he'd made a beeline for the liquor store and was now fairly fucked-up.

Didn't help.

Maybe made it worse.

He couldn't get his head to shut off. Replay after replay.

Flashes.

Beth. Fat. In an orange jumpsuit. A slimmer Beth, at the door, holding Isobel.

Christian.

David could feel the dead weight of his son in his arms.

He let out a sob. He bit the back of his hand, smothering the sound.

Fuck, fuck, fuck.

It's over now, he tried to tell himself, rocking back and forth on the floor.

Over, over, over.

Christian. Dead. Dead. Dead.

Another sob was wrenched from deep inside him.

Knock, knock, knock.

Dead, dead, dead.

"David?"

Voice at the door. Woman's voice. Who? Beth?

"David, are you in there?"

Not Beth.

He shoved himself up from the floor. How had he gotten there?

Barefoot, he shuffled to the door and looked through the peephole. Somebody with long, dark hair. Who?

He undid the chain, unlocked the door, and opened it.

Oh. *Her.* Flora.

"Hi," she said.

It was dark in the hallway. It was dark behind him.

"I went to the SCAD art fair in Forsyth Park," she said, lifting something in a frame. "I picked this up for your apartment." She swung it around.

Lots of color. Bright reds. Bright blues. Was that a cat? He liked cats. Swirly, spinning cats.

"Howdy," he said, stepping backward. The room slanted and he had to grab the kitchen counter for support. "Shit," he muttered, closing his eyes and resting his heavy forehead against the cool Formica.

Flora closed the door, leaned the framed print against the wall, pulled her purse strap from her shoulder, and dropped the bag on the floor. "What are you doing to yourself?"

She'd seen a lot of wasted guys in her life, but the man she'd been fantasizing about for the last several days was about as wasted as a person could get while still remaining conscious.

He was dressed in a pair of black pants that matched a jacket slung over the back of a nearby chair. Along with the jacket was a leather holster and gun. His shirt and tie had been removed, leaving him in a white, V-necked T-shirt.

"Oh, no, you don't," she said when she saw him lifting a fifth of something to his mouth. She snatched it away and read the label. "Gin. No wonder you smell like a Christmas tree." She walked to the sink and dumped the rest down the drain.

He frowned and regarded her as only a drunk person could, through his eyelashes, chin down. "Was I expecting you?"

"I just stopped by. Guess it's a good thing because you seem to be in need of a baby-sitter."

She didn't know what was going on in his life, but he was hurting. Bad. She should have had Strata Luna put together an unfuck-my-life spell for him.

He continued to stare, and she wondered if he even recognized her.

"I like you," he finally said.

"That's nice. I'm sure you'll feel the same way to-morrow," she said dryly.

He let go of the counter and moved toward her, reaching and fumbling for the buttons of her blouse. "Let's just make you more comfortable."

She brushed his hands away. "No."

"Why not?"

She slid his metal watch from his wrist. "You're the one who is going to get more comfortable." She undid his belt buckle and slipped it from his pants. "Follow me." Walking backward, she pulled him toward her, moving in the direction of the bedroom.

He minded as best he could.

When they reached the bed, he fell across the mattress, pulling Flora with him. And immediately passed out.

How much had he had to drink? she wondered. More than what was missing from the fifth?

She gave him a little slap on the cheek. No response. She slapped him again. Nothing.

Her plan had been to undress him before putting him in the shower. That wasn't going to work. "David! David, come on. You have to get up."

He groaned.

"Come on." She pulled him by the arms. "Stand up."

Amazingly, he managed to get himself upright. With his arm draped over her shoulder, she walked him to the bathroom and stuck him in the shower, his back to the tiled wall. Somehow he stayed there, even though his eyes were closed and his mouth was slack.

Everybody in the world was a mess. Doctors. Priests. Prostitutes, and cops. Didn't matter who you were, what you did, or how much money you made. Living was tough.

She turned the cold faucet.

At first, David didn't even respond as icy water poured over his head, soaking his clothes. He finally let out a loud, shocked gasp. His eyes flew open and his arms flailed.

"Jesus!" he shouted. "Are you trying to kill me?"

Mercilessly, she let the water continue to pour over him. "You're doing a good job of that by yourself."

Chapter 18

"He's cute." Audrey stared into the distance as she sucked sweet tea through a straw.

"Our waiter?" Elise asked, following the direction of her daughter's gaze.

"Yeah. Think he goes to SCAD?"

"Most of the people who work here go to SCAD."

They were sitting in wooden schoolroom chairs at a marble-topped table in the front window of the Gryphon Tea Room, overlooking Madison Square. The Gryphon was one of the many buildings owned and renovated by SCAD, Savannah College of Art and Design. The renovation had involved retaining most of the original features, from the pharmacist cabinets and apothecary tile to the mahogany walls and Tiffany glass.

Audrey loved the place, and Elise tried to take her there several times a year for a mother-and-daughter tea.

"Here he comes again," Audrey whispered, leaning forward.

Audrey was the age when moods changed so rapidly it almost seemed like sleight of hand. Now you see it; now you don't. At the moment she was up, almost euphoric—a direct combination of the tearoom, caffeine, and their waiter. Elise was smart enough to know she herself didn't even register in the equation.

The waiter breezed past with a tray of decadent-looking desserts, bound for another table. Elise found herself much more interested in what the young man was carrying than in the young man himself.

"Don't you think he's cute?" Audrey asked once he was out of earshot.

Audrey was wearing makeup now. Fairly conservative if you discounted the powder blue eye shadow that matched her long-sleeved T-shirt. Her normally curly hair was parted in the middle and had been tamed with some kind of straightening tool. Her face still held baby fat, her cheeks soft and slightly rounded. Her short nails had been carefully painted with silver, glittery polish.

Would she be tall? Elise wondered. Thomas was fairly tall. And what about her grandfather? Because more and more Elise found herself believing that she was the daughter of Jackson Sweet. She'd read that Jackson Sweet had been over six feet. Very few pictures had been taken of him, but Elise had once come across two blurry photos at the Historical Society. Brooding, with a long, thin face. He'd been wearing the glasses Strata Luna had given her.

Elise reached for the teapot. "Not my type, I guess," she replied in answer to Audrey's question about the waiter.

Audrey took one of the bite-size sandwiches from the tiny three-tiered tray. She examined it carefully, pulling back the bread to make sure the filling didn't contain something she would consider gross. Which could be almost anything, because Audrey's definition of *gross* changed with her mood. "Was Dad your type?" The question was presented in a sneaky, casual way.

Elise poured tea and put the pot back on the tray. "At one time."

"But not anymore."

"Well . . . no."

Elise knew Audrey blamed her for the divorce. Maybe she *was* to blame, more than anybody knew. It was a question that had haunted her since she and Thomas had married.

"Is David Gould your type?" Audrey asked with a sly smile.

"Gould?" Elise made a face and picked a red grape from the top tier of the serving tray. "*David* Gould?"

"Yeah. He's about your age, isn't he?"

"I guess." She popped the grape in her mouth.

"And single."

"Divorced, I think he told me."

"See. You're divorced; he's divorced."

Elise laughed and shook her head. "Audrey, we are nothing alike."

"You're both cops. Both detectives. You told me once that the reason you and Dad broke up was because you were too different. So you need a guy with the same lifestyle."

Elise thought it in poor taste to mention that her partner had a drinking problem and that beyond work their lives were nothing alike. But then, she knew how a young girl's thoughts could take off, and she didn't want Audrey to start thinking she and Gould could ever be *anything*. As it stood, they were barely even partners. "It's not going to happen," Elise said. "So get that out of your head."

"But you married Dad thinking you were so right for each other. Then you found out you weren't. Maybe you need to find somebody who seems wrong for you. Maybe then it would work."

Teenage logic. "Not all women need a man," Elise told her.

A couple of patrolling Guardian Angels walked past the window dressed in red berets and vests.

"How old do you have to be to be a Guardian Angel?" Audrey asked.

"Sixteen," Elise said. "Do you have an interest in being one?"

Audrey suddenly looked confused, then embarrassed, as if her own curiosity had caught her unaware. "No way," she stated, once again the annoyed, bored teen. "Why would I wanna do that?" And of course she wouldn't want to show interest in a profession that remotely resembled her mother's.

Elise had brought Audrey to the tearoom hoping to talk to her about Jackson Sweet, but suddenly the timing didn't seem right. When Audrey was up, you didn't want to risk bringing her crashing down. Why spoil the afternoon?

Their tea finished, Elise paid and left the waiter a nice tip. Then she and Audrey walked up Bull Street, through Madison and Chippewa Squares in the direction of the police station, where Thomas was scheduled to pick up his daughter.

The temperature was perfect. Not too hot or too humid. A white horse-drawn carriage moved lazily past, the Morgan's huge, shaggy feet clumping slowly and rhythmically against the brick street. Azaleas were blooming, and for a few short moments Elise could almost believe everything in their lives would be fine.

They were preparing to cross the street when Audrey halted abruptly. "Look!"

Turning the corner was a black car, its back windows tinted so nobody could see inside. The charming Enrique was at the wheel.

"Strata Luna," Audrey whispered in awe, her eyes glued to the long vehicle, her mouth hanging open. "They say she killed her *daughters*. That she drowned one and strangled the other. That is *so creepy*."

Elbows at her sides, Audrey rapidly waved her hands as if she might flutter off. "Oh-my-God," she gasped. "She's coming this way!" She pinched the sleeve of Elise's jacket and tugged. "Hurry! We have to run!"

The car pulled to a stop and the blackened electric window glided down. In the darkness of the backseat, Elise could make out the vague shape of a hat and veil.

"Elise." Strata Luna's melodic voice came from the murky interior. "Is this the daughter you were telling me about?"

Audrey stiffened. Elise could sense her shock, maybe even her disapproval.

Elise introduced her naive, innocent daughter to the woman who had feasted on her own mother's heart and ran a whorehouse. A nice wrap for a mother-daughter outing.

They were caught in the middle of a no-win situation. If Audrey chose to keep the encounter from her dad, then she'd be hiding things; if she chose to tell him, he'd be extremely upset.

"Are you skilled, child?" Strata Luna asked, choosing to keep her face hidden by the black veil.

"S-skilled?"

"Has your mother taught you anything? Passed on her root knowledge?"

"N-no."

"Elise, it's your duty to pass the mantle," Strata Luna said.

Audrey glanced at her mother. "That's okay. I don't want to know any of that root stuff."

"Then what do you do, child? What keeps your mind and body busy?"

"I play ball. Softball."

"Are you good?"

"Pretty good."

"Do you win?"

"Sometimes."

"I'll make a charm so you'll be always winning. Something you can wear around your neck."

"Audrey doesn't need a charm," Elise said firmly, while at the same time thinking of the herbal pouch Strata Luna had given to her. At that very moment, it was in her shoulder bag. "She's an excellent player."

"My ears hear what you're telling me," Strata Luna said with a sly smile in her voice. "Every mama knows what's best for her girl." She lifted a gloved hand and made a motion like a blown kiss. The electric window silently closed, leaving Elise and Audrey regarding their own reflections.

As they watched, the car glided away.

Beside Elise, still clinging tightly to her arm, Audrey whispered, "*Sweet kitty.*"

Chapter 19

Gary Turello's grave was labeled with a cheap metal marker. The kind with nothing more than a piece of paper slipped behind thin plastic. The family had given consent to exhume the body under the condition that they wouldn't be responsible for any fees incurred, including the cost of reburial. Elise was relieved that they'd had no desire to witness the event.

"He was seventeen," she told Gould, who stood beside her in shirtsleeves and loose tie.

"A kid," he agreed.

She'd done a little investigating and had found that Turello had been a runaway. And like many runaways who were broke and scared and homeless, he'd turned to prostitution. It had probably seemed an easy way out.

The exhumation was taking place in midafternoon of an overcast, shadowless day, hot and humid, with a heat index above ninety degrees, the air so heavy and wet it had wilted the fabric of Elise's suit. The smell of magnolia blossoms hung in the air. Bees buzzed among the tombs decorated with dying flowers while digital cameras silently recorded the event.

Laurel Grove Cemetery had been laid out in wide carriage lanes. Back in the days when early death was a part of life, relatives desired the comfort of constant communion, so the mausoleums had porches where people could sit and visit.

Savannah PD had tried to keep the exhumation from becoming media fodder, but as with all things tantalizing, people whispered secrets that could not be kept, and pretty soon news teams and press reporters were there from as far away as Atlanta.

Earlier that day, Cassandra Vince, the state medical examiner from the GBI in Decatur, had arrived. Casper had picked her up at the airport, and now the MEs stood side by side. Abe Chilton, crime scene specialist, was also there with a team.

The backhoe was loud and threatening as the bucket maneuvered into position above the grave. As everybody stepped back, Elise heard the whine of hydraulic cylinders. The bucket shifted, shuddered to a stop, then moved again in a jerky, awkward ballet until the teeth made contact with the ground and began to peel away the sod.

Georgia earth had a distinctive smell. Highly loamy and peaty, with hints of woodiness and stagnant water.

When she was little, Elise had picked up a library book called *Tales of the Grave*. Inside was a drawing of a cadaver clawing its way from the coffin to the surface of the ground. Not a comforting bedtime story.

"Stop!" The man in charge waved his arms, signaling to the backhoe operator.

Leaving the coffin's gray protective outer case in the ground, they broke the seal. Sticky, gummy residue trailed off the lid as it was lifted away. It took another piece of large equipment to hoist the coffin from the case.

Elise had helped Thomas pick out a casket for his grandfather. The mortician had talked about the different models as if they were cars. Elise and Thomas had looked at each other and burst out laughing. Completely inappropriate, but hysterical humor came at just such highly emotional moments. Thomas still talked about it. "Remember when we laughed our asses off at the coffin salesman?" he would sometimes say.

Abe Chilton broke away from the crowd and approached the casket, taping down evidence seals where the double lid met the body of the box. Two of his assistants documented the entire process—from the first bit of ground broken by the backhoe to the final seal—with a video camera and 35-mm film.

The casket was loaded onto a flatbed truck and secured with chains.

"Show's over," Gould said, hands in the pockets of his dress pants.

They were met by a wall of news junkies, cameras running, shutters clicking. A reporter from the *Savannah Morning News* jumped in front of them, took their photo, then asked for their names.

Elise didn't dislike the media the way some police did. She felt they could have a healthy, symbiotic relationship. She paused and told the reporters who they were. But when the questions turned to the body and exhumation, she put up her hands. "There'll be a press conference at police headquarters. The time will be announced later today."

In her faded yellow SAAB, Elise drove carefully,

getting Gould and herself through the crowd while the air conditioner blasted away and Spanish moss dragged across the windshield.

She took 516 to the Southwest Bypass in order to avoid the lights and traffic on Abercorn. The route probably didn't save them any time, but it was less stressful and didn't require idling in congested traffic. Fifteen minutes later, she swung into the small parking lot located directly in front of the new one-story building. She and Gould headed inside the morgue.

Elise had attended two autopsies of exhumed bodies. One had been a child who'd died unexpectedly, the other a case where a woman's third husband was found to have ingested rat poison. That led to the exhumation of her previous mates and the discovery of poison in both husbands' tissue samples.

The suite was packed.

Abe Chilton was there, along with his team. Conducting the autopsy was the state medical examiner, Dr. Cassandra Vince, along with John Casper and his crew. Two assistants sat on ladders with video cameras running so they could record from a good angle when the coffin lid was cracked open. There were even a few student interns, hoping to learn something or just looking for entertainment.

Everybody wore disposable yellow gowns.

"You never know what you're going to find when you open one of these," John Casper told the crowd. "Sometimes the body will be as fresh as the day it was put in the ground. Other times—it's mummified. All depends on the mortuary and how much embalming fluid they used."

He took a deep breath. "Here we go. Meet Mr. Turello."

Casper sliced through the chain of evidence tape, then swung open the divided lid, one section at a time.

Cameras clicked and flashes went off.

He was in fairly decent shape, Elise decided. There were a few areas on the face where the skin had fallen in and the color had darkened.

Gary Turello was dressed in shiny black leather pants and a black Ramones T-shirt. On his wrists were studded leather bands, on his tattooed fingers a multitude of rings. Beside him in the coffin were a pack of filterless cigarettes, a Zippo lighter, plus a red CD player, along with several CD jewel cases. His hair had been so heavily gelled—or glued—that it was still sticking up around a somewhat shrunk face.

Abe Chilton and his crime team moved in to collect and bag what they could.

"It seems a shame to disturb him," Elise said quietly.

A soft murmur of agreement followed her comment.

"Is that what I think it is?" Gould pointed.

Wedged between the body and the satin lining of the casket was a small glass tube. Using a pair of tweezers, one of the crime techs lifted the object out and held it high.

"A one-hit pipe." He checked out the end. "Complete with one hit."

A titter moved through the crowd.

"The funeral must have been open casket," Elise said dryly.

"A little something for the road."

The young technician bagged the glass pipe and marijuana while another person listed the items on a piece of paper.

Next came the CDs.

"We'll dust everything for prints," Chilton said.

"Does anybody else notice anything unusual about the CDs?" Casper asked.

The technician read off the band names as he bagged them. "INXS. Joy Division. Gin Blossoms. Better Than Ezra. Ministry."

"What are you getting at?" Elise asked.

"They're all groups in which a band member committed suicide," Casper told her.

"Whoa. You're right," commented the technician.

Elise glanced at Gould. She could see her own question in his eyes. Had the CDs been left as a joke by a friend? Or had Turello's killer attended the funeral?

There were too many people in the room. It wouldn't be wise to discuss the case in front of them.

We have to talk about this, Elise wanted to tell him.

He lifted his eyebrows. *Later.*

Casper and the technician were still chattering.

"But hey, didn't they think Michael Hutchence maybe died of autoerotic asphyxiation?" the technician asked.

"I think his case was finally ruled a suicide," Casper told him.

"Are you sure?" The tech tapped a finger to his chin, then pointed to Casper, his head tilted. "Maybe you're thinking of that guy from Max Under the Stars. What was his name?"

"Jerome somebody."

"Yeah. He hung himself too."

"Then there are all the ones who died of drug overdoses. Some of those had to be suicides."

"And think of all the guys who just disappeared."

Casper nodded. "Suicide."

"Creativity spawns instability. Or is it the other way around?"

"Boys, boys, boys," Dr. Vince said with humor in her voice. "Would it be terribly rude of me to suggest we quit discussing rock trivia and get back to the autopsy?"

Casper's face turned red. "Yeah. Sure. Sorry." He sheepishly scanned the room.

When all possible evidence was collected, attendants jockeyed for position in order to lift the body from the wooden box to the stainless steel exam table.

In a normal autopsy, every item of clothing was tagged and cataloged, but this wasn't a normal autopsy. John Casper and two assistants began removing the clothing. First the laced red tennis shoes.

The room was silent except for the ticking of a large, industrial wall clock and the downdraft fan.

The human body is so frighteningly fragile, Elise thought.

Beginning at the hem, the state ME cut the pants. The scissors were sharp, and it wasn't difficult to get through the leather.

The material fell away.

"No underwear?" Casper said. "What the hell's wrong with that mortuary?"

The T-shirt followed, revealing the Y autopsy stapled incision across the sunken chest.

Elise recognized the body for what it was: a vessel that had harbored the spirit of Gary Turello.

The autopsy couldn't be as extensive as the original, but every one followed a rigid blueprint, which the ME adhered to as closely as possible.

They took a series of X rays, which were sent to a technician. Then Dr. Vince began her external exam.

"As far as physical evidence," she said, "it would be almost impossible to find anything on an embalmed body like this. Certainly nothing that would stand up in court."

Organs that had already been removed and replaced once before were lifted free of the body cavity and weighed, with samples taken. The liver, the organ that would be most important if they were to find any toxins, had shriveled to less than half its original size.

Two hours later, they were done.

"When can we expect results?" Elise asked.

"It depends on a lot of things," Dr. Vince told her. "We'll start by running some of the cheaper, more rapid tests, like the radioimmunoassay and enzyme-mediated immunoassay. If those don't show anything, then we'll have to pull out the big, expensive guns, like mass spectrometry and gas chromatography. That would take quite a bit longer."

"How much longer?"

"A week. Maybe two. Sorry, but we have to adhere to a certain protocol."

Elise and Gould thanked her and left the autopsy suite.

"I know how anxious you are about this," Gould said when they were alone in the adjoining supply room, "but I'm actually impressed with how quickly we got that guy out of the ground and to the morgue."

Elise untied her gown and tossed it in the biohazard

container. "If Turello is a victim, then our killer goes back a lot farther than we think. And it will also give us a whole new thread of clues to follow. And what about those CDs? What significance do they have?"

"You're getting ahead of yourself. We have no idea if this guy is connected to the recent crimes."

"But what if he is? What if the CDs were left by the killer?"

"Justification for the killing, maybe. Someone could reason that a prostitute is killing himself. Committing slow suicide. And our killer just helped him along."

"Or it could be a death obsession."

She looked through the glass, to the body still on the table. Two workers from a Savannah funeral home were there, signing paperwork.

"The family is going to have a memorial service," she said. "Then he's to be reburied."

Gould wadded up his gown and tossed it in the bin. "That's just sad as hell."

"I don't know," Elise said. "Years ago, it wasn't unusual for Gullahs to bury their loved ones twice."

"A second burial? I don't get it."

"The body decomposed so quickly in the heat that they would bury the deceased, then dig him up a year or two later at a more convenient time when all of the family and friends could gather."

"Ah," Gould said with exaggerated satisfaction. "Just another quaint local custom."

Chapter 20

"I've heard people aren't getting embalmed and are holding three-day wakes," Gould said as he and Elise walked side by side in the direction of the Savannah Police Department conference room.

It was the day after the exhumation, and Major Hoffman had called an impromptu meeting. Elise was suspicious, because so far nothing had really changed. Except for Harrison's unconnected death, they were still dealing with one prostitute, maybe two, and insufficient evidence. And the police department was still broke and short of officers.

They missed the elevator. Already late, Elise headed in the direction of the stairs. "Funeral homes are complaining because of the smell and potential health risks."

"When I die," Gould said, jogging up the steps beside her, "be sure to bury me with a bell."

"Not a cell phone?" Elise asked. "I just saw an advertisement for a company claiming to offer crystal clear service six feet under."

"Cell phones are undependable. We need to get

back to basics. I want one of those contraptions they sold back in the days when the definition of death was even murkier than it is now. We should think about going into a new business," he told her. "Those are going to be a hot commodity. We won't be able to make them quickly enough. What could you call them? Let's see. . . . Death bells. Coffin bells. I like that. Or burial bell. How about burial bell?"

"And the slogan would be 'For whom the burial bell tolls.' "

They were bantering. Gould paused at the fire door and beamed at her as if she'd suddenly given him a long-desired gift. "Exactly."

In the conference room, Elise recognized a couple of agents from the Georgia Bureau of Investigation, Abe Chilton, a woman from the crime lab, plus the local FBI and the press liaison. Starsky and Hutch— or rather Mason and Avery—were also present. But the majority of occupants were uniformed police officers there to be briefed on the TTX case.

Things were just about to get under way, so Elise and David grabbed two empty seats near the door.

"The way I understand it," Major Hoffman told the crowd, "is that TTX poisoning is like having the wrong key in a lock. It blocks the keyhole, so nothing can get through. And because TTX cannot cross the blood-brain barrier, the victim remains conscious while the peripheral nervous system shuts down."

"That sounds like science fiction," Detective Mason commented.

"Simplified, TTX is nothing more than poisoning that puts people in a state of suspended animation," Major Hoffman said. "It mimics death. Reputable doctors have been fooled into thinking a victim is dead."

A beat officer wanted to know about the warning stages. Someone else asked what people could do to protect themselves.

"The most important thing is to be vigilant," Major Hoffman said. "With the recent budget cuts, we're hurting for manpower. This means we need community involvement. Savannah residents have to be our eyes and ears. If someone sees anything in the least suspicious, something that doesn't seem right, he needs to call the police. Same thing goes for police officers. When you're out on patrol, be aware. Keep your eyes open. Trust your gut, and follow up on anything that doesn't seem right."

"Is it true that this stuff is used to make zombies?" Detective Avery asked.

"That is exactly the kind of reaction I want to discourage," Major Hoffman said sternly. "It's my understanding that it's one of the ingredients, along with some less toxic poisons. Something to keep in mind is that in Haiti, zombification is often used as retribution for wrongdoers. It's possible someone is doling out sentences for things he sees as crimes, possibly against himself, possibly against others."

Major Hoffman rolled out a media cart. She popped a tape into the deck, picked up the remote, and turned on the television and VCR.

Gould borrowed Elise's pen and jotted something down on his tablet.

"I just had a visit from the mayor," Hoffman said. "He's extremely concerned with the TTX case and left something I want everybody to see."

It was well known that the mayor of Savannah never commented on crime other than to say that Savannah was no worse than any other city of its size. But now that an election year was coming up, he must have decided it was time to display concern.

The tape rolled.

Poor quality. Something that had been filmed with a bad camera, in a bad public-access studio, with bad equipment.

Elise and David simultaneously let out low groans as they recognized the face on the screen.

Harvey Ostertag, of *The Ostertag Show*.

The Ostertag Show was filmed in Atlanta on a small budget. One camera. Horrid lighting. Crappy microphones that produced muffled voices. It was both embarrassing and mesmerizing as only awful TV could be.

"As promised," Ostertag announced, "here are Katie Johnson, Twila Jackson, and Mercury Hernandez, all the way from Savannah, Georgia."

The girls moved into position. Two twirled a thick, heavy rope while the third jumped. All three chanted in unison:

> *Draw a circle on the floor*
> *Whisper secret words*
> *The city sleeps*
> *The mayor weeps*
> *Speak the final dirge.*

Aha. No wonder the mayor had taken a sudden interest in the TTX case, Elise thought.

The camera closed in on the host.

"Mysterious ditties like the one you just heard have

been popping up all over Savannah," Ostertag said. "Some people have compared these to nursery rhymes. But others claim they bear a striking resemblance to the meter used in spells. In black magic. One theory is that by the repetitious chanting of these spells, children are unknowingly calling forth the powers of evil upon an unsuspecting city."

Major Hoffman shut off the VCR. "Lovely, isn't it? We're accustomed to being ridiculed by the media," she said, "but I think ridicule on *The Ostertag Show* is a new low."

Elise pulled Gould's tablet close and read the question he'd written earlier: *Are we going to watch porn?*

He ripped the paper from the spiral and wadded it up, making a great deal of noise.

"Mr. Gould," Major Hoffman said. "Since you've played a fairly passive role in this meeting, perhaps you'd like to share some of your feelings about the case."

Christ. He was in third grade all over again. *Is there something you'd like to share with the class, David?*

A titter moved through the crowd. Several people twisted around to give David smug smiles. Starsky and Hutch were grinning with evil delight.

Oh, this place was its own vicious small town, David thought. Half the people in the room were salivating.

"Actually, I've had some profiling experience," David said calmly.

Hutch let out a snort. Major Hoffman looked his direction; he turned the snort into a cough. "I'd like to hear what Detective Gould has to say," Major Hoffman said. "For the sake of discussion, let's assume these deaths are murder, all by the same hand."

David wasn't thrilled at being put on the spot. On the other hand, he knew his stuff and wasn't afraid to brainstorm and theorize. "For starters," he said, leaning back in his chair, "the killer is an egomaniac."

Starsky and Hutch looked at him with annoyance. If they weren't in such good company, David was sure they would have had some sarcastic comment like, "Tell us something we don't know."

"He sees himself almost as a puppeteer, someone controlling the show," David continued. "Many people kill out of self-hatred and a lack of confidence. This person is killing because he thinks it's his right. He probably doesn't even consider the victims as people."

"Could he be doing it for his own amusement?" Elise wondered aloud. "Simply from boredom? Otherwise, why doesn't he kill them outright? I don't get it."

"Some derive sexual pleasure from torture," someone offered.

"But where's the pleasure if they're comatose?" Elise asked. "Wouldn't it come from hearing them scream? From watching their suffering faces? These people can't respond in any way."

"He's getting off on their *inability* to respond," David said.

"That could be the key," Elise said thoughtfully. "He may have experienced a time in his life when he was unable to defend himself." Her gaze cleared as her idea solidified. "Possibly at the hands of an adult figure." She leaned forward. "Think about the way siblings will pass various childhood cruelties down the line."

"This is a little more than a childhood cruelty," Major Hoffman pointed out.

"Of course, but the principle is the same," David

said. "The logic, or lack of logic, behind it is the same. They are passing the sin, that sin growing from one person to the next."

His comment was followed by a long communal silence.

"That makes sense," Elise finally said.

"What do you think about age? Race? Occupation? Education?" Those questions came from Starsky.

"I'm unsure about race, but I feel he's highly intelligent and fairly well educated, although he may have stopped short of receiving a degree. Possibly successful within his field of expertise. Age, somewhere between twenty and thirty-five. He's probably harbored a hatred of humanity for years, possibly since childhood."

"Hatred combined with ego is a dangerous combination," Elise said.

"Thank you very much, Detective Gould," Major Hoffman said with a gracious smile. "My grandmother would have said you've been hiding your light under a basket."

David found her praise in front of Starsky and Hutch to be extremely gratifying.

"I'd like a copy of your profile on my desk ASAP," the major added.

Which meant he would have to actually type one up. David hated reports. He hated typing.

"Detectives Avery and Mason." Starsky and Hutch gave Major Hoffman their attention.

"I'm putting you both on the TTX case on a part-time, as-needed basis. I want you to assist Detectives Sandburg and Gould in any manner they see fit."

David looked at Elise in dismay. Starsky and Hutch looked at each other in dismay.

Oh, boy. Just one big, happy, dysfunctional family.

Chapter 21

"It's the necromancer spirit!" the TV evangelist shouted from behind a pulpit. "Hanging over the city of Savannah! A spirit that is praying to the dead! Worshiping dead spirits! Voodoo curses, brought by servants of the devil! Creating mindless people who have no pulse, who breathe no air, but are alive!"

A font showed up on the bottom of Elise's TV screen: BROTHER SAMUEL, OF THE CHURCH OF SAMUEL. It was late. Almost midnight, but Elise couldn't quit thinking of the theories that had been tossed around that afternoon at police headquarters.

"A curse put on our fair city!" the man on the TV continued to shout. "We must pray! Children of the devil. A demon spirit we've allowed into our homes! Caused by rejecting Christianity! I plead with you to come forward now and beg forgiveness, to denounce the devil. Denounce the necromancers!"

Another message appeared at the bottom of the screen: a P.O. box where people could send their donations.

Elise clicked off the TV, picked up her portable phone, and called David.

He answered after one ring, sounding wide-awake.

"What do you know about necrophilia?" Elise asked.

"Necrophilia. A pretty word for a really sick sickness."

"I keep asking myself, why would the killer drug someone with TTX in the first place?"

"You think the guy could be a necrophiliac? An interesting theory. But a necrophiliac gets off on dead people, not zombies."

"As we all know, a dead body begins to do nasty things pretty damn quickly, especially in a hot, humid environment like Savannah," she said.

"So he simulates death. So he can romance the body until the victim eventually really dies."

"Then tosses it like so much garbage."

"What a sweetheart."

"I think we need to check local funeral homes and cemeteries. The morgue. Get a list of employees. See if any of them have ever shown a particular fondness for the dead."

"Sounds like a good job for Starsky and Hutch."

"You read my mind."

The flashlight beam sent cockroaches scurrying for darkness in one giant black wave. There were billions of them, packed into every crack and seam. The walls of the tunnel were made of brick, with a rounded ceiling. Years ago someone painted them white, but now the red was bleeding through.

Tunnels are everywhere under Savannah. Nobody

talks about them much, but they're here. Some have collapsed; some have been filled in. All have been sealed, most with bricks and mortar, others with a grate that can still be opened if a person knows where to look.

I knew where to look. I made it my business to know.

The tunnels are a black, rotten, infested world that lurks just below the feet of the gentlemen who frequent the exclusive Oglethorpe Club. Sometimes when I was walking along President Street and passed a sewer grate, I would get a whiff of that fetid, rotten stink and know decay was near.

It was easy to blend with the homeless.

And there are a lot of homeless in Savannah. They like to hang out downtown, in the square nearest Martin Luther King Boulevard.

When you're homeless, you're invisible. People, even cops, look right through you. Tourists don't want to make eye contact for fear you'll hit them up for cash or say something crazy. . . .

Right now I was in a section of tunnel near the old Candler Hospital. It was no longer a hospital but some kind of home for old people. I could always get my bearings near Candler, because the tunnel was littered with discarded and forgotten hospital debris like old wooden wheelchairs and rusty gurneys.

I reached in my pocket and pulled out a map dating back to the 1800s that I had lifted from the Georgia Historical Society.

Finding my way around in the tunnels was a little like playing Monopoly, only with bigger pieces.

I traced my finger along the path leading to the

Hartzell, Tate, and Hartzell Funeral Home. A left, then a right, then a left.

Advance to Boardwalk.

I slipped the map back in my pocket, grabbed a gurney, and continued my journey.

The funeral home was located in an old mansion with a catacomb-like basement that seemed miles from the rest of the building. Like everything else about the tunnels, the sealed entrance was crumbling.

I'd been this way before.

It didn't take long to dig out the bricks and make a hole large enough to crawl through—and I'm not a small person.

But once inside, I got a little turned around—it was such a maze! Room after room of embalming para-phernalia. Shelves of embalming fluid. Boxes of drainage tubes and expression formers. Yes, that's right. They could actually make a dead person smile. But then, I could do that too.

I moved silently up a flight of stairs. I'd also been here before, so it was easy to locate the cooler.

And locate my friend, Mr. Turello.

He looked good, considering. And lucky for me he was a little bit freeze-dried. Much lighter than the night I dumped him in an abandoned lot off Skidaway Road.

But he was still heavy.

I wasn't exactly sure why I decided to collect him. For one thing, I thought it might be fun. Stir up the cops. Those two detectives. Elise Sandburg. David Gould.

David Gould. He was kind of sexy. Really sexy, ac-tually. I'd seen him running and running. As if some-one, or something, was after him.

I had to drape Turello over my back to carry him. He was stiff, but pliant at the same time. A little like a cheap leather jacket you know is never going to soften up no matter how many times you wear it.

When I originally dumped him, he smelled. Dead-rat awful. Now he smelled . . . mysterious. Like the sweet odor of embalming fluid, but also maybe a little like compost.

Downstairs, I dragged him through the opening, sealed it back up, put him on the gurney, and we were off.

"Somebody's going to be shocked as hell," I told Gary as I shoved him along the rough floor.

Anybody who's ever had to deal with a shopping cart with a bad wheel will know how bone jarring it can be. Not fun. Not fun at all.

Then I forgot about my struggle and laughed softly to myself. I couldn't help it as I pictured the chaos tomorrow morning when they couldn't find Gary.

Psychiatrists might say I was starved for attention. That I didn't get enough as a child.

They would be right.

Chapter 22

A little after midnight mortician Benjamin Ming arrived for work and unlocked the delivery door of the Hartzell, Tate, and Hartzell Funeral Home. He reached around the corner and flipped on the overhead lights while allowing the heavy door to close and lock behind him.

He went straight to his desk to look over his shift orders. Old man Hartzell had already called to fill him in, but Ben always double-checked.

Two bodies.

One straightforward embalming, one just a basic sprucing up.

Gary Turello. The guy who'd been exhumed.

Ben had heard about him on the news. He was being reburied, and Hartzell, Tate, and Hartzell had donated a marble headstone. It was advertising, but still a nice gesture, Ben conceded.

The embalming order was a thirty-two-year-old woman who'd died of cancer.

Ben wheeled her from the cooler and began preparations. He undressed the body, then gently stretched and massaged the limbs in order to limber them up. After the body was washed, he sliced open an artery in the groin and one in the neck. While the blood drained into the table gutters, he returned to the walk-in cooler to retrieve Mr. Turello.

"Finch. Austin. Johnson," he said, checking the toe tags.

He straightened, hands on his waist, and perused the small room.

Hmm.

He rechecked the tags.

He lifted the sheets.

Old lady.

Middle-aged lady.

Fifty-something man.

All fresh. The women were scheduled for cremation after their funeral service; the guy was to be done tomorrow.

Where was Turello?

Ben's heart started to slam in alarm.

Had Hartzell, Tate, and Hartzell lost a body?

The soles of David's running shoes pounded against the sidewalk as he ran a familiar route through town.

There were three reasons he was running at four a.m.

One, he couldn't sleep.

Two, he hadn't had a chance to run for several days.

Three, he thought the odd jogging time might help him avoid Flora—who suddenly seemed to think she owned him because she'd convinced herself that she'd saved his life the other night.

She stopped by too often. She left messages on his cell phone.

David found her company easy. And certainly a distraction . . . but was she good for him? Was he good for her? Or were they just two smart but extremely messed-up people clinging to each other for comfort?

Yep.

As he neared Mary of the Angels, he slowed to a walk and cut to the left, stepping off the sidewalk and into the shadows of a magnolia tree. Keeping to the edges of the darkness, he stealthily approached his apartment, scanning the area for any sign of Flora.

He caught a shifting of shadows beneath the overhang at the front door.

Damn.

He glanced up the side of the building, to his room, where a dim light burned, and briefly considered trying to scale the stones and crawl in the window. That idea was quickly but reluctantly tossed out due to its lack of cool and a slant toward the juvenile.

He stepped from the shadows and approached the ivy-wrapped building. "What'll it be?" he asked. "Sex or conversation?"

Someone emerged from the recesses.

Dark, straight hair. Dark eyes. Pale skin.

Elise.

"I'm guessing you were expecting someone else."

"Forget what I said. Just an old Yankee idiom." He waved his hand in insignificance. "Roughly translated, it means 'Who goes there?' "

He wiped an arm across his sweaty forehead. "Now that I know the *who* answer to that question, what about the what? As in what are you doing here?"

"We've had another interesting development. Come on." She nodded her head toward the building. "Let's talk inside."

He unlocked the door with a key that was heavy and worn smooth. Side by side, they hurried up the marble steps and down the hall to his third-floor apartment.

Once inside with the door shut, she turned and faced him, her arms crossed.

"Remember how Gary Turello was supposed to be taken to a local funeral home?"

"If you're going to tell me Turello woke up in the morgue, I will then know that this is all a madman's dream, and that Mary of the Angels is really a mental institute."

Isobel came strutting from the bedroom, trying to appear casual while at the same time extremely interested in their guest.

"Turello didn't wake up, but he disappeared from the funeral home."

David tugged his sweat-soaked T-shirt over his head and used it to wipe his neck and chest. "You think he may have been accidentally cremated?"

"Seems logical, doesn't it?"

Isobel circled Elise's legs. She bent to pet her.

She was doing it wrong. Isobel didn't like to be lightly stroked down the middle of the back.

"Since when has anything about this case been logical?" He headed for the shower. "Give me five minutes," he said over his shoulder. "You can entertain Isobel. She likes to be scratched on the stomach."

"Yankee idiom, my ass," Elise said once she and Isobel were alone.

Had he been lying about the stomach petting too? Elise was a little afraid to try it. Every cat she knew clawed the hell out of you if you touched its stomach.

She scratched Isobel's chin.

Liked that.

Behind the ear.

Didn't much like that.

Down the spine.

Seemed to hate that.

Stomach.

Isobel dropped heavily to the floor, purring and stretching for more.

The cat was every bit as strange as its owner.

"It's not safe to jog in the middle of the night," Elise told David when he returned from the shower, his hair wet. "Your being a cop doesn't mean anything. A jogger, male or female, alone at night is a target."

He ignored her and looked down, buttoning his shirt. "What'd I tell you?" He pointed to Isobel, who was purring madly. "She likes it on the stomach."

Elise straightened away from the cat. "Savannah is a port city. It has a long history of street crimes against the unwary and the foolish, going back to pirate days. Are you listening to me?"

He tucked his shirttail into his pants. "I'm listening."

"I don't want you jogging at night anymore." It wasn't an order; it was a plea.

"I won't promise you that."

"Why do you do it? You have to know it's dangerous. Do you get some kind of thrill out of it? Or do you just not care about yourself?"

For an instant, something seemed to fall away from him. She saw a bleakness in his eyes, and despair.

Then it was gone.

"I have trouble sleeping," he said, sitting down on the couch, pulling on socks and shoes. "Running helps."

"How long have you had this sleeping problem?"

He tied his shoes and stood up. "Ever since I got here, but it's been a lot worse lately."

"How many nights a week?"

"Every night."

He grabbed his apartment key and stuck it in his pocket. He shrugged into his black jacket. "All night." Before she could respond, he pushed the conversation away.

"Come on," he said. "We can talk about this later."

The streets were deserted, and it took Elise and David only a few minutes to get from his apartment to the funeral home. When they arrived, two police cars were parked in front of the green, arched awning above a wide walkway.

Officer Eve Salazar was guarding the door.

"What's the story?" Elise asked.

"The guy who does the embalming came in to get the body ready for the service. I guess dress it and stuff." She pressed her lips together and fatalistically shook her head. "Couldn't find the body."

"Any sign of a break-in?" David asked.

"Nope. The building has a top-of-the-line security alarm that wasn't tripped. No sign of anything. Nothing knocked over. Nothing out of place. Just a missing dead guy."

"What about the crime scene team?"

"We're holding off." She leaned closer. "Until you verify that a crime has been committed and we're not dealing with just a misplaced body."

"Good call."

"Everybody else is downstairs where they keep the bodies."

Officer Salazar pointed across a deep red carpet. "Take the steps to the basement. Then make a right. You can't miss it."

"These places certainly have a distinctive odor, don't they?" David whispered as they headed downstairs. "Kind of heavy. Kind of sweet."

"Like a rich dessert, only deader?" Elise asked.

"Exactly."

There were three uniformed police officers in the room, along with the owner of the funeral home and the mortician who'd alerted everyone to the missing body. The funeral director, a man named Simms, had managed to throw on the obligatory dark suit.

The partners introduced themselves.

"I can't explain it." The director's frantic gaze went from Elise to David, and back again.

The detectives perused the room. "Anything out of place?" Elise asked.

"Nothing."

They interviewed the mortician, an earnest little man named Benjamin Ming. He didn't have much to tell them that they didn't already know.

Elise strolled into the adjoining crematorium. David and the director followed.

The room temperature was cool. She examined the heat gauges on the machine.

Nothing registered anything.

"How long does it take for the oven to cool down after use?"

"Hours," the director told her. "The oven hasn't been used in days. The police officers already asked me about it. Why are you trying to point the finger at me? Ever since the ugly business with the funeral home that had uncremated bodies stuck in every corner, we're all suspect. I resent it. I'm the one who's the victim here. Along with poor Mr. Turello."

"Nobody's trying to accuse you of anything," David said. "We have to consider every angle so we know what to rule out. Once we've eliminated accidental cremation, then we can focus our investigation on other possible scenarios."

The director grabbed a tissue from a nearby box and wiped it down both sides of his face. "Sorry. We pride ourselves in having an impeccable reputation. I'm the third generation in this establishment, and we've never had this kind of thing happen. Ever."

Elise felt sorry for him. Normally he was the one who remained calm and collected, who soothed the upset patrons. "Mr. Simms," she said in a voice that was soft and serious, "have you ever had any employees who seemed particularly . . . *fond* of the dead?"

He frowned. "What are you talking about?"

"We're talking about necrophilia," David said. "Being in this line of business, you've surely heard of it."

"Of course." The director was flustered. Angry. "But I'm here to emphatically tell you that no one— NO ONE—in my employ has ever . . ." His words trailed off. He seemed unable to continue.

"We will need a list of everyone who now works

for you," David said. "Plus everyone who's worked here in the past three years. Cleaning people. Lawn care. Everybody."

Elise called in a crime scene team to collect evidence, then moved on to the more traditional questions.

Anybody suspicious around?

Anybody who might be doing it to make Hartzell, Tate, and Hartzell look bad?

That was followed by an exchange of cards and phone numbers. "Call us if you think of anything," Elise told Simms. "We'll be checking back."

"You know what people are going to be saying about this, don't you?" David asked once they were outside, both of them squinting and flinching like vampires against the bright morning sunlight.

"That Gary Turello got up and walked out of there all by himself?" Elise asked.

"You got it."

"We need to talk to Strata Luna again," she said. "Find out if she knew Turello. My guess is she did."

"Go ahead. Give her a call." David pulled a pair of dark glasses from his jacket pocket and slipped them on. "But this time I'm coming along."

Chapter 23

"Is this your store's logo?"

The scruffy-haired kid behind the cash register examined the CD in Elise's hand. "Yep."

Next to her, Gould spread more bagged CDs on the glass countertop. "Notice anything strange about these?" he asked.

The kid looked them over. "This some kind of test?"

"Look closely," Gould insisted.

The kid fiddled with the hair on his chin. "Well . . . oh, hey. I get it. They're all suicides! Is that it?"

"That's it," Elise said. "But more important, they all have your sticker on them. Would you or any other employee possibly recall someone making a purchase of this sort a year and a half ago?"

"Wow." The kid scratched his head. "I have a hard time remembering what happened last week."

Another guy wandered out of the back room. He was heavily pierced and wearing spiked leather wristbands.

"Hey, Tobias. Come 'ere." The kid at the counter

looked at the detectives. "Toby's the manager. He's worked here a long time." Then back over his shoulder, he shouted, "Take a look at these, will you?"

The sleepy-looking kid took his time getting there.

The clerk pointed to the CDs. "You remember anybody buying these?"

"Who're you?" The manager eyed Elise and Gould with suspicion.

They flashed their badges and introduced themselves. That settled him down a little.

"I don't remember. Sorry."

"Would it be possible for you to locate a record of the sales?" Elise asked. "Especially if they were all purchased at the same time?"

"I dunno. . . ."

"Maybe in your tax files?" Gould prodded. "I'm sure you keep cash register tapes."

"You're talking about a lot of stuff," he said doubtfully. "And it could take a long time."

"It's extremely important," Elise told him.

"I'll try, but I don't know. . . ."

Gould presented the photos of Winslow, Turello, and Harrison.

Negative.

Elise handed the manager her card. "Call if you find anything or happen to think of something you forgot." She thanked them both for their time. Then she and Gould headed for the parking lot, passing a small playground on the way. In the center of the basketball court, three girls jumped rope.

Lady in a black veil
Babies in the bed

Kissed them on the forehead
Now they're both dead.

"What a serendipitous segue." Gould looked at her over the top of the car. "Isn't it about time for our meeting with the priestess of death?"

Elise had been able to schedule another appointment with Strata Luna, this one at the woman's home. When she'd asked if her partner could come along, Strata Luna had surprisingly agreed.

The detectives hopped in the car and drove to the Victorian District, where they parked on the street and approached the mansion on foot. Elise announced their arrival to the intercom and they were buzzed in, the black iron gate swinging wide.

The partners stepped through the opening, broken shells crunching underfoot.

"Where no man has gone before," Gould said.

"Person," Elise reminded him. "They upgraded *Star Trek: TNG* to the politically correct *person*."

"That was because the vainglorious James T. Kirk was of the martini-swilling, swinger generation, where women were conquests and trophies," Gould added.

"With large breasts."

"A requisite."

They were conversing with neither giving much attention to what they were saying, both taking in the lush surroundings as they paused side by side at the start of a straight drive lined with live oaks, their sweeping branches creating a curved canopy. At the end of the lane stood a pink antebellum mansion trimmed in black.

Breathtaking.

Behind them the gate clicked shut.

"An ominous sound," Gould muttered.

The ever-present Enrique met Elise and Gould at the door. He gave them a serene smile, then led them down a dark hallway to a secluded courtyard, where they found Strata Luna sitting in the shade at a round café table. She wore her signature long black dress minus hat, veil, and gloves.

Elise introduced her partner.

Neither seemed terribly impressed with the other.

"I hope you like hot tea," Strata Luna said, introduction over and Gould's importance quickly minimized. She seemed to be tolerating him because he was with Elise.

A china teapot had been placed on a tray in the center of the table. Beside it was a plate of shortbread cookies, sugar cubes with a pair of tiny silver tongs, and cream.

They were being treated like visitors, not detectives, something that made Elise feel slightly uncomfortable. She shot a glance at Gould, wondering if he was thinking what she was thinking—that this had a tinge of a Mad Hatter's tea party.

He missed her glance, distracted as he looked beyond the courtyard to a massive, ornate fountain.

The fountain where Strata Luna's daughter had drowned?

In the center was a statue of a young girl. Elise had heard that a life-size memorial of the drowned child had been erected somewhere on the property.

As they drank the dark exotic tea, Elise questioned Strata Luna about the prostitute Gary Turello. Gould pulled out the dead man's photo.

"He worked for me at one time, but I can't tell you anything about him." Strata Luna passed the photo back.

"Did he have any friends we might be able to speak to?" Gould asked.

"I don't know. That's the truth. When did you say he died?"

"A year and a half ago."

Strata Luna frowned, appearing puzzled. And for the first time, maybe a little worried. "You think his death has something to do with these recent ones? But that doesn't make any sense, does it? It was so long ago."

"We believe they're connected," Elise told her. "We just haven't come up with the evidence necessary to link them."

Gould remained focused on Strata Luna. "You seem worried," he observed bluntly.

"Of course I'm worried," she said in a defensive tone. "Everybody in this city is worried."

"Can you give us names of anybody he may have associated with?" Elise asked. "Or people who may have known the slightest thing about him?"

Strata Luna shook her head. "I wouldn't know, darlin'. I don't socialize with my employees."

"What about Enrique?" Elise asked in an attempt to trip her up. "You seem on fairly good terms with him."

"That's different." Strata Luna waved a long-nailed hand. "He's more like family."

"And Flora Martinez?" Gould asked, an unusual note in his voice.

"She's like a daughter."

Before Elise could give the episode much thought, Strata Luna continued. "There is one person you might want to talk to. I thought about him a few days ago. His name is James LaRue. He comes to Black Tupelo sometimes, sniffing round my girls, asking questions."

"What kinds of questions?" Elise asked.

"About me."

"I wouldn't think that would be so unusual. People are curious about you."

"Newspeople, yes. Reporters, yes. But a retired scientist? What does he wanna know? I ask myself. I finally agreed to speak to him on the phone."

"And?" Elise asked.

"Said he was studying tetrodotoxin. Writing a book. But I think he was looking for a place to *buy* tetrodotoxin. He insinuated I use it to get high." She lifted her chin and looked down her nose. LaRue was unworthy of her. "People wanna see me for many reasons. Some are curious. Some want a story. Others just want their fortunes told."

"You tell fortunes?" Elise asked.

"Used to. Years ago, when I was hardly more than a child. I gave a few people some good advice on stocks and lottery numbers. People who've heard 'bout my early success have offered large amounts of money for advice. But I don't do that no more."

"Why'd you quit?" Gould asked. "I'd think fortune-telling would be less unpleasant than . . . escort service."

"Humans are intuitive, but few know how to channel that power, including myself. I couldn't foresee the deaths of my own children. I could pick stocks and lottery numbers, but I couldn't save the people who meant the most to me."

All three fell silent. Strata Luna finally looked across the table at Gould. "It's a beautiful fountain, isn't it?"

Gould was once again staring past the potted plants, creeper vine, and magnolia tree, to the fountain. Strata Luna's direct statement caused his cup to slip. He caught it as it rattled against the saucer.

"Do you have any children, Detective Gould?" Strata Luna asked in a way that seemed deliberate as well as elusive. "Alive or dead? Because we must always remember the dead."

Did she question everyone about offspring? Elise wondered.

Gould pulled his gaze from the statue. He stared at Strata Luna for a long time before attacking her question with one of his own. "You lost two children, didn't you? Two girls?"

"I had two daughters," Strata Luna said. "Both are dead. Deliliah drowned, and Marie hung herself." She glared at him, her voice angry. "But you would have already known that, so why talk about it to me?"

"Just my job," Gould said, refusing to be intimidated.

"I know what people say. They say I killed them. Is that what you think? Is that what you're implying? Are you looking for a confession?"

Gould blinked, apparently figuring he'd gone too far. "The question was out of line. I'm sorry."

His words might have fooled anybody else. But Strata Luna was a perceptive woman. She would know he didn't mean them.

"Would a mother kill her own child?" Strata Luna asked.

"It happens," Gould said flatly.

The sudden tension and hostility between the two was palpable. Should she jump in? Elise wondered. Or let the scene play out?

"Not this mother." Strata Luna jabbed a finger at herself. "This mother would never kill her own children."

"I said I was sorry."

"Words are real. Even if you can't see them, or hold them. Once you send them out in the world, they have power. Never speak words you don't mean."

Gould was trapped. There was no response that could placate the woman. Elise had decided it was time to intervene when Strata Luna spoke again.

"You need to stop your self-destructive ways," she told him.

The eye lock was broken.

Gould suddenly made a big deal out of peering into his empty cup. "Did I miss something? Did you read my tea leaves?"

Always turning everything into a joke.

"I try to guide people," Strata Luna said. "I try to keep them from being foolish."

Gould replaced his cup on the saucer. "Thanks for the advice." His voice may have been level, but Elise didn't miss the underlying sarcasm.

He stood. "I have a couple of questions for Enrique."

"He should be in the house unless he's left for the grocery store." Strata Luna waved behind her, clearly glad to be rid of Gould. "Feel free to look around. I have nothing to hide."

"I'll catch up in a minute," Elise told him.

Gould nodded and strode away.

"He could use some lessons in self-discipline," Strata Luna said once he was gone.

"Detective Gould's okay," Elise said, surprised to find that her opinion of him had changed for the better. He was more than holding his own, and sometimes a detective had to ask tough questions to get the right answers. His tactic had been a good one, just misplaced.

"Thanks for agreeing to see us," Elise said, getting to her feet.

Strata Luna reached out and grabbed her arm, fingers squeezing tightly. "Sit down."

Elise remained standing. "Remove your hand." Now it was her turn to confront Strata Luna.

The woman released her hold, apparently realizing her forceful nature hadn't gone over well.

"Have you thought of something about Gary Turello you forgot to tell us?" Elise asked, her voice now remote and businesslike.

"No."

Elise checked her watch. "Then I have to go. You have my card. Call if you think of anything." She began to walk away.

Strata Luna's next words stopped her. "Your mother was one of my girls."

Elise felt a heavy thud in the pit of her stomach. She pulled in a breath and swung around.

"Her name was Loralie," Strata Luna said. "She was beautiful. Exotic. Popular with the men. Oh, I'm sorry. You didn't want to hear that."

Elise waited.

Strata Luna picked up a cookie, turning it this way and that. "Did you know that when I heard you'd been left in a cemetery, I thought about adopting you myself? But I knew they wouldn't give a baby to somebody like me. Not even a baby with devil eyes."

Was she being intentionally cruel? Elise wondered. "Why didn't you come forward when the police were requesting citizen help?"

"What good would that have done, with a prostitute for a mama? Your best chance was to remain a mystery. And Jackson Sweet was dying. . . ."

"Where is she now?" Elise's heart pounded. Her palms were clammy. "Loralie?"

"She has a new life that has nothing to do with who she once was. A life that has nothing to do with you."

Elise would have felt differently toward her birth mother if she'd been given up for adoption in the normal way. What kind of cruel legacy was a cemetery to leave a child? "I want her full name."

"I can't give it to you. Not without asking her permission." Strata Luna took a casual sip of tea that had to be cold. "Would you like me to do that for you?"

Do that for you?

Her word choice was particularly disconcerting. "What's this about? What do you want from me? First you tell me about Jackson Sweet. Now you bring up the name of a woman you claim is my mother. Why exactly did you agree to this visit?"

Strata Luna's haughtiness fell away. "My daughters are dead." She looked up at Elise. There were tears in her eyes. "You're a connection to my past. To a better time. A time before evil came to Savannah."

*   *   *

"Do you know what this is?" Flora touched the ruffled green edge of a red leaf attached to a bushy plant sitting atop a stalk that was at least two feet tall.

David glanced nervously over his shoulder, expecting Elise to appear any second. He'd left the tea party to get away from Strata Luna and her painfully accurate insight. Instead of finding Enrique, he'd run into Flora—who'd apparently been watching for him.

"It's called a lollipop coleus," Flora told him, even though he hadn't asked. Even though he wasn't remotely interested. "They don't normally grow like this."

"I see."

"It took Strata Luna a year to cultivate this particular plant."

"That's weird," David said. "Kind of Tim Burton."

"Tim who?"

"The director," he said, seeing he'd already lost her.

"It's called a topiary."

"Don't talk to Strata Luna about me, okay? No matter how mundane the information might seem."

"I don't have to tell her anything. She just knows."

He let out a snort of disbelief.

"Let's not fight." Flora smiled and moved close, backing him up against the wall. She put her hands on his hips and pressed against him.

He whipped out the photo of Gary Turello and held it in front of her face. "Ever seen this guy?"

"Da-vid." She laughed.

"I'm serious."

"It's Gary Turello. Now put it away." She snatched the photo and tossed it over her shoulder.

"You knew him?"

"We didn't hang out or anything. He was into the punk scene, always getting a new piercing every week."

"Remember anything else about him?"

"He didn't mind the weird shit. If a client was into kinky stuff like beating or bondage or drinking blood, we always sent them Turello."

"Do you remember any of the clients?"

"I never saw them. And unlike you, my naive man, those kind of people always use false names, and the meeting places always change. It might be an abandoned warehouse one night, the basement of an empty Victorian the next."

"Anything else?"

"Should I come by tonight?" When he didn't answer, her hands moved up his body to finally link behind his head, her fingers digging into his hair. She pulled his face close.

At first he put up a fight, but then he bent his head and pressed his lips to hers.

He was kissing Flora when Elise caught up with him.

"Gould?"

He and Flora sprang apart.

Flora gave him a wicked smile. "I'd better go." She scampered off, leaving David alone with Elise.

"Were you just making out with Flora Martinez?" Elise asked, clearly shocked.

David wiped at his mouth and pulled his hand away. "Kissing," he said, distracted by the red lipstick on his fingertips.

"Did she attack you?"

"We . . . have kind of a relationship."

That announcement was followed by a long span of silence.

"You're dating one of Strata Luna's prostitutes?" Elise finally asked.

"*Dating* isn't really the right word. . . ."

"What is the right word? *Paying?* For services rendered?"

"Seeing each other. That would be more accurate."

"I'm not one of those people who has big issues with prostitution unless it involves innocent children," Elise said. "Under those conditions, I'd be looking for a death sentence if such a thing were possible."

"Flora's a good person."

She picked up the photo of Gary Turello and handed it to him. "Moral issues aside, she's too close to the case."

"It just happened." He pocketed the photo.

"Did she approach you after our visit to Black Tupelo?"

He could see she might be able to accept that.

"I knew she liked you," Elise said.

"I called her. Before Black Tupelo."

"What?"

"I called for a prostitute."

"Jeez, Gould! Are you crazy?"

"Possibly." He thought a moment. "Probably."

"You're a cop."

"I was drunk." Out of his mind, that's what he was.

"That should never be an excuse."

She was right. "I know." He looked down. Anywhere but at Elise.

"Isn't this great?" he asked, cupping a ruffled coleus leaf under his fingertips. "It's called a topiary."

"I didn't know you were a master gardener."

"Wouldn't you say it's a little Tim Burtonish?"

"Pre–*Sleepy Hollow*?" she asked.

"Goes without saying, doesn't it?"

He wasn't tricking her with the diversion, but she still played along. He liked that about his partner. She knew when to push and when to stop pushing. But then he regarded her more closely and realized she seemed preoccupied with something more than just his relationship with Flora.

"You okay?" he asked.

She pulled in a deep breath. "Just one of those days when I've been given a little too much information."

Chapter 24

James LaRue wormed his hand through the T-shirts and underwear in his top dresser drawer until his fingers made contact with a box the size of a cigarette pack. It was said that the underwear drawer was one of the first places burglars looked when robbing you. If they found James' stash, they would most likely think it cocaine, snort a little, and be dead within a minute.

He carefully extracted the box from its hiding place and carried it down the hallway, through the living room to the kitchen, where he lifted the lid.

Nestled against cotton batting was a small glass vial filled with white crystalline powder. Beside it, a sewing needle. James removed the glass container and held it at eye level.

Tetrodotoxin. TTX. The tiny vial contained enough to kill the inhabitants of a small city.

Carefully, he removed the rubber stopper, then slipped the fine, sharp tip of the sewing needle inside, tapped it free of residue, and lifted it out, recapping the vial. He swirled the needle in a glass of water, wiped the needle clean, and replaced it and the vial inside the box, which he left on the counter.

A dangling chain brushed against his temple. He pulled it, turning on the ceiling fan.

He held the glass high, noting the clarity of the water.

James had never been a big one for extreme sports. Growing up, he'd been a little on the geeky, frail side. No rock climbing or cave diving for him. But he'd found a way to compensate for that lackluster past without leaving the comfort of his own home.

One of the biggest drawbacks of tetrodotoxin was its lack of consistency. No two grains were alike; no two grains held the same amount of poison. But for James and for a handful of other thrill seekers, that was part of the appeal. Nature was the one in control. Not man. And coming up with the right dosage, no matter how careful you were, was always a crapshoot.

James lifted the glass to his mouth. Cool liquid touched his lips. One, two swallows.

He'd taken five once and almost hadn't lived to tell about it. Since then he'd built up a tolerance. Five would probably be a pretty cool experience, but right now he was just looking for a buzz.

Then again, he'd been drinking all day. He wasn't sure what an overload of alcohol would do to the mix.

His lips began to tingle, and a familiar warmth seeped through his veins. With a slow, deliberate movement he put the glass down on the counter. A wave of sweat broke out on his body, and he had a sudden urge to vomit.

This too shall pass, he told himself, physically unable to laugh at his little biblical joke.

His ears rang, and his breathing became quick and shallow. His legs buckled, and he dropped straight down, knees crashing to the floor. He continued to fold and unfold until he was flat on his back, paralyzed.

His tongue filled his mouth. He tested it, trying to speak.

He couldn't produce even a faint vibration in his throat. He lay there, staring up at the ceiling fan that circled slowly above his head. The edge of every blade was coated with a thick layer of dust.

Rotating.

Turning.

Spinning.

If he concentrated hard enough, he could slow the fan down with his mind until he could see the individual blades. Or he could let it go, let it become one blurred but solid object, cutting into the air.

It made him think of aerodynamics and airplane wings, the amazement of flight. He was a scientist, but such things still wowed him.

His research had sparked a controversy within the scientific community that was still going on years later, with over half the scientists he ran into treating him as if he were a joke. He'd once believed tetrodotoxin could save the world. With it, he'd imagined being able to slow down the disease process. He'd hoped to put an end to severe, chronic pain and needless human suffering. He'd even hoped TTX could eventually be used to induce a state of suspended animation in astronauts while they snoozed their way into deep space.

Now he used it to get high.

The dream was over. Finished. The end. His life had been nothing but a waste. A fucking waste.

As he always said, what doesn't kill you makes you bitter.

With one hand on the steering wheel, Elise allowed herself a quick glance at the map on the passenger seat beside her. It was the morning after her visit with Strata Luna and she was following up on the James LaRue lead. It didn't seem that he owned a phone, and the Internet uncovered only a few scientific articles, no address.

Research had finally turned up an acre of land belonging to a J. T. LaRue on Tybee Island, and she was now bumping along a dirt road overgrown with vegetation. Spanish bayonet and cabbage palmetto flared out from beds of holly and wax myrtle. Sprawling live oaks were ensnared by thick muscadine vine, the languidly streaming moss creating pockets of deep darkness.

Inside those pockets, fireflies moved like tiny ghost lights, and confused crickets chirped frantically, thinking day was night. The earthy scent of stagnant water seeped slowly through the car's air-conditioning unit until the interior smelled like a bog.

Much of the South Carolina and Georgia coastland was being overdeveloped. Tybee Island had escaped to some extent when people woke up and realized that all of Chatham County would soon be a golf course if somebody didn't do something about it. But prices of real estate had escalated over the years until Tybee was now inhabited exclusively by the wealthy or by longtime residents like LaRue.

She'd ditched Gould without telling him where she was going. The whole Flora Martinez thing was still freaking her out, and she needed more time to process it—although an infinite number of hours might never be enough. Gould's coming along would have been a waste of manpower anyway. The person she was seeking was a retired scientist who could helpfully supply them with some much-needed information on tetrodotoxin; he was not a criminal.

She came to a Y and followed it to the right, continuing for a half mile. There the road ran into a cabin that wasn't much more than a shack, and ended. The poor souls with a Ph.D. in mathematics or science fields seemed to fall the hardest, but given the sketchiness of her directions, she leaned toward thinking she'd taken a wrong turn.

She shut off the car and walked up the bowed wooden steps to knock on the screen door. The inner door was open, the interior vague shadows of an overstuffed chair, the edge of a table. The smell of mold and mildew hung in the air.

She slipped a hand inside her jacket pocket, her fingers coming into contact with the rough cloth of the *wanga* Strata Luna had given her. Had she been reaching for the reassurance of the charm? Or her gun? Elise the cop would say her gun, but the daughter of a conjurer wasn't so sure that was the truth.

From the belly of the house came the sound of a fall, followed by a muffled curse and footsteps. A silhouette appeared on the opposite side of the screen. The door swung open on creaking hinges.

A man.

About thirty, shirtless, barefoot, wearing a pair of

ancient jeans hanging on a thin frame. The smell of sweat and alcohol wafted from his pores. His hair was dark and wild and matted. Despite his appearance, he somehow managed to exude something—a kind of strange, patronizing superiority, if one could call it such a thing when he was so lacking in personal hygiene.

He was one of those lovely occurrences of nature that sometimes came from mixtures of light and dark blood. His skin was golden; his eyes were blue. And red at the moment. He continued to stare at her as he clung tightly to the door, quite obviously stoned out of his mind.

Elise pulled out her ID, introduced herself, then folded and pocketed the leather case. "I'm looking for Professor LaRue," she told him. "He lives in the area, but I'm afraid I may have taken a wrong turn. Do you happen to know how to get to his place from here?"

"LaRue?" the man asked, thick dark eyebrows drawing together in puzzlement while his hand rubbed an unshaved chin. "Nobody around here with that name." He was sweating profusely. Water globules clung to the tapered ends of his hair.

"Perhaps I was given the wrong information. I was under the impression he'd retired on a family lot here on Tybee Island. James LaRue."

"LaRue. Sounds familiar, come to think of it. Maybe we can figure it out."

He gestured with one hand, waving her inside, then turned and shuffled into the dark interior, walking as if he had stomach cramps.

High as hell.

She caught the screen door, but remained in the

doorway. Instinctively she felt the urgent need to leave, but logically he'd given her no real reason to be afraid.

There was a darkness coming from him that often accompanied drug addicts. It was a crippling, frightening hopelessness. The man in front of her was a mess. A much bigger mess than David Gould.

"He's an expert on tetrodotoxin," she explained. "Maybe you've heard about the poisonings we've had in Savannah."

While she talked, her ears strained to hear any sound that would signal the presence of another person. Her gaze swept the small room with practiced ease and nonchalance.

She took two steps inside and was immediately in the kitchen and living area. Off the kitchen was an open doorway that appeared to lead into a bedroom.

Were there any other rooms? From outside, it had been hard to tell.

He shuffled to a wooden table strewed with food wrappers and trash, stopped, and glanced over one hunched shoulder. "I don't get a paper and I don't listen to the news."

This time she felt for the reassurance of not the *wanga* but her gun. In his present condition he seemed fairly harmless, but she could have inadvertently stepped into the middle of a crank-making enterprise. People were killed for that kind of thing. Killed and fed to the alligators. She was beginning to regret her strictly emotional decision to leave Gould behind.

"It's hot," the man stated, acknowledging the obvious in the way of someone drunk or stoned.

"If you don't know where LaRue lives, then I'd best be going."

"I'll draw you a map."

"So you do know where he lives?"

"Sit down." He motioned toward the table.

"That's okay. I'll stand."

He walked to the sink and turned on the water. "Why'd you say you were looking for LaRue?"

"He's an expert on tetrodotoxin."

He filled a glass with water, then handed it to her. "You look like you could use a drink."

"Thanks." She accepted the glass. It looked clean.

He shuffled around a little more, found a coffee mug, dumped the contents, and filled it with water from the tap. He drank and refilled it twice before pulling up a chair at the table.

He dug through the litter to tear off the corner of a brown grocery bag, then used it to draw a map.

"It's easy to get all twisted around back here," he explained, penciling heavy dark lines to signify roads.

"This is north." He pointed to the top of the paper. "Here's the road you came in on that runs along the sloughs."

The water seemed to have revived him a little. His movements weren't as sluggish, and his voice seemed stronger.

"Here's the Y where you turned right. Remember that spot?"

"My directions said to turn right. Was I supposed to go left?" She lifted the glass to her mouth and took a swallow. Then another.

He stared at her much longer than was socially polite. "No," he finally said.

"No?" She didn't get it.

That's when she became aware of a strange tingling on her lips and in her mouth. The tingling in her mouth created a searing heat that rushed down her esophagus to her belly.

Sweat erupted from every pore, and in a matter of seconds a rivulet was trailing along her spine, soaking into the waistband of her pants.

From what seemed an observer's position, she was aware of the glass slipping from her fingers. She tried to clench her hand tighter, but her body failed her.

The glass shattered to the floor.

It was hard to breathe; her lungs didn't want to expand.

She imagined lifting a hand to her throat, but was unable to do so.

The floor shifted beneath her.

The room slanted. And kept slanting . . . until her face was smashed against the gritty wood of the kitchen floor, her body pressed down, seeming ten times its weight.

It was such a relief to be horizontal, such a relief to be over the fall.

Her eyes were wide open. She tried to blink but couldn't.

LaRue—because of course the disheveled man in front of her had to be LaRue—arranged himself beside her on the floor so he could look into her open eyes. With his face inches away, he said, "I've found that the best way to learn about TTX is to experience it firsthand."

She was going to die.

How strange.

For some reason, she found the whole situation hysterically funny. She would have laughed if it had been physically possible. A shame, because she needed a good laugh.

"I'm not what you expected, am I?" LaRue asked. "Not what you expected from a Harvard graduate? That's okay. Don't feel bad. I've never been what anybody expected. I don't take it personally."

She knew people were often chameleons, ever changing, never what they seemed, even to themselves. She would have liked to apologize, explain that it wasn't his appearance or circumstances that had thrown her; it was his age. She'd been expecting someone much older.

"Close your eyes," he said, still on the floor beside her.

He reached out and forcefully pushed her eyelids down with his fingertips.

"Don't fight it. Fighting makes it worse. Just close your eyes and enjoy the ride. That's it," he said in a soothing voice, coaching her, guiding her through new terrain. Her own Timothy Leary. "There you go. That's better, isn't it? Much better. The first time's the toughest because you don't know what to expect, and because you're scared shitless. Kinda like sex," he said with a laugh. "The second time will be better. You'll see."

Second time?

She felt something against the side of her face, a sensation she couldn't quite place, then realized he was stroking her numb cheek as he mumbled soothing nonsense, whispering words meant to calm and hypnotize as if trying to talk her down from a bad acid trip.

It worked.

She began to relax.

She began to float.

Float out of her body, up, up to the ceiling, where she could see herself on the floor with James LaRue beside her, one arm looped around her head, his fingers stroking her cheek.

"It's like playing dead, isn't it?" he whispered seductively.

She was looking down on them both, but his words were tickling her ear, stirring her hair. "As close as a living person can get to the real thing."

He was insane. Completely, totally insane.

"Let go," he coaxed. "You have to let go."

She let go.

Chapter 25

Elise gave a scissors kick and broke the surface of the black-water swamp. A stale breeze skimmed her cheek. The hypnotic croak of frogs floated to her in waves.

She collapsed faceup on shore and lay there breathing hard. Fan blades circled above her, struggling to push the heavy, stagnant air.

She was where she'd always been: in the kitchen of LaRue's cabin, a hard floor beneath her, pressing into her shoulder blades.

She tested herself, lifting her head a couple of inches, then letting it drop. She shifted her arm and heard something scrape, vaguely recalled the broken glass.

LaRue.

Where was he?

Her head was thick as she automatically reached for her gun.

Still there.

Fumbling, she slipped her hand inside her jacket.

Her fine motor skills suffering from the effects of

the drug, she struggled with the snap of the leather case to finally pull the weapon free. She rolled to her side and shoved herself to a half-sitting position, steadied by one hand.

The sudden movement sent nausea washing over her.

She strained to listen for peripheral sounds, her ears ringing. With her gun drawn, she made an assessment of her surroundings, then staggered to her feet, gun hand trembling.

"LaRue?" Her voice came out a faint croak.

She slowly made her way through the cabin, making sure the bathroom and bedroom were empty, doors banging as she shuffled from one room to the other. Returning to the kitchen, she looked outside.

Her car was still there.

She checked her pocket and felt the rough edge of her keys.

Her fingers were sticky.

She lifted her hand to find a shard of glass embedded between two knuckles. She pulled it out and shook more glass fragments from her jacket. On the floor where she'd been lying was dried blood.

She'd let LaRue get the better of her.

Shameful.

She wanted to go home, shower, crawl into bed. Instead, she made herself take another pass through LaRue's house. Without a search warrant, she couldn't touch anything. She had to suppress the urge to open the books that lined the walls, to read his e-mail.

Her phone rang.

She pulled it out and stared blankly at it for an undetermined length of time before finally lifting it to her ear.

Gould.

The signal was weak, and his voice broke.

"Where the hell are you?" was what she finally deciphered.

"Gone where the goblins go . . ." The words came out a harsh whisper.

"What? I can't hear you."

He went on to say something about trying to reach her all afternoon.

She looked at her watch; she'd lost four hours.

The signal fell from one bar to none and the phone went dead.

She tried to call him back but couldn't connect. She shut off the phone and dropped it in her pocket.

An enormous amount of energy exerted for nothing.

She slid her gun into the shoulder holster, jacket open and the leather strap free. Before leaving the house, she collected several pieces of broken glass and wrapped them in the fake map LaRue had drawn.

Then she stepped onto the front porch and scanned the area. Was he out there watching? Waiting for her to leave?

Her tires were okay. He hadn't slashed them or let the air out.

With the shards of wrapped glass in her pocket, she slipped into the driver's seat.

It was getting late.

It would be dark soon.

After locking the doors, she forced herself to proceed at a sedate pace. The nausea had passed and she felt she was thinking clearly until she found herself half asleep at the wheel in the middle of the deserted road with no sense of how long she'd been there.

She turned up the air-conditioner of the idling car, letting it hit her full in the face, and continued to Savannah. At one point, she deliberately stopped and pulled out her mobile phone. The signal was strong. There were at least ten messages from Gould, left over the course of the afternoon. The latest said he was heading home and to get in touch with him as soon as she got his message.

She called his cell phone, then his home number, getting voice mail at both.

She'd been to his apartment only once, but Mary of the Angels was easy to find. A place all Savannah residents knew about. A bleak, compelling piece of architecture with a dark past, clinging to the edge of the Historic District.

Time was weird, and it seemed she'd just made the decision to head for Gould's when she found herself there—pulling into the parking lot adjacent to the four-story building.

Darkness had arrived.

There were no stars.

At the front door, she found Gould's name on the intercom and buzzed his room.

No answer.

She leaned against the stone wall and closed her eyes, legs trembling. Why had she come here? Why hadn't she driven to the police station?

She couldn't think.

Sleep. She just wanted to sleep. Could she even

make it back to her car? Could she drive herself home?

She pressed the button again . . . and kept pressing.

A voice crackled over the intercom.

"Yeah."

Gould. Annoyed.

Elise leaned close to the speaker. "Let me in."

"Elise?" His annoyance was gone, replaced by confusion. "I was in the shower. Come on up."

The entrance door buzzed and Elise stumbled inside. She took the elevator to the third floor, went down a dark hallway of red carpet and wall sconces, to 335. The door was unlocked.

Inside the apartment, she heard a shower running. A puddle of water had been left on the wooden floor near her feet. The only illumination was a small light attached to the hood of the stove. Nearby, a window air conditioner hummed.

The apartment was a corner unit that probably would have been light during the day if the windows hadn't been covered with ivy. Near those windows was an overstuffed rocking chair. She shot straight for it and collapsed, tipping back her head with a deep sigh.

Something landed on her lap. She looked down to see Gould's Siamese cat. What was its name?

The cat began to purr loudly. Elise stroked its soft fur and closed her eyes.

What a lovely, peaceful place . . .

David dried off and put on a white T-shirt and a pair of jeans, then wandered back into the living area. Elise was sitting in a dark corner, Isobel on her lap purring like crazy. There was actually something tranquil and domestic about the little scene.

David opened the refrigerator. "Wanna beer?" he asked over his shoulder.

She mumbled a negative.

"Soda?"

Another negative.

"I have some news." He retrieved a diet cola, popped the top, and took a drink. "There have been four other confirmed cases of poisoning in the area in the past year, all by undetermined toxins. All in different jurisdictions, so nobody compared notes."

He sat on the stool at the kitchen counter, one bare foot braced against the crossbar, leaving the length of the small apartment between himself and Elise. "Unless it involves a case that's going to trial, most morgues don't keep tissue and blood samples over a certain amount of time, but I asked them to double-check just in case. If they come across anything like liver tissue, they're going to retest it for a broader range of toxins, then get back to us."

He took another swallow of soda. "Alcohol can be a toxin. If some alcoholic showed up dead and his liver was toxic, chances are they didn't look any deeper, thinking he simply died of acute alcohol poisoning."

His partner seemed completely disinterested in the information he was relating.

"I can't remember your cat's name."

"Isobel."

"Isobel. That's a nice name."

"Let's forget about the cat a minute. Where have you been?"

"To see the TTX specialist."

"Without me?"

"Bad idea, I know."

"Is he willing to help? Did he have any relevant information?"

"We didn't get around to discussing it."

He frowned. Was she acting a little weird? A little out of it? "So, what happened? What did he say?"

"He offered me a drink of water."

She rocked and continued to stroke the cat. "In hindsight, I can see it was foolish of me to accept, because I believe it contained tetrodotoxin."

Everything stopped.

David replayed her last sentence in his head.

I believe it contained tetrodotoxin.

That's what she'd said. Exactly what she'd said.

He put down the soda can and slipped from the kitchen stool.

He rarely used the ceiling light because it was so blinding and unforgiving and made his place look stark and shitty.

He flipped it on now.

Elise raised her arm to shield her face. "Do you mind?"

He crossed the room and crouched in front of her, every cell focused on Elise. "Tell me what happened," he said levelly.

The cat let out a little meow of alarm, jumped from her lap, and disappeared down the hall.

"You scared Isobel," Elise chastised.

She had a gash on the back of one hand. It was no longer bleeding, but it looked as if it might need stitches. "Why didn't you say something?" He picked up her hand. "How did you get this?"

"I only took a swallow. I dropped the glass. It shattered. I fell on it. That's where I was when you were trying to call me. Paralyzed."

"Jesus."

The overhead light was still bothering her. She squinted against the brightness.

He grasped her chin with one hand and turned her face toward the light, examining her eyes. Her face, framed by dark hair, was ashen. Even her lips were colorless.

She pulled away.

"Your pupils are dilated."

"My system is messed up, but I'm not high."

He nodded. She seemed lucid. Exhausted, but lucid. "You should be in a hospital."

"And let the media get hold of this story? No, thanks. I'm fine."

He wanted to believe her. "That hand might need stitches."

She looked at it, turning it back and forth. "Think so?"

"Have you filed a report?"

She shook her head. "Not yet."

"Where's LaRue now?"

"I don't know. He was gone when the drug wore off four hours later."

David's emotions had been shut off for so long that now, when a wave of despair and anger hit him, he didn't know how to deal with it.

He sprang to his feet and turned away, hiding his

face. Too much reality. If LaRue had stepped into the room at that moment, David would have killed him.

The intensity of his reaction scared him.

Get a grip, Gould.

Focus.

Put it away for now and do what you have to do.

He pulled in a deep breath and turned back around.

"Elise . . ." He paused, swallowed, then asked, "Do you need a rape kit?"

She looked surprised, as if it was something she hadn't considered. "N-no."

"Are you sure? Can you remember what happened during those four hours?"

She seemed uncertain. "Yes . . . and no."

She struggled to pull everything together. He imagined she was going over possible signs of rape in her head.

"I was there, and I wasn't." She gave it more thought. "No," she finally said. "It didn't happen."

"Okay. Good." He let out a breath and relaxed a little. "We've got to get you to the police station. You have to file a report. We need to catch this guy. Bring him in. Jesus. He's probably the one killing all these people."

"I don't know. Seems too easy. Too obvious."

"Every crime doesn't have to be hard to solve. Not if the perpetrator is a fucking idiot."

She closed her eyes and leaned back. "Too much anger," she said, her voice weak with exhaustion. "I don't feel like arguing."

"Right. Sorry." He raised his hands as if to choke an invisible person in front of him. "I'm upset." He dropped his hands.

He crossed the room, grabbed the phone receiver, and began punching numbers. "I'm ordering a crime scene team to LaRue's. They have to scour—" He stopped midsentence to direct his attention and dialogue to the person on the other end, making the arrangements that needed to be made.

"You should go to LaRue's and oversee the search," Elise said once David disconnected.

"I'm taking you to headquarters." He picked up the receiver again. "A late night visit to LaRue's seems just the thing for Starsky and Hutch."

After telephoning Starsky to give him an abbreviated version of what had happened, he packed Elise in his car and drove to the police station.

She wasn't accustomed to being on the victim side of the desk. It felt strange and a little surreal, the remnants of the drug in her system giving everything the sensation of a waking dream. After she signed the forms she needed to sign, they sent her to the crime lab to get six tubes of blood drawn.

While Gould waited in the break room, residue swab tests were taken of her mouth, lips, hands, and random places on her body. After that, she was stuck in a shower for fifteen minutes in case any small grain of TTX remained on her skin. That done, she was given a set of clean scrubs, her own clothes kept as evidence.

Butterfly bandages took care of her hand.

On the way home, Gould swung by a Chinese restaurant, left the car idling by the door, and ran inside. He reappeared two minutes later with a white paper bag. "I called ahead," he explained, getting back in the car and passing the bag to her.

At Elise's house, they sat on the floor in the living room and ate from carryout containers.

She wore the green scrubs the lab had given her, hair still damp from the shower. Gould was dressed in jeans and the T-shirt he'd thrown on. His hair had dried funny.

Elise opened her fortune cookie.

Ah, she thought. Generic Fortune Number 75. *Good deeds bring rewards.* She should write fortunes. She could come up with much better ones.

"Damn," she said. "Too bad I didn't read this earlier."

Gould paused, chopsticks in his hand. "What?"

Elise pretended to read the slip of paper. "An unquenchable thirst leads to an overabundance of knowledge."

He put down the cardboard container and chopsticks, then opened his fortune cookie, popping half of it in his mouth while smoothing out the tiny strip of paper. "A wise person refuses candy from a stranger.".

"Ha-ha." She pulled the paper from between his fingers. "You always have to one-up me, don't you? What does it really say?"

He tried to get it away, but she turned her back to him, the paper clutched to her stomach. " 'The past is never really the past.' "

"Hmm," Gould said. "A fortune cookie that paraphrases Faulkner. I think the actual quote is 'The past is never dead. It's not even past.' "

"Do you think that's true?"

"Unfortunately, yes."

It was late. After midnight.

"Where do you sleep in this place?" Gould asked, looking around.

"Upstairs. On the third floor. Why?"

"I'm not leaving you alone with TTX in your system."

"That's completely unnecessary." The thought of Gould holing up in her house was a little too personal. They'd gone from I-hardly-know-you to a sleepover in a nanosecond.

The phone rang. It was crime scene specialist Abe Chilton.

"I'm at LaRue's place right now," he explained. "We're almost done collecting evidence."

"Find anything that could be TTX?" Elise asked.

"Nothing obvious."

"Any sign of LaRue?"

"Nope. But how are you? Would you like me to come by? Do you need company?"

"My partner's here," she said.

"Gould?" Chilton sounded puzzled. "Keep an eye on him. I've heard things."

She couldn't believe he was joining the conspiracy. "What kind of things?"

"That he's unstable as hell, for one."

She glanced over at Gould. He was gathering up the empty carryout containers, stuffing them in a bag. At the moment, he looked as stable and domestic as a fifties sitcom dad.

Chapter 26

The edges of Elise's dream were dark and blurry, like looking through a camera lens with no depth of field. She was walking down an alley with a brick, graffiti-covered wall. Water ran across the ground. She stepped in a hole and was submerged to her knees.

The streetlights were off, and the scene had a dark, apocalyptic feel.

She felt something brush against her leg and looked to see a floating body gently bump against her.

The corpse attached itself, wrapping its arms around her ankle. Elise shook herself loose and began moving through the dark street.

Now she noticed that the silhouettes she thought were unlit streetlights were really people.

Like something choreographed, they fell into step beside her as she drew even with them—until the street was full of dark forms, moving toward the river.

What did it mean? She felt the answer was there somewhere in the dream. If only she could reach the river . . .

She woke up, suddenly aware of her bedroom, her bed, the open doorway. The pillow beneath her head.

David lay in the dark of Elise's house, listening.

Had he been asleep? He didn't think so, but wasn't sure.

Somewhere a clock ticked and a small motor ran.

Her place was dusty halls and broken plaster exposing a wooden skeleton. Very little furniture. A few rugs here and there, but not enough to keep the echo down.

A work in progress.

He strained his ears for sounds of her breathing.

Silence.

"Elise?" he whispered.

No answer.

He tossed back the light blanket and rolled off the inflatable mattress they'd set up in the corner of her room. In the murky darkness, he reached across her bed.

Nobody.

In the haze of a blue night-light, he made his way down the hall, then the stairway, with its curving banister, to the first floor.

He stood there a moment. Light from the street fell through tall, curtainless windows.

He smelled cigarette smoke.

He followed the smell to a small sitting room at the front of the house.

"Come on in," Elise said from the depths.

He heard a rumble from beneath his feet; then a cool breeze hit him in the face as the central air kicked on.

The room was dark, with light filtering through lace curtains, falling on a patterned throw rug. The tip of a cigarette glowed red. As she inhaled, her face appeared, then fell back into shadow.

"I didn't know you smoked," he said.

"I don't."

She flicked an ash in a nearby tray. "Not very well, anyway. It's something I do occasionally."

"For enjoyment?"

"Not enjoyment exactly. More as a way of thumbing my nose at the grim reaper."

"I'd say it's more like inviting him in. Mind if I turn on a light?"

"I'd rather you didn't."

There was enough illumination to see that she was sitting in an overstuffed chair, bare legs dangling over the arm, and she wore some kind of bulky robe. The furniture was dark and shapeless, littering the room like large, indistinct rock formations.

He felt around until he came in contact with the couch across from her. She seemed a mile away, sitting there quietly smoking.

"I've owned this house five years," she said. "This sitting room and my daughter's bedroom are the only things I've managed to finish."

"Restoration is a helluva job."

"I guess I lost my initiative once I realized Audrey didn't want to come here whether her room was done or not."

The air conditioner shut off, and the house grew quiet.

She picked up the ashtray, bringing it close, flicking the cigarette, taking a drag, flicking it again. "Life is full of surprises," she said. Her voice sounded a little on the husky side. "Wouldn't you agree?"

"Things happen we can't be prepared for."

"Some people would say that's what makes it worth living."

"I've had some surprises I'd rather not have had," he admitted reluctantly.

"Such as?"

"Nothing I want to talk about."

"Oh, really? I've found that darkness allows me to say things I can't admit in the light."

"I'm the same person, day or night."

"That's not very mysterious."

She stubbed out the cigarette. He could see the tip break into several smaller chunks of red, then go out.

He shrugged, even though it was too dark for her to see his response. "I'm a boring guy."

She laughed. "That's what you want people to think."

She was acting strange. And why not, after what she'd just been through? And with what she still had in her system.

"You feel okay?" he asked.

"Couldn't sleep. Here's a tip: Never take a four-hour nap. It really screws you up."

Tell me about it. Sleep didn't come knocking on his door very often.

"I belong to a dream analysis group," she said. "We meet a couple of times a month, and we analyze our dreams."

"That sounds a little too New Age for me."

"Some people think you can see the future through dreams. I don't believe that, but I think you might be able to unlock your subconscious mind. I'd like to be able to use dreams to help solve problems. Maybe even crimes."

"How would you do that?"

"Before you go to sleep, you ask yourself a question, or focus on a puzzle, and sometimes the answer will come to you while you're sleeping. But the answer comes from within."

He nodded. "That makes sense. Harnessing the power of the untapped mind."

She paused, struck a match, and lit another cigarette, then shook out the match.

He really wished she wouldn't smoke.

He watched the tip of her cigarette. He couldn't take his eyes off it. "You shouldn't smoke. It's bad for you."

She took a drag, the glow briefly illuminating her face. "You're one to talk. Somebody bent on self-destruction. What's your story, Gould? Why'd you quit the FBI?"

David realized he'd been hiding. Taking comfort in his new life, the life of Savannah and the police department and Elise. Because the new life had nothing to do with the old.

But it did. That's what he hadn't understood. It was all connected. Everything was connected.

Suddenly he wanted to tell her. Not because it was dark and darkness made things easier. He wanted her to know.

I might cry. Cry like a baby.

What would his partner think of that?

His heart pounded in his chest so hard his shirt moved.

In the end, he just said it. Because that was the only way to handle such things.

He told Elise about his ex-wife. And then he spoke words he'd often thought but never vocalized. "I found my son dead. In the bathtub. Drowned. She did it. My wife. She deliberately murdered him."

For a long time, Elise didn't respond. And what could a person say? Really? Silence was better than telling lies or speaking words that meant nothing.

Outside, a street cleaner passed. Savannah had to have the cleanest damn streets—and the dirtiest closets. Ha-ha. Who said he'd lost his sense of humor?

"Why haven't I heard about this?" she finally asked, her voice sounding normal.

Thank God. Because if she'd been choked up, if she'd told him how sorry she was, and what an awful tragedy it was, he would have fallen apart. And he didn't want to do that.

"You know the FBI." He struggled for nonchalance. "They didn't want anything to reflect poorly on them, so they covered it up. Beth had been using her maiden name. My name was never released to the press. Easy. Didn't happen, at least not to me."

And as far as everybody was concerned, he'd never had a son.

"Thanks for telling me," she said quietly.

"I don't want your sympathy." Please, God. Not that.

"I know."

Did her voice crack? Just a little?

Don't do that. I can cry like hell when I get going. I can cry like hell and never stop. "Business as usual?" he suggested hopefully.

"Business as usual."

Elise listened as the street sweeper turned the corner, the sound comforting, like hearing the city quietly breathing, quietly watching over residents while they slept.

Such a public denial of what had happened couldn't have been healthy. David had never been allowed to adequately grieve. His self-destruction finally made sense. The antisocial behavior. The drinking. The way he'd been acting at Strata Luna's. Strata Luna, who'd also come upon the body of her drowned child.

Elise could now even understand his calling a prostitute. It actually seemed a bit noble in a twisted way. He'd craved human contact but knew he couldn't give of himself—so he'd called someone who would expect nothing of him. Except that his plan had backfired. Except that Flora Martinez had responded to the sadness and desperation in him. Women, even prostitutes, were looking for a man to nurture and heal.

"You keep trying to put it someplace," he said, his voice tight. "You keep trying to find a place that makes even a little bit of sense, but that place doesn't exist."

Elise thought of what Strata Luna had said the afternoon in the cemetery. About evil not needing a reason to exist. It was true. "The murder of children can never, ever make sense," Elise told him.

He must have detected sympathy in her voice. "Don't feel sorry for me," he said quietly out of the darkness. "I don't want you to feel sorry for me."

"I won't," she lied.

She wondered what he'd been like before.

"I used to be different," he told her. "I used to be funny."

"You're still funny."

"I don't mean funny strange."

"Neither do I."

"This thing with Flora. I'm going to tell her I can't see her anymore."

Maybe this marked a turning point for him.

"I haven't been a very good partner," he said sadly.

"You've been all right." She had to be truthful.

"Like your going to LaRue's by yourself. That shouldn't have happened."

"It's over. I'm alive. And it was my decision."

"I'll do better," he promised. "From now on. I swear." He paused, thinking. "We'll be a good team," he said, suddenly sounding enthused. "We'll kick some Starsky-and-Hutch ass."

Chapter 27

"How are you feeling?" David asked.

He was sitting at the kitchen table, where he and Elise had spent the predawn hours brainstorming, his laptop open in front of him.

With her back to the porcelain sink, Elise put her coffee mug down on the blue-tiled countertop and gave him a determined smile he suspected was to head off any protests he might be inclined to make. Because honestly, she looked like hell. Not hell in a bad way. More of a Virginia Woolf way.

He'd always had a thing for women with dark circles under their eyes.

Before Elise could answer, David's cell phone rang.

"I just heard," Major Hoffman said, concern in her voice. "How's Detective Sandburg?"

"Here, I'll let you talk to her yourself." David passed the phone to Elise.

David eavesdropped while Elise assured the major she was fine and that she didn't need any time off. After a lengthy silence followed by a rolling of eyes, she hung up.

"Problem?"

"It seems the *Savannah Morning News* wants to do an interview this a.m. with the detective in charge of the TTX case."

"Why can't the press liaison handle that? It's her job."

She handed the phone back. "I don't mind. Plus this way I can be in control of the information we need to get out to the public."

David closed his computer. "Nothing like an encounter with the press to start the day."

Elise went upstairs to change while David made a feeble attempt to tidy himself in the first-floor bathroom.

Water splashed on his face. Washcloth to the armpits.

He needed a shower. He needed to shave.

He longingly and suspiciously eyed the two toothbrushes in the cup on the sink. One was red. The other had a plastic alligator for a handle. After a moment's consideration, he opened the bathroom door. He was filling his lungs to shout a toothbrush question at Elise when she appeared in front of him.

"You have a spare toothbrush?" he asked within normal voice level.

She squeezed past him, opened a drawer, and presented him with a new toothbrush, package and all.

"I'm eternally in your debt."

"Absolutely."

Two minutes later they were heading out, planning to swing by David's apartment so he could grab some fresh clothes and Elise could pick up her car.

Or at least they *appeared* to be heading out until

Elise pulled open the front door. If she'd made any tracks, she would have frozen in them.

David bumped into her, halted, and peered over the top of her head.

Standing on the step was a tidy man in khaki pants and a white polo shirt. Next to him was a girl of about thirteen, headphones around her neck, a panda backpack, a stuffed elephant tucked under one arm, and a portable CD player in her hand.

Audrey. Elise's daughter. David had met her once. No, twice. The biggest resemblance between mother and daughter was a certain air of suspicion.

In direct contrast to David's wrinkled T-shirt, old jeans, and unshaved face, the people before them looked as if they'd stepped out of a department store ad. Their clothes were fresh and crisp and new. Audrey's strategically scuffed jeans were expensive, and her sparkling white jogging shoes had never been jogging.

Elise let out a little gasp, sounding like someone who'd just remembered she'd left a burner going after the plane had taken off.

"Audrey!" She inhaled. "Thomas."

The man's gaze shifted from Elise to David. And locked there. "Did you forget Audrey was coming today?" he asked, his voice vague and perplexed, his brows drawn together in puzzlement as, with reluctance, he forced himself to break away from David to focus on Elise.

David was fascinated. So this was Elise's exhusband. God. No wonder she'd left him. Which brought up the question, what had she ever seen in him in the first place?

David couldn't quit staring.

The guy was almost pretty, but Elise didn't seem the type to be taken in by a pretty face.

And then there was Audrey. . . .

Thirteen. David did some quick mental math. Elise would have had her when she was about seventeen or eighteen. A vulnerable age. A foolish age. He knew about such things.

"I didn't forget," Elise said quickly. "Of course I didn't forget."

As she talked, Thomas' gaze kept drifting back to David.

He thinks Elise and I are having sex, David realized.

That was funny as hell. If Elise's daughter hadn't been standing there, David would have played it up a little. Instead, he laid everything out, plain and concisely. "This—" David pointed a finger at himself, then at Elise, then back again. "Strictly business."

Elise had been so flustered over forgetting her daughter's visit that she hadn't caught Thomas' reaction to David. Now she jumped in to add her own version, introducing her partner.

"But it's not even seven o'clock," Thomas pointed out, clearly still suspicious. "And where's your car? I didn't see your car when we pulled up. It hasn't been stolen, has it? I told you this neighborhood was rough. Every time I see the crime map in the *Savannah Morning News*, the Historic District is loaded with burglaries and assaults."

"My car is fine."

Would she tell them what had happened? David

wondered. Would she explain why he was there and why her car was at his place?

"We've been working on this case . . . ," Elise said.

Thomas frowned, studying her face. "You look exhausted. I thought you were going to slow down."

"I know, I know. It's just that we have this . . . *situation*—"

"There's always a case. Always a situation."

The disapproval was gone. The suspicion was gone. The only thing left was concern.

Why, the guy still loves her, David realized. *He doesn't get her, but he loves her.* David's opinion of Thomas did an about-face.

"What happened to your hand?" Thomas asked.

"I cut it." Elise tucked the hand behind her. "It's nothing."

"Is the case the voodoo, zombie thing?" Audrey asked. Her eyes were huge.

"It's not voodoo," Elise said. "And there are no zombies."

"Kids at school said somebody is turning people into zombies."

"That's not true."

David jumped in, hoping to back her up. "Absolutely not true," he said, shaking his head.

"Yesterday, a girl fainted in PE class, and everybody freaked out. They said she was a zombie. And now boys are going around putting fingers to their wrists, screaming, 'I have no pulse! I have no pulse!'"

"That's enough, Audrey," Thomas broke in. "You know what I told you earlier."

Audrey's brief moment of animation ended. "Sorry, Dad," she said, her shoulders slumping.

"Where are you off to now?" Thomas asked Elise.

"Headquarters."

Audrey let out a low, I'm-already-bored groan.

"You can come too," Elise told her daughter with that kind of mock enthusiasm mothers used when they knew the kid wanted nothing to do with what was being offered. "We'll pick up some Krispy Kremes on the way. You love those. We'll have a breakfast picnic in the cemetery."

As they stood on the porch, the vile stench of the pulp mill wafted in their direction, the stink permeating David's sinuses. He'd heard that years ago the fumes had actually eaten paint off cars. Just another one of those lovely Savannah rumors nobody could seem to substantiate.

"I don't want to go to the police station." Audrey looked up at her father with pleading eyes. "Do I have to?"

"Audrey—"

"Dad." She twisted her feet to stand on the sides of her shoes. "*Please?*"

She stared at him, as if trying to communicate telepathically. When that failed to get any response, she was forced to say the words aloud, whispered through gritted teeth. "Remember what you told me at the house?"

It was suddenly embarrassingly obvious that the child hadn't wanted to visit her mother in the first place. That she'd come only because her father had made her.

David stood just behind Elise and to her right. He couldn't see her face, but he could feel her stillness.

He put a hand to her shoulder. Thomas followed the

movement with his eyes and stared. David dropped his hand.

"Another time would be better," Thomas said. "When things are slower."

Audrey's body relaxed, and her face lit up. She shot her father a look of gratitude.

"You're probably right," Elise said woodenly. "When things are slower."

"I'll call you." Thomas reached for Audrey. "Let's go, honey. So your mom can get to work."

Audrey spun around and began to walk away, her panda bear backpack bobbing. They were halfway up the sidewalk when Thomas bent his head toward her and said something. Audrey turned and gave a big wave. "Bye, Mom." And then to David, "Bye, Mr. Gould!"

She turned and caught up with her dad, then passed him, galloping to the white SUV parked at the curb.

Elise stared at the vehicle as it pulled away. "A stay of execution."

"She probably wanted to do something with friends," David said, searching for a fragment of truth that might make her feel better. "Friends are more important than family at her age. Family doesn't even count."

Elise didn't answer. Instead, she turned and locked the door behind them.

He hoped she wasn't going to cry.

He hated it when women cried. It made him feel useless. And it hurt. He didn't like to hurt.

"Oh, fuck, fuck, fuck!" he shouted as soon as he reached the street and saw his car.

The driver's window was broken.

He looked inside.

The CD player was gone.

"Fuck, fuck, fuck!"

He stomped around in a circle, finally coming back to the car.

Nope. He hadn't just imagined the broken window.

"What *the hell* is it with the burglaries in this town? Thomas was right. You people have a problem. A real problem. And right in front of a cop's house. How blatant is that?"

"Do what I do," Elise said calmly, as if this kind of thing happened every morning. Maybe it did.

"What's that?" he asked.

"Don't get the CD player replaced, and quit locking your car. It keeps them from breaking the window."

"So you adjust your life to accommodate criminals? That's insane."

"Insane but effective."

"I'm calling my insurance company today. I'm getting a new window *and* CD player. And a car alarm."

She looked at him with skepticism.

"Oh, I suppose the sound of a car alarm is like a lullaby around here."

"I was going to say like the chirping of crickets."

He dug a towel from the trunk, took a few swipes at the crumbled glass, then tossed the towel over the front seat. Two minutes later, they were heading for his apartment. David reached for the radio, then clenched his fist at the black hole staring at him from the dash. He liked to listen to the local station on the way to work in order to keep up on the hysteria level of the city.

"You had to get married, didn't you?" David asked,

giving Elise's profile a quick glance as he fought morning traffic.

"Had to get married? What time period did you transport here from? Nobody has to get married anymore."

"You know what I mean."

"Do you find that amusing?"

"I'm surprised, not amused. You come across as someone who knows exactly what she wants, who doesn't make mistakes."

"Audrey wasn't a mistake."

"I'm not talking about Audrey. I'm talking about Thomas."

"Don't trivialize my life."

"I'm not."

"You are."

He stopped at a red light. "How long were you married?"

"A year."

"Did you ever love him? Or was it just a teenager crush kind of thing?"

"That's none of your business."

"I think it is. You're my partner."

"When did that finally occur to you?" she asked, secretly glad he'd finally noticed. This was good. Things were progressing. He'd spilled his guts last night; she was more than ready to share. "I thought I loved him," she admitted. "I was confused."

"You were a kid yourself."

"Seventeen."

"A confusing age."

Not that life was any less confusing now.

The light turned green. He checked for traffic and

pulled through the intersection. "I've heard some interesting things about you," he said casually. Too casually.

"Like what?"

"That you're some kind of voodoo priestess or something."

She let out a strangled laugh. "Who told you *that*?"

"People talk."

"Well, they talk shit. What you should know is that the Savannah Police Department is like an eccentric aunt with a multitude of stories to tell, most of them lies."

"That's just a romantic way of saying the place is infested with gossips," David said.

"You Yankees are so blunt. What would Savannah be without romanticism? Just another port city."

"Do you know that some people are actually a little afraid of you?" he asked.

"Are you afraid of me?"

"No."

"*Were* you? At the beginning?"

"Of course not."

Time to tell all. "I'm surprised you haven't heard the whole story." She suspected he had by now, or at least some variation of it. But with any departmental gossip, it was always best to go to the subject.

"I heard you were abandoned as a baby. In a cemetery. That you're the daughter of some famous witch doctor."

"*Root doctor* is the accurate term, but most people say conjurer or witch doctor. No one really knows exactly where I was found. In a cemetery? Yes. On a grave? Maybe. Whose grave? Nobody knows."

"That's very cool."

"Cool? I've never had anybody say that before. *Weird. Creepy. Scary.* That's what I usually get."

"So then you were adopted?" he asked, prodding for more information.

"The story quickly grows boring," she confessed. "I was adopted by a nice religious family and raised in a traditional household. My father worked as an accountant until he retired, and my mother was a stay-at-home mom."

What she didn't tell David was that people were freaked out by her. Her family had adopted her because nobody else would take her and they'd thought it was the Christian thing to do, not because they'd wanted another child. And even though her parents were kind and tolerant, she was still a charity case, never a real part of the family.

"Brothers? Sisters?" He hit Whitaker and took a left.

"Two sisters, and a much older brother. All of them are married now and have moved out of the area. My parents retired, sold their home, and moved to Tucson." They stayed in contact. Christmas cards. The occasional phone call. "But we're not extremely close."

Another left and he was circling Forsyth Park. "Never felt like you fit in?"

"Exactly. My adoption wasn't a secret, but I never knew the details. When I was seven, my sister Maddie and I had a fight and she told me I'd been found in a cemetery, on a grave. At first I didn't believe her, but she didn't have much imagination and it was a pretty wild story, so eventually I asked my mother and she said it was true."

He turned into the lot next to Mary of the Angels, slid into a spot near Elise's car, and shut off the engine. "And the conjurer?"

"His name was Jackson Sweet. When I heard that he might be my father, I became obsessed with finding out everything I could about him. I suddenly had a history, and a damn interesting one. By the time I was in high school, I'd learned a lot of incantations from an old woman who lived down the street."

While her sisters occupied themselves with after-school projects, Elise pursued what at the time she'd decided was her life calling. The old woman didn't have any living relatives, so she was glad to teach Elise everything she knew. In bad health, she'd been looking for an apprentice in order to pass the mantle.

She lived in a shanty with the doors and window trim painted blue to repel evil spirits. Elise had never known the woman's real name. Everybody just called her Peppermint, because of the peppermint sticks she always had in her mouth.

The ability to perform spells, whether they worked or not, became Elise's best line of defense when it came to her siblings. All she had to do was gather a few ingredients together, and they became loving and well behaved.

"I used a Barbie—well actually Skipper, Barbie's little sister—to cast my first real spell."

He laughed.

"Spells are a serious thing. Spells are real. Or at least some are."

He turned to face her, his left arm draped over the steering wheel. "How can you say that? You're a cop.

A detective. Your daily performance is based on logic."

"Not everything in the world makes sense. Not everything can be explained. Our eyes and our memories constantly deceive us. A good detective knows that."

"Did you ever cast a spell that worked?" he asked, still smiling. Still a nonbeliever. That was the big difference between a Northerner and a Southerner. A Southerner would believe.

Elise had been a seventeen-year-old lovesick girl just playing around. Thomas had passed her again and again with unseeing eyes. But once she cast the spell, he had looked her way . . . and kept looking, as if unable to help himself, as if his eyes were locked on her.

After entrapping Thomas and getting them both tangled up in a disastrous marriage that should never have happened, Elise got rid of every notebook, every herb, every scrap of paper that spoke of any kind of conjuring, no matter how innocent. At the time, she tried to convince herself that there wasn't such a thing as root doctoring and spell casting. Thomas had noticed her because she'd been staring at him with the fever and intensity of a passionate crush.

"I'm not talking about something vague, like making someone's headache go away," David said. "Come on. You can't honestly tell me that you ever cast a spell that actually worked. Something you could be a hundred percent sure of."

"Oh, but I did. On a person."

"Who?"

"Thomas."

"What'd you do to the poor guy?"

"Made him fall in love with me."

Chapter 28

David stared out the office window that overlooked Colonial Park Cemetery.

An interesting place. A sign near the entrance told of the yellow fever epidemic that accounted for a high percentage of the graves. Probably occupied by some of the same people who'd been hospitalized at Mary of the Angels.

He spotted Elise and a photographer from the *Savannah Morning News*. Of course they'd wanted a photo in the cemetery to go along with the TTX article.

"This is Savannah," Elise had said with a smile when she'd tried to talk him into joining her for the photo. "Where else would they take the picture?"

Not far away, a group of children were jumping rope. He couldn't hear what they were saying, but he could easily imagine the content of the chant.

Lady in a black veil
Babies in the bed
Kissed them on the forehead
Now they're both dead.

The office door opened and closed. He turned to
see Elise tossing a stack of papers down on her desk.
"Hot today," she said.

He looked back out the window, to the cemetery,
half expecting to see her there too.

Was he losing it? Sometimes it felt like it. Like his
mind just seemed to slip.

"How did that go?" he asked, regarding a cluster of
ancient, mildew-covered tombstones.

"Okay, I suppose. You know how those newspaper
things are. I gave her the information. All she has to
do is copy it, but tomorrow I'm sure I'll read some nonsense I never said."

"They can't get it right. I don't think they're supposed to. Part of the job description."

She dug in her bag, pulled out a Polaroid, and
handed it to him.

"Test shot."

Elise stood in front of a tombstone. Seeming to
float somewhere off her shoulder was the name Christian.

Too much reality. The cemetery. The name. Following on the heels of his coming clean to Elise.

Christian had been buried in a little Ohio cemetery
in a special section just for children. Playland, or
some such horror. It had all happened so fucking fast
that David hadn't known what to do. His mother had
suggested another place, but nothing seemed right.

David had wanted him close, even though he hadn't
been able to make himself visit the grave. But Playland was all wrong. He could see that now. So frivo-
lous. Naive.

He tacked the Polaroid to the bulletin board, next to

the photo that had been taken of him and Elise on his first day.

So he had some unresolved issues. There were sometimes events in a person's life that could never be accepted.

He would never get over the death and murder of his son. He didn't want to get over it, but he knew he had to find a way to allow his painful past to dwell within his present life, to bring it out of hiding so his child, alive or dead, could be a part of who he was now.

So far his way of dealing had been to slam the door, but in so doing, he'd been unable to experience emotions in life as they unfolded. He'd also set himself up for a hard fall, because whenever he was forced to relive what had happened, or whenever his mind wandered unsupervised and took him back there, the shock was intense.

A surprise attack. That's what it was. And surprise attacks were never good.

He dealt with death on a daily basis, but couldn't deal with the death of his own child.

"You feeling okay?" Elise asked.

"Headache."

"Probably the heat. Want a couple of Advil?"

"Thanks. I have some."

Shortly after the funeral, while he was out of the house, his sister and mother had packed up all of his son's belongings. Toys. Clothes. Books.

All just gone.

Where were Christian's things now? On a shelf in a secondhand shop? In a landfill? The thought made him feel physically ill.

The floor slanted.

He felt bad about so many things.

Black began to creep into the edges of his vision. He ignored it, caught up in the sudden sweep of misery.

"David?"

Elise's voice came from the end of a long tunnel.

He suddenly realized he was falling, but couldn't seem to do anything about it. He heard Elise's shout of alarm, and was distantly aware of her running for him.

Then he was on the floor, looking up at the ceiling.

The handcuffs he kept on his belt were biting into his spine. His gun and holster were jammed against his rib cage.

"Should I call an ambulance?"

She sounded scared. Cool, calm Elise. She was a cop, a detective; she shouldn't sound so scared.

Everything's going to be okay. Everything is going to be fine. Fine and dandy.

When he didn't answer, she made the decision for him. "I'm calling an ambulance."

"No!" He grabbed her by the arm, maybe a little too firmly. He released his grip. "No. I'm okay."

"Does your mouth feel weird and tingly?" she asked, her voice breathless. "Are you having trouble breathing?"

No wonder she was in such a panic. She thought it was tetrodotoxin—when in fact he'd apparently fainted.

"It's not TTX," he said slowly. "It's nothing like that."

"What is it, then? Do you have any pain anywhere? In your arm? Your chest?"

"Actually, I believe I—" Could he make himself say *fainted*? "I got dizzy, and my vision got blurry. . . ."

She leaned back on her heels. "Gould, are you telling me you *fainted*?"

"Let's just call it *blacked out*, shall we?" he whispered weakly.

One of his nemeses, this one happening to be Hutch, showed up in the open doorway. "Hey, that was one filthy place you sent us to." He was all revved up. "That LaRue guy's supposed to be some fancy-ass scientist who graduated from Harvard, and here he's living out there like an animal."

David closed his eyes.

The detective finally spotted him on the floor. "For chrissake, Gould. Are you taking a nap?"

Chapter 29

He walked toward me.

A shadow among the shadows.

He always came to me at night.

Sweet boy. Sweet, sweet boy. Such a pretty face.

He couldn't see me, because I was hiding.

Nobody could ever see me. I was invisible.

It had been easy to lure Enrique to the fountain. He was used to these assignations, and suspected nothing.

He always did what I told him to do.

When he was close, I stepped from the shadows, frightening him.

"Those two detectives," he fretted. "I'm afraid they might start asking questions I won't know how to answer."

"You worry too much."

"You didn't kill them, did you? Gary Turello and Jordan Kemp?"

"Of course not. How could you think such a thing?"

"I'm sorry."

"I'm not mad at you. I should be, but I'm not."

He smiled. Enrique of the pretty face. The pretty

teeth. He always did what he was told, but Enrique was weak. If the police brought him in for questioning, he would talk. In the end, his loyalty would be to no one but himself.

"I'll never ask you to do anything you don't want to do ever again," I said.

I used to pretend that something had come over me. That a spell, a curse, had turned me into something else, a new species. But then I realized. This is what it's like to be human. What it's like to be alive.

The smells.

Glorious.

The *hunger*.

The *cravings*.

So much time had been wasted.

"Come and play," I whispered. "Wade with me in the fountain."

A smile hovered near the corner of his mouth, but he made no move.

The tabby brick wall was wide. I ran, landing on the top, silent and smooth as a cat, then I slipped quietly into the water.

He would follow.

I heard a splash behind me and smiled to myself.

The water wasn't deep. No more than three feet.

I dropped to my knees, then rolled to my back and floated. Something brushed my hand, and I realized it was a fish.

Stars. In a black velvet sky.

"I haven't told anybody," Enrique said. "And I won't. Ever. You know that, don't you? Your secret is safe with me."

"Shhh," I whispered. "Look at the stars. Just look at the stars."

"They're beautiful," he whispered.

I rolled to my stomach. "Keep looking." With my feet on the bottom of the pond, I pushed and floated to Enrique's side. "Don't stop looking."

He always did what he was told.

I could see his eyes, see the stars in his eyes. The eyes in his pretty, pretty face.

I pulled out the knife. "Are you looking at the stars?" I asked him.

"I'm looking."

I could hear the echo of the smile in his voice as I slit his throat.

Your secret is safe with me.

Hot blood ran across my fingers. Sticky. Smelling sweet and bitter and metallic, all at the same time.

I'd been planning this moment for days so I knew what to do. I worked diligently, and soon everything was exactly the way I'd seen it in my mind. I filled his clothes with rocks, so he would sink. So he wouldn't be found for at least a few days.

Finished, I climbed from the fountain, water pooling from my clothes. I was hot and tingly, my nerve endings singing. I could smell the worms living in the soil beneath my feet. I could taste salt in the air, from the marshes miles away. I could hear people fucking in the safety of their homes and beds.

I stroked myself through my soaked clothes and thought about the detective David Gould.

The salt in the air became the taste of his skin; the whispers, his soft encouragements and groans of sexual satisfaction.

I hurried through the darkness. In my bed, I stripped off my wet things and slipped under the covers, putting my arms around Mr. Turello, pulling him close, whispering sweet tales of death in his ear.

Chapter 30

James LaRue was on the run.

On the run.

He liked the phrase. It sounded important.

His frantic escape from Savannah had been harrowing, with cops everywhere, all of them eyeing his car with suspicion. One hour into his panicky flight to the Big Easy, he'd exited Highway 95 and taken the back roads the rest of the way.

Exciting.

Like a movie.

Or television.

James LaRue, badass.

To someone who had been teased and humiliated his entire life, it had a nice ring.

Not that he'd always been a straight edge. Hell, no. As early as eleven years old he was doing a bit of walking on the dark side.

Always a curious kid and never one to pass up an opportunity to get something for free, he'd been digging through the trash behind a funeral home one day and had come upon a mother lode of Polaroids.

Of dead people.

The family funeral business was folding and they'd cleaned out their files.

One person's trash was another's treasure.

He took off his hooded sweatshirt and filled it with photos, then tightly bundled the sleeves together. He pedaled home, dumped his treasure in his bedroom closet, then returned at night with garbage bags to fill with more loot.

The photos were a hit with his school buddies.

He could have unloaded them for five bucks a pop. Instead, he kept them all, every one of them. They filled four shoe boxes that he hid in the back of the closet. His favorite was a full-frontal nude of a teenage girl whose face had been smashed in, but whose body had remained flawless.

He sometimes let his buddies take a look at his private collection, which was something he learned to never do again.

Never let anybody else in on your secret or it won't be a secret anymore.

The photos gave one of the kids, Shawn Hill, nightmares and he ended up telling his dad about the stash in the closet. Big trouble. A life-altering moment.

All because of some snapshots that had been thrown away. Trash was trash. Public property, if any of the public wanted it. He hadn't done anything wrong.

His father was shocked. Disgusted. Confused. Embarrassed.

His old man had been reading the latest parenting book, written by the latest self-proclaimed expert on child rearing. In the chapter "Punishing the Wayward

Child," the author suggested that the punishment should always be related to the crime. Say, if you had a dog that killed a cat, then you would beat the dog with the dead cat.

As punishment for his Polaroid crime, James was locked in his bedroom closet for two weeks *with the Polaroids.*

Cunning.

Sick.

James' father wasn't an evil man, just misguided. How was he to know that the person who'd written a book on child rearing would end up in prison for child pornography?

In adult time, two weeks wasn't much. For a kid, it was a lifetime.

Things became confused in that closet. Even though it was dark, James could see the photos in his mind. He could see the dead people.

They became his friends. His comfort.

Things were never quite the same after he got out.

He was never quite the same.

Which wasn't necessarily a bad thing.

A psychiatrist would probably say that his time in the closet had twisted him, maybe even damaged him. Not true. It had cleared his head. Made him strong.

And just maybe a tad obsessed with death.

But one thing hadn't changed. He wanted to please his dad. *Needed* to please him.

James would have enjoyed his present notoriety more if it hadn't been for his dad. James kept imagining him sitting in the living room in front of the TV. James' face would suddenly fill the screen. His dad's heart would leap, because he'd long expected James to gain international attention as a famous scientist, someone who'd used his knowledge to better the world. Not as a fugitive from the law.

James had tried. He'd really, really tried.

He knew he should call home, tell his dad everything was okay, but cops would be watching the house. That was the first thing they'd figure he'd do. They'd also be watching previous associates and members of the academic community. Friends, if he had any.

Funny how you could be an outcast even among your own kind.

He had to go it alone.

He had to disappear.

New Orleans was perfect for that. After things cooled down, he would hitch a plane to the Bahamas, then on to Haiti. Once there, he'd call his dad. Tell him he was okay. Try to convince him he hadn't really done anything wrong.

Shouldn't have done it. With hindsight, he could see it had been a bad idea. But he'd been a little out of his mind at the time. And when he was out of his mind, he did unpredictable things. Crazy, foolish things.

Sometimes, when he looked back after a particularly wild encounter, he couldn't remember what he'd done, where he'd been.

Who he'd been.

When he reached New Orleans, James referenced movies he'd seen, as a blueprint to disappearing.

He didn't use his credit card. He cut his hair. Bleached it blond. Quit shaving. Wore dark glasses. Different clothes.

A whole new persona. It felt good. Great to reinvent himself. Step into a new life . . .

But not many days into being a fugitive, the novelty began to wear thin. He grew tired of trying to find places to sleep, tired of being dirty, tired of wandering the streets of New Orleans.

Then he was mugged.

The last straw. The last fucking straw.

"Don't spend it all in one place!" he shouted after the three hoodlums as they ran down the alley with his billfold.

Enough.

He wandered into the New Orleans Police Department Headquarters.

"I'm James LaRue," he announced to the female officer at the front desk.

His new persona must have been good, because nothing about him registered with her. She stared blankly, waiting for him to state his purpose.

"If you look up the name on your computer, you'll see that I'm wanted in Savannah, Georgia, on a felony charge."

She called for assistance.

Two more officers showed up, one huge black guy and a white guy who looked as if he spent every free second in the gym.

"James LaRue," the female officer confirmed when she checked the computer. She eyed him, then the screen. "But you don't look much like the guy in our database."

Another officer wandered by, glanced at the screen, then back at James. "Could be him. What about prints?"

"No prints in the system. Never been in trouble before."

"Got any ID?" the black officer asked.

James patted the pockets of the baggy tan shorts he'd picked up at a thrift store and shrugged, his hands spread. "I was robbed."

"Did you report it?"

"I'm reporting it now. And aren't we getting a little off track?"

"I think we'd better get one of our facial-identification specialists down here," the black guy said.

"Why would I say I'm somebody I'm not?" James asked. "Especially somebody who's wanted for a felony?"

"Happens all the time," the woman told him. "You could be a Confessing Sam, looking for some attention your parents didn't give you as a child. Or you could just be looking for a free ride to Savannah."

Ingenious. He'd stepped into a whole new sick world.

"You could have run into LaRue somewhere. You could be pulling this switch for LaRue."

Until they could make a positive ID, they put him in a holding cell, fed him, and gave him a pillow and blanket.

After what James had been through, it felt like a five-star hotel.

Chapter 31

Elise folded the newspaper and tossed it on her desk. The cemetery photo was kind of campy, but the reporter had done a good job on the TTX article, getting her facts straight and displaying the Savannah Police Department tip line in large numbers on the front page.

Smack. Smack. Smack.

The sound came from beyond her office window.

Elise looked out to see David and Audrey in the cemetery, playing catch. She zipped her computer in its carrying case and went down to meet them.

"The pitcher hurt her arm," Audrey announced. "So I'm going to pitch a few games. Isn't that cool?"

"Isn't pitching a dangerous position?" Elise asked. "Didn't somebody break a nose last season?"

"I have to practice." Audrey lined up her fingers on the softball. "A lot." She tossed the ball to David, who was crouched in white shirtsleeves, his jacket and tie draped over a tombstone.

He caught the ball and straightened, shaking his bare hand. "That's enough for me without a glove."

"Mom, will you practice with me? Maybe tomorrow or the next day?"

Elise had never tossed a ball in her life. "What was her name? The girl who broke her nose? Camille? Didn't they say if it had hit any harder, her nose would have been shoved into her brain and she could have died?"

"Mom!" Audrey let out a laugh of exasperation. "Will you practice or not?"

"Okay." Since life made no sense, Elise would probably be the one to end up with the broken nose.

She eyed her partner. He obviously knew quite a bit about gloves and balls. "Need a ride home?" she asked. His car was still in the shop.

"Love it." He grabbed his jacket and tie.

It was late afternoon and traffic was heavy getting from downtown to the suburbs. They hit every red light and breathed in enough carbon monoxide to kill all of the canaries in the state of Georgia. Audrey, still excited about pitching, chattered the entire way and bailed out of the car as Elise pulled to the curb in front of Thomas' house.

"I'm going to pitch!" she shouted, dropping her glove in the grass and running toward Vivian, who was strolling around the yard, a baby on each hip.

Vivian passed off Toby to Audrey, then came over to sit cross-legged in the grass so that she could chat through David's open window. In the background Audrey put her mouth against Toby's belly and blew, making the baby grab fistfuls of her hair and laugh hysterically.

"We're having a neighborhood block party and cookout in two weeks," Vivian said, bouncing baby

Tyler on her knee and making faces at him. "Please come. Both of you. You need to have some fun, Elise," she added as if anticipating an argument.

"Oh, I have fun," Elise muttered. "Lots of fun."

Block party. It meant a bunch of strangers milling around, struggling for common ground. Elise didn't fit in that kind of world. A world that pretended bad things never happened. But then, was her world any more real? A world where horrendous things happened on a daily basis?

Vivian attempted a new tactic. "Try to get her to take some time off," she begged David. "Try to get her to come."

David was slouched in the passenger seat, eyes squinted against the setting sun, arm braced on the window. "Sounds nice to me," he said congenially. "But I don't have any influence over her."

Everything seemed way too normal all of a sudden. It made Elise feel a little queasy. "We'll try to make it," she lied.

After a lot of waving and too much baby talk, Elise and David drove away, heading back toward civilization and a higher crime rate.

"You have no intention of showing up, do you?" David asked.

"I don't know. . . . I might. Depends on what's going on at work."

"Sure." He made a sound that implied he knew better than that.

Was she getting more transparent with age? "I love Vivian dearly," Elise said, "but I'm no good at that kind of small talk. I hate it."

"What you really mean is you're afraid of it."

"I can't believe you're lecturing me. You. Mr. Anti-social."

"I'll go if you go. That way we can talk shop if things get too awkward."

"Oh, that would be a hit. Maybe we should bring along some crime scene photos to pass around while we're at it."

"Eight-by-ten color glossies. I can see it now."

Elise veered to the left and pulled into the parking lot of a sporting-goods store. "I need a glove," she explained in answer to David's look of inquiry.

Inside, David made a tight fist and punched the center of the leather baseball glove.

"This one seems pretty decent." He pulled it off. "Here. Try it."

Elise wiggled her fingers into the glove. Her hand was healing nicely. The butterfly bandages were gone, replaced by two small Band-Aids. "It doesn't go all the way on."

"It's not supposed to."

"It's stiff."

"It'll soften up. You have to work with it. You don't want to get one that's too soft, or it'll start folding up on you. How does that feel?"

She made a fist and smacked it against the padded palm of the glove. "I don't know. How's it supposed to feel?"

"Okay." He let his shoulders sag, his arms dangle. "I can accept that you never played softball, but you surely played catch."

She smacked the glove again. "Nope." The ball fit so nicely in the glove. She rolled it around, pressing her fingertips against the stitching.

"What'd you do instead? Don't tell me you actually *played dolls* with those Barbies."

Elise thought about the time she'd tried to put a spell of silence on her sister. She'd found a doll with brown hair. She cut the hair so it resembled Maddie's. She superglued an X of black thread across the mouth, burned some herbs, and read a spell she'd been taught by the old lady conjurer down the street. It had been one of her many early failures.

"Yeah," she told David. "I played with dolls."

"Hmmm." He squinted his eyes and appraised her. "There's something you're not telling me."

"So, you think this glove's okay?" She pulled it off and tucked it under her arm. "What about this one?" She lifted a red glove from the shelf hook. "I kind of like it. Or what about that pretty blue one?"

"The brown glove is better."

"It's more expensive."

"With a glove, you get what you pay for."

She put the red glove back and picked up a ball.

"That's a hardball. You need a softball. Here." He plucked two from a wire barrel. "One more thing . . . " He perused the shelf until he found a small brown bottle. "Glove oil. You have to oil the glove, put the ball inside, then tie it closed so it will get a good shape to it."

"How has this gotten so complicated?" She shook her head in bafflement. "We're just going to play catch. *Play.*"

"Play takes work."

David picked out a glove for himself. Something that took a little longer, because he was even more particular about his purchase than he'd been about Elise's.

"Stay where you are."

He gave her a slow, lazy throw.

She had no choice but to try to stop it, just snagging the ball with the top of her glove. She didn't toss it back.

"I'm assuming you played a lot of ball, so why don't you have a glove that already fits you?" Elise asked as they walked to the checkout area. "That's already formed to your hand?"

"I do, somewhere. It could be at my mother's in Ohio, or in storage in Virginia."

"I can't imagine my life being that scattered."

"They're only *things*. Material possessions."

He tossed the ball straight up and caught it in the glove. "You don't strike me as materialistic."

"No, but I become attached to my possessions in an emotional way. Like my car. It has over one hundred fifty thousand miles on it. I know I should get a new one, but emotionally I'm not ready. I can't let it go. I've had it so long that it's a part of me. An extension of who I am."

He got in line and put the glove with the ball inside on the conveyor belt. "Your car is a piece of shit."

"But it's *my* piece of shit." She thought over what she'd just said. "Figuratively speaking."

"Of course."

"I'll probably get attached to this ball glove if I use it long enough. Especially if it eventually forms to the shape of my hand and only my hand."

She was already feeling herself becoming fond of it. She particularly liked the way it smelled.

Their items were rung up separately.

"Some people believe objects take energy from

their owners," Elise said once she'd paid and grabbed the noisy plastic bag. "And when they absorb so much, they begin giving it back."

David paused as the automatic door opened. "So does that mean there's a part of me packed away in the bottom of a box, in a shed in my mother's backyard along with my Matchbox cars and microscope?"

The image he suggested gave her a strange, sorrowful feeling in her chest. "I think you should find the glove."

He laughed.

"I'm not kidding."

"I know you aren't."

Elise's phone rang.

Headquarters. Their brief foray into normalcy was over.

James LaRue had been caught and was at that moment being escorted back to Savannah.

Chapter 32

"Your visitors are here."

James LaRue stuck his hands through the small rectangular opening in the cell so the guard could slip a pair of handcuffs around his wrists. The heavy cage door was unlocked, the sound of metal against metal reverberating hollowly.

LaRue shuffled out, his slippers making a shushing sound against the glossy cement floor. He was led through a series of locked doors to a small, brightly lit room with surveillance cameras high on three walls and an inner observation window of reinforced glass.

Sitting at the table was Detective Elise Sandburg. With her was a guy with dark hair and an angry face.

They were both dressed like they were ready for a funeral.

An omen?

He sat down across from them, annoyed to find that the chair was difficult to get into gracefully because of the short chain used to anchor it to the floor.

So. There she was. The woman he'd drugged.

For a moment he found himself distracted by her

strange eyes. They were multicolored, with dark lines going through them.

She was attractive, something he didn't recall because he'd been so fucked-up at the time. She was also very cool. Very together. Just like you'd think a detective would be, only prettier.

The guy . . . he was rougher around the edges. With the look of someone who needed some kind of fix. Maybe alcohol. Maybe drugs. Maybe even legal medication prescribed by a doctor who liked to keep his patients happy.

LaRue experienced a wave of panic.

He'd been panicking a lot lately.

What a stupid thing for him to do. A stupid, stupid thing. But it had seemed so logical at the time. Funny how that kind of thing worked. The guy—he would surely understand that. He'd surely done some stupid things while under the influence.

Now there was a good chance LaRue himself might end up in prison with murderers. With pedophiles. Where beasts with shaved heads and tattoos raped guys like him.

He looked from one to the other, hoping he didn't appear as desperate as he felt.

"Hey—" He glanced up at the guard.

She was a large, tough-looking woman he'd managed to coax a smile out of a few times. "Would it be possible to get something to drink?" he asked. To his visitors, he said, "Would you like something? Soda? My treat."

Detective Sandburg shook her head and, with a twist of her lip, said, "I'll pass."

LaRue inwardly cringed. Oh, shit. Last time he'd

offered her something to drink, it had been laced with tetrodotoxin.

"Me too," said the guy.

She was pissed. Of course she was pissed. They were both pissed. Why wouldn't they be? But it wasn't as if he'd killed her. It wasn't as if he'd meant her any harm.

"Okay."

He waved his linked hands nervously in the air, as if to shoo away his bad idea and the time he'd already wasted. These were important people. Busy people.

"Stop wasting our time, LaRue."

Wow. Apparently the guy was a mind reader.

"I'm sorry," LaRue said. "And you are?"

"Detective Gould."

"Nice to meet you." He slid his hands across the table, cuffs jingling.

Gould leaned deeper into his chair. "I don't shake hands with people who poison my partner."

Double shit. "I don't know what you're talking about." LaRue pulled back his hands.

"You don't remember giving my partner a glass of water laced with tetrodotoxin?"

LaRue shook his head.

"But aren't you an expert on the stuff?" Gould asked.

"Well, yeah."

"Don't you sometimes have it in your house?"

"Hey, I can't help it if she somehow came upon some when she was snooping around my place."

"You mean, a glass laced with TTX just happened to bump into her mouth? Didn't you in fact offer her a drink? Didn't you in fact hand her the glass?"

This was bad. Really bad. Whatever happened, LaRue had to make this convincing. The rest of his life could depend on it. . . .

"You have no proof of anything."

"I collected pieces of broken glass," Elise said. "Took them to the lab. Guess what they found?"

He let out a long breath. Shit, shit, shit.

"Tetrodotoxin," she said. "On a glass from your house. A glass you handed to me."

"Don't lie to us," Gould said. "Because we already know all the answers."

"Not everything. You can't know everything."

"We'll see about that."

They interrogated him for three hours.

Thank God nobody smoked. That would have been bad, because the room was small, and something like that could have really gotten LaRue's asthma stirred up.

The interrogation was pretty much what you'd expect. They bullied him. Especially the guy. LaRue could feel the hatred coming from him.

He was asked the why, where, who.

As the hours progressed, he could sense their growing frustration. They'd entered the room hoping to find him guilty of the tetrodotoxin murders, and he'd given them nothing to substantiate their theory. They were disappointed.

Sorry to let you down, peeps.

The interview shifted.

"What can you tell us about tetrodotoxin?" Detective Sandburg asked.

LaRue would have crossed his arms if it had been possible. Instead, he leaned back in his chair, hands in his lap. He stared from one to the other. "Nothing."

"Nothing?" Detective Gould asked in mock disbelief.

"I don't want to talk about tetrodotoxin."

Gould tensed up again. He leaned forward. "What you want has nothing to do with this conversation."

"I'm not going to talk about tetrodotoxin," LaRue said, shrugging his shoulders.

"What would I have to do to convince you?" Gould asked.

"Is that a threat?"

"Of course not," the guy lied, glancing up at a corner camera. "I would never threaten someone who poisoned my partner."

"My expertise has a price," LaRue said.

Gould made an impatient sound.

"I'm the most knowledgeable person in the country when it comes to tetrodotoxin," LaRue said smoothly. "And you should be taking advantage of such expansive knowledge. My education wasn't cheap. This is the U.S. We thrive on capitalism. I have a product. I sell the product. You buy the product."

"You want *money?*" Gould asked incredulously. "People are being murdered, and you want money?"

"Oh, and I suppose you're a *volunteer* detective."

Elise crossed her arms. "He wants the felony charge dropped."

LaRue smiled at her. She was a doll. A complete doll.

"Your ego is awe-inspiring," Gould said. "But you aren't the only tetrodotoxin expert in the country. Don't you think we've been in touch with other specialists? You have no bargaining power. Nothing to stand on. You can't tell us anything we don't already know or can't find out from someone else."

He was bluffing. Either that, or misinformed. Nobody knew as much about tetrodotoxin as LaRue. He looked up at Gould through his lashes. "You don't know anything about tetrodotoxin. *Nothing*. You think you do, but you don't. There's a secret society, a huge underground network of people who are addicted to TTX."

"Why would someone take poison for entertainment?" Detective Sandburg asked.

"At first, it's for the thrill. Like somebody else might go skydiving, or drive too fast. But then . . ."

He ran his tongue over his lips, then inwardly berated himself. They would think he wanted out because of his own addiction.

"It's not a physical addiction," he quickly said. "It's a mental one. It's a high like nothing else, because it is one step away from death. I understand that. I know all of the sweet corners, the stages TTX takes a person through."

He shifted in the slick chair. "You know what it's like. You know what I'm talking about," he said, addressing Detective Sandburg. "Don't you feel as if you've cheated death? You've mastered death? Doesn't it give you a feeling of power in a world where so much is beyond our control?"

"You know, Mr. LaRue, I wouldn't have described it as a pleasant experience. But maybe it's because it didn't involve free will."

Would she ever let that go? "I was a mess that day. A total mess."

"That should never be an excuse," Detective Sandburg said.

He was losing them.

"I have an idea," Gould said. "Why don't you stay here, and if we need your help, we'll know where to find you?"

This wasn't working. Not working!

Tears of fear and frustration welled in his eyes and everything got blurry. He couldn't end up in prison with creeps watching as if he were some tasty morsel they hadn't yet sampled. Or worse, had sampled. Why had he turned himself in? Why hadn't he seen where such action would lead? God, he was as naive as a ten-year-old.

He leaned close and whispered, staring directly into Detective Sandburg's eyes—because he felt that was where any chance of sympathy lay. "Can you imagine what it would be like for me if I go to prison? Where the animals are running the zoo? Look at me! I'm a scientist! I'm a geek! I haven't any street smarts."

Did they want him to beg? At this point, he didn't have a shred of pride left. He'd beg, if that's what they wanted. Fucking cops.

His nose was running. He had no choice but to lift his parallel hands and wipe mucus on the orange sleeve of his jumpsuit.

Using some spooky, silent form of communication, the detectives nodded to each other and got to their feet.

Detective Sandburg leaned forward, hands braced on the table. "This is what we're proposing," she said. "If you cooperate with us, if you answer all of our questions, then I'll *consider* dropping the felony charge." She pushed away from the table. "We're going to leave you alone for a couple of minutes. Give you a chance to think about it."

*   *   *

"He could still be involved in the killings," Elise said once they'd stepped into the hall, and the interrogation room door had closed firmly behind them. "He could even be working with somebody else."

"That's a possibility," David said.

"We could have him released and put a tail on him," Elise suggested. "If he is involved, we'll find out fairly quickly while he leads us to his accomplices. If he isn't involved, he could actually help us with the case."

"Are you forgetting what he did to you?"

"It might be worth the risk. I'm willing to drop the charges in order to find out what he's up to."

"Maybe you won't have to." David turned toward the door. "Maybe the little shit will be ready to spill everything."

LaRue was exactly where they'd left him.

"Shall we continue our little chat?" Elise asked.

He stared silently at the shiny surface of the table.

She and David took their seats.

Rather than asking LaRue if he'd come to a decision, Elise took a less humiliating approach. "Why don't we start over?" she suggested in a friendly tone.

He didn't answer.

She began questioning him anyway.

Just normal, conversational things, to get him to relax. Where he was born. His education. Where he'd gotten his degrees.

Ego was a perplexing and amazing thing, and it always surprised Elise to discover how much people enjoyed talking about themselves even when being interrogated by the police.

There was usually a point when something fell

away and suddenly the interview took on a life of its own. As soon as they got on the subject of LaRue's research, he tumbled through the hole and seemed to forget whom he was talking to.

Twice she'd seen killers reach that point and become so engrossed in telling their own story that they confessed without even knowing it.

"I expected to be famous by now," LaRue said. "Tetrodotoxin was going to be a new, better morphine, the answer to severe pain. A new way to sedate patients. Even a way to send astronauts into space in the state of suspended animation."

"What happened?" David asked.

"Budget cuts. My University of North Carolina funding got pulled."

"Ouch."

"That was three years ago. I can't believe I've been basically doing nothing since then."

He let out a heavy sigh. "My research was my life. All I knew. But I didn't realize how important it was to me until I lost it. I'm going through an identity crisis. If I'm no longer that guy, then who am I?

"Do you have any idea what it's like to spend years moving toward a goal, focused completely on that goal, certain that if you worked hard enough, it would finally be attained, only to have everything you've worked for taken away? It's fucking heartbreaking, that's what it is. It's a fucking tragedy."

"What about tetrodotoxin?" Elise said. "What can you tell us about it other than the obvious?"

"People are afraid of what they don't understand, and people were afraid of tetrodotoxin. That's why my funding was pulled. They blamed it on a lack of finances, but things were happening too quickly."

"Maybe they didn't appreciate the fact that you were using it to get high," David suggested dryly.

LaRue frowned at him. "I'll admit to taking it even then, but I couldn't get it stabilized enough for human trials. And I couldn't ask my students to be guinea pigs. My colleagues kept arguing that it would never be controlled enough to use on humans. I had to prove them wrong."

"We're going to need the names of everybody you know who's involved in this underground movement of TTX use. Every single person."

"Most of them are college students. Just harmless kids."

He was backpedaling, unwilling to turn anybody in. Actually, an admirable character trait.

"We just want to talk to them," Elise said. She slid a piece of paper across the table, followed by a pen. "Write down every name you can think of."

It took about five minutes. When he handed the paper back, there were six names on it. "Is that all?" Elise asked.

"All I can think of right now."

David stiffened. She could see he was ready to press LaRue for more names. She folded the paper. "This will give us a place to start."

Then he talked about tetrodotoxin, telling them things they did and didn't know.

"The poison attacks sheathed, peripheral nerves, but doesn't cross the blood-brain barrier, which means the victim's mental functions are unimpaired. In the wrong hands, TTX could be the perfect method of torture. Imagine being able to do and say anything to someone while that person remained fully conscious and aware."

"Maybe that's why your funding was pulled."

"TTX is everywhere. Anybody can get it. Anybody can produce it. I was doing something worthwhile. I was trying to harness it."

Elise opened her briefcase and pulled out a five-by-seven of Truman Harrison and placed it on the table in front of LaRue. "Recognize this person?"

"I saw his picture in the paper."

"Ever meet him?"

"No."

Next came the black-and-white of Jordan Kemp, taken in the cemetery.

"Oh, man. This is some evil shit." He pointed to the photo. "You don't think I had anything to do with this, do you?"

"Did you know him?" David asked.

"Was he someone you sold TTX to?" The question was slipped in on the sly. Elise suspected LaRue of selling the poison, and hoped she could trip him up.

"I never sold TTX to anybody. Let's get that straight."

"Did you know Jordan Kemp?"

"I saw him a few times."

"Where?"

"Black Tupelo."

"You go to Black Tupelo?" David asked.

"Not for the reason you might think."

"What about Strata Luna?" Elise pressed. "Have you ever met her?"

"No."

"Sure about that?"

"I tried to. I wanted to meet her. Who doesn't? I finally convinced the kid, Enrique, to call her for me."

"So you talked to her on the phone."

"Yeah."

"What about?"

"I'd heard rumors that she knew how to make zombies. Total bullshit, I'm sure, but I thought she might know something about tetrodotoxin that I didn't. It can be mixed with different ingredients with varying results. Depends on the cocktail. It's hard to regulate the dosage of straight TTX, since the strength is all over the place. But it always does one of three things: gives a person a buzz, paralyzes, or kills."

"So what's your professional opinion about the Savannah cases?"

"Not straight TTX. Straight TTX paralyzes, yeah, but not for *days*. With tetrodotoxin, the user wakes up after a few hours or dies."

Elise took note of the instant when he realized he'd incriminated himself. On camera. In front of three people.

She looked at her partner. He was smiling.

Elise felt a little alarmed now that she realized just how close she'd come to dying that day at LaRue's place.

"That's about all we need for now, wouldn't you say?" Gould asked.

"I *knew* the strength of the tetrodotoxin I gave you!" LaRue said in a panicky rush, his handcuffs rattling. "I *knew* it wasn't enough to kill you!"

"That sounds like a confession," Gould said, mockery in his voice. "Shall we get some people in here for a deposition?"

"I thought you were going to drop the charges."

"I said we'd think about it," Elise said.

"I told you everything you wanted to know."

"Yes, but you also admitted to almost killing me. You're a smart man. Surely you can't expect us to responsibly release someone with your history."

"A history of attempted murder," Gould added.

"You need me!" LaRue said. "You know you need me!" He glanced up at the guard, then back to Elise. "This isn't over, is it? You'll be back, won't you? I helped you today. I can help you again."

"We'll consider it and let you know."

He jumped to his feet.

Gould shot upright, prepared to hit him if the occasion called for it. The guard stepped forward to stand to LaRue's left.

"When?" he asked, looking from Gould to Sandburg. "When will you get back to me?"

"Hard to say," Sandburg told him.

LaRue glared at her.

BITCH!

She was enjoying this, enjoying keeping him in the dark, toying with him. His anger shifted to Detective Gould. What did that reject know? LaRue thought with resentment. He'd never been picked on, never had anyone laugh at or make fun of him.

As if in silent communication, the detectives turned and began walking away.

LaRue held his cuffed hands toward their retreating backs. "I'm going to be fucked in the ass!" he sobbed.

Chapter 33

The evening of the LaRue interview, Elise picked up Audrey from school. In the courtyard behind the old Victorian, they grilled kabobs made with mushrooms, tofu, and mangoes, then walked to a nearby café for frozen yogurt. Afterward, Elise helped Audrey with her pitching in Pulaski Square.

On the way back to Elise's, they passed a vendor selling a child's sleeveless dress with a no-puffer-fish design on the front.

Kinda cute, Elise thought.

The red-and-white sign had appeared seemingly out of nowhere. It could be found on the windows and doors of every eating establishment in town, even McDonald's. It was a version of the no-smoking sign, only instead of a cigarette, it sported a puffer fish with a red diagonal line through it. Underneath, it read: NO EXOTIC FISH SOLD HERE. Many restaurants had removed fish from their menu completely.

"This is so cool." Audrey held up a T-shirt, checking for size. VISIT SAVANNAH. WE DARE YOU.

How did these things appear so quickly? Elise wondered. Was there a secret factory somewhere in the United States, always on standby in order to pump out souvenirs for every disaster that came along?

An even hotter item was the latex glove. Since the mode of TTX delivery hadn't yet been determined, people were being warned to wash their hands thoroughly and often, and to keep all cuts covered. The public had taken it upon itself to stock up on disposable gloves.

Last Elise heard, the gloves were a fashion fad, with the purple and red ones being *the* gloves to be seen in. The local supply had been depleted, even the boring flesh-colored gloves, and now people in other parts of the country, even the world, were putting up boxes on eBay, where the bidding could often go as high as fifty bucks. Which went to prove you could never put a price on style or health.

"How much?" Elise asked the vendor.

"Thirty dollars."

"*Thirty?*" For a T-shirt?

"Twenty."

Elise pulled out her wallet and extracted some bills. "How about fifteen?"

The woman quickly pocketed the money before a tourist happened by. "We have charms to go with the shirts," she said with a sweep of her hand.

A basket in the corner held *wangas*. With the white T-shirt draped over one arm, Audrey picked up a *wanga*, sniffed it, and recoiled. "Ugh." She held it to Elise's nose.

Sulfur.

Elise was familiar with sulfur—a main ingredient in most root work.

She'd seen people on street corners selling *wangas* for much less, but a person had to be careful. Those supposed *wangas* could be filled with leaves and grass out of the backyard. Not the real thing, with no powers of protection. Wearing a fake *wanga* would be like driving with a faulty seat belt or defective air bag. Unfortunately, there were always vultures out there ready to make a buck on someone else's misfortune.

"How can people wear these?" Audrey made a face. "They smell awful."

"It's worth it if it makes you feel safe."

"Dad says this kind of stuff preys on people's fear."

"It's not always a bad thing for people to believe a bag of herbs will protect them," Elise said. "It gives them a feeling of control in a situation in which they have none."

Audrey tossed the charm back in the basket. "Thanks for the T-shirt, Mom." Audrey slipped the shirt with the puffer fish design over her tank top and they resumed their walk.

Elise reached into her pocket and pulled out the *wanga* she'd been carrying for the past several days.

Audrey stared at it. "Where'd you get that?"

"Strata Luna made it for me."

"She *did*?"

"Would you like it?"

Elise realized she might feel better if Audrey had the charm. It could offer her some protection.

Audrey picked it up and sniffed it. "It doesn't smell as bad, anyway."

"The herbs she used help cover up the sulfur."

Audrey handed it back. "No, thanks."

The fact that her mother carried a *wanga* obviously

made Audrey uncomfortable. What would she think when she learned about Jackson Sweet?

That line of thought reminded Elise of her last visit with Strata Luna. Would she come through with her birth mother's full name? If so, what would Elise do with it?

Three more blocks and they were home.

Their evening together had been somewhat of a success, but as Elise returned Audrey to the suburbs, she thought of her daughter's reaction to the *wangas* and was once again reminded of the differences between them. Not that she expected her daughter to be like her. That was egotistical and unrealistic. Audrey lived in a traditional, practical world while Elise continuously found herself straddling two cultures, neither of which fit. She could say she didn't believe in spells and *wangas*, but on a more primitive level she did. She also understood the power of the myth, a power that could never be discredited.

Elise dropped Audrey off, then drove back downtown through dark, silent streets. Arriving home, she found a manila envelope with the Black Tupelo logo stuck in her door. Just a single sheet of paper with the name Loralie and the address of the Savannah Carmelite Monastery printed in large black letters.

Chapter 34

Elise's phone rang in the middle of the night.

It was a Savannah Police Department dispatcher.

"I know this is your night off," she said, "but there's a sticky note here saying we're supposed to call you if any dead bodies make an appearance."

Elise took down the information, thanked the woman, and hung up. Then she called Gould. His car was still in the shop, his apartment on the way. "I'll pick you up," she told him.

Gould was waiting on the front steps when she got there. He ran for the car and slid into the passenger seat as she pulled away.

Heading toward the address given to her by the dispatcher, Elise filled him in on what little details she could. "The body was discovered in the courtyard of the Secret Garden Bed and Breakfast, currently unoccupied and under renovation."

"Sex of the victim?"

"Male."

"Approximate age?"

"Nothing on that."

Elise knew they were getting close to the site before they reached it. Emergency lights flashed silently. Streets had been barricaded, and traffic was being redirected.

After parking two blocks from the perimeter, Elise and David jumped from the car, flashlights in hand, doors slamming, the pounding of their shoes sounding hollow against the cement sidewalk as they walked rapidly in the direction of the lights.

Even though it was the middle of the night, people had wandered out of their homes to watch. They huddled together on sidewalks and in the street, snatches of conversation floating toward Elise and David.

"Did you see anything?" a young female voice asked.

"I heard somebody found a body."

"I heard the head had been chopped off."

"I heard somebody was wading in the pond and tripped over it."

"Oh, man. That's sick! Really sick!"

"Not the head, you retard. The body."

"That's sick too."

To someone outside law enforcement, the scene may have appeared chaotic, but Elise automatically took note of the dividing lines that had been made to partition off witnesses, keeping them corralled until their stories could be taken down. Savannah Police Department used what they called the two-barrier method. The outer barrier was for press and gawkers, the inner barrier for the few people who were given permission to pass. Detectives and police officers were questioning people, tablets in hand.

One of the officers spotted Elise and Gould. "Weird

as hell," she whispered. "The place was dark. The gates were locked, but some kids sneaked in and went wading. One of them tripped over the body and thought it was a friend joking around until it just stayed there. Turns out, it had been weighted down with rocks."

"Headless?" Elise asked.

"No, but the throat's been cut."

Elise glanced at David. *Not our guy*, they were both thinking.

"What about lights?" Gould asked. Randomly placed police cars with spotlights were parked at odd angles, but it wasn't enough to adequately illuminate the crime scene.

"Getting a generator set up."

"Where's the body now?" Elise asked.

"Still in the fountain," the officer said. "Or maybe I should say pond. It's huge—that's all I know. In the middle is kind of an island with a stone bench. I dragged him up there." She aimed the flashlight on herself. "Look at me."

Her pants were wet from the thigh down. When she shifted her weight, her black leather shoes squeaked and water oozed out.

"These shoes will never be the same. I wish I'd known he was dead. I wouldn't have gone to the trouble. And now I keep smelling him. Don't know if it's in my sinuses, or my clothes."

The detectives thanked her and made their way up the brick walk.

Elise turned on her flashlight as they stepped through the wrought-iron gates decorated with cherubs. "I've always loved this place." She'd visited a few times during the annual spring tour of gardens. "It's breathtaking under normal conditions."

But not now . . .

The first thing that hit them was the sweet smell of magnolias mixed with the stench of death. Water trickled and ferns grew from damp stone walls. There were boxwoods and trumpet vines, water poppies and hibiscuses. Nestled amid plants and trees were various kinds of statuary, from angels to frogs.

David scanned the area using a high-powered flashlight beam. "Wow," he said, pausing to admire the twisted trunk of a Jerusalem tree. In the distance, crickets chirped and chimes made a soft, delicate sound.

Elise was relieved to see that Abe Chilton was on duty. With some crime scene specialists, she had to tell them what to collect. Abe knew what he was doing.

She and David had arrived so quickly that the preliminary preparations were still under way. It wasn't their shift, but Mason and Avery hadn't yet arrived, so Elise and David temporarily took charge.

"Ready for daylight?" someone shouted.

The sound of a generator drowned out the crickets and chimes. Everybody turned their backs. One second later, brilliant, blinding light flooded the area.

Two EMTs stood in the center of the fountain, staring at the body at their feet. They looked up when the light came on, flinched, and raised their arms against the glare.

"Water," Chilton muttered. "I hate water."

Water destroyed evidence.

"We've been trying to decide if I should go there or they should come here," Chilton said.

"Best to go to the body," Elise said.

Since the victim had initially been pulled from the water, it probably made no difference, but Elise always felt it was better to have too much information than too little.

"Here they are."

Chilton's intern ran up, as happy as a puppy, a pair of hip waders in his hand. Chilton grabbed them and raised them into the air. "Are we going to draw straws for these?"

Elise heard a splash and turned to see Gould wading toward the center of the fountain, water hitting him above the knee, darkening his jeans.

"You go ahead," she said.

Chilton was wearing a suit and dress shoes, Elise nylon sandals and the kind of drawstring cotton pants a teenager might lounge in. Almost proper swimming attire.

She swung her legs over the stone barrier and stepped into the water.

"You doll," Chilton said.

He let out a satisfied sigh and put on the hip waders. Then he positioned himself on the cement wall surrounding the fountain, swung his legs over, and began sloshing through the water carrying a large gray case that resembled a fishing tackle box.

"I need more light," Chilton said when he reached the center. The foliage was dense and the single generated light stationed near the wrought-iron gates couldn't penetrate it. Immediately, powerful flashlights were directed on the body.

Nude.

Male.

Late teens, early twenties.

Moss was wrapped around the torso. A water lily clung to a forearm.

"We've got some serious deterioration going on." Chilton poked around with a gloved hand. "Our guy's not a fresh fish."

But then, a body could decompose fairly quickly in tepid shallow water under warm, humid conditions.

"Did he move?" someone asked. "Did anybody else see that? Because I thought he moved."

One of the EMTs jumped back and fell with a splash, water spraying.

After everything that had occurred lately, it wasn't surprising to find people jumpy and suspicious about true and absolute death. But if the body had a slit throat and had been submerged. . . . not much room for doubt there.

The EMT came sloshing out of the pond, bringing with him gallons of water.

"He isn't going anywhere," Gould said. "Look." He waved his flashlight back and forth quickly across the victim. The shifting beam tricked the eye and made the body appear to move.

Light and shadow.

Someone sighed in relief.

Not Elise. She directed her own flashlight beam on the victim. Even though the face was swollen, it was one she'd seen before. One she'd seen fairly recently.

Enrique Xavier.

Chapter 35

There were times when the historic brick building that housed Police Headquarters seemed to inhale and exhale. Seemed to have a rhythm and heartbeat. You got used to it after a while, but when that rhythm was upset, you noticed. It was similar to a flock of blackbirds suddenly stopping their chatter. Or when a heart monitor flatlined.

It was the change that got your attention.

Elise was in her office with the phone to her ear, hoping the third time would be the charm and Strata Luna would pick up.

She didn't.

Were they going to have to issue a court order to bring her in for an interview?

At that point, Elise became aware of a hollowness in the air. She hung up and sat there, testing the moment.

The sensation reminded her of the stillness that came when the eye of a hurricane passed overhead. After hours of unending noise, after hours of the wind creeping under rafters and whistling through window cracks, finding and banging every tiny loose bit of anything—silence.

Then you knew you had time to open the door and run outside into the hollow, echoless void.

Elise opened her office door.

The halls were silent and empty.

The elevator motor kicked in. From downstairs, a beehive of sound began to build.

People.

Talking. Whispering.

The elevator stopped on the third floor. The door opened and Strata Luna stepped out.

"Detective Sandburg." The agitated words were spoken through a black veil. She hurried over, dress billowing. "You must do something. You must catch the person who did this terrible thing. Enrique's killer can't be allowed to enjoy one more second of freedom."

So much for a court order. "We're doing everything we can," Elise told her, knowing her words wouldn't be nearly enough to calm the upset woman. They were waiting on the lab results, and of course they were looking for TTX, but at the moment all involved were treating the Xavier case as nonrelated.

David Gould turned the corner and appeared at the end of the long hallway. Upon catching sight of Strata Luna, he stopped, coffee cup halfway to his mouth.

The noise downstairs increased. Pretty soon people would be making their way to the third floor with a sudden need to use the copy room.

"Let's go into my office," Elise said.

When they were all three inside, David closed the door and Elise pulled a chair around for their guest while the overhead fluorescent lights cast them in a green, twitching glow.

Strata Luna sat down, then lifted the veil with both hands. Her face held the expected signs of stress and grief.

"Would you mind if we took your statement?" Elise asked.

"That's why I'm here."

It wasn't common practice to take a statement in the privacy of their personal space, but considering the circumstances and Strata Luna's notoriety, Elise thought it wiser to remain where they were. Since they weren't set up to videotape, David called downstairs and was able to recruit a stenographer so Strata Luna's statement would hold up in court. Five minutes later they were questioning her, a young male stenographer clicking away while a small tape recorder ran silently on the desk in front of Strata Luna.

The interview began with the usual name, age, address, and phone number.

Then Elise moved on to questions relating to the case. "Did Enrique Xavier work for you?" she asked.

"Of course he did."

"Do you know anyone who may have wanted to harm him?"

Strata Luna pulled a tissue from a deep pocket of her black dress. "I keep asking myself that question." A tear ran down her cheek. "Could it be somebody he knows?" She wiped the tear away with a trembling hand. "Can you tell things like that? By how the body was found?"

"You mean like a crime of passion?" David asked.

"Yes."

"It's a little early for that kind of speculation," Elise said.

"Do you have someone in mind?" David pulled a pen and small notebook from his shirt pocket. "Someone you think could have been capable of such an act?"

The appearance of the notebook seemed to ground Strata Luna. The tears vanished and she pulled herself together. "No."

"When did you first notice Enrique was missing?" Elise asked, steering them back to the traditional questions.

"Three days ago."

"Three days?" David asked in exaggerated surprise.

Elise added her own question. "And you didn't report it to the police?"

"I have little faith in the Savannah Police Department."

"Then what are you doing here?" David asked.

"Enrique is dead!"

"Let's go back," Elise said, hoping to placate her. "You said he was gone for three days. Didn't you think that was strange?"

"He goes away sometimes. But he always returns to me."

"He leaves without telling you?"

Strata Luna tucked the tissue in her pocket, then admitted, "We had a fight."

"What do you mean, fight?" David broke in.

"An argument born of passion."

David caught Elise's eye. *Okay. Wasn't expecting that.*

"Are you saying Enrique was more than your employee?" Elise asked.

"Yes."

"He was your boyfriend?" Elise asked.

"What a stupid word."

"Okay, how about *lover*? Was he your lover?"

"I hate that word almost as much. We sometimes had sex." She shrugged. "That's all."

"You lost two children, isn't that right?" David asked slowly, as if contemplating and setting up his next question.

"I told you that before," Strata Luna said.

"And one of those children was found dead in a fountain—isn't that correct?" David continued.

Strata Luna frowned, beginning to appear uneasy and annoyed, her grief pushed aside. "That's right."

"And now your lover is found dead in a fountain. Wouldn't you say that's a rather strange coincidence?"

David didn't trust Strata Luna. Everything about the woman was a flamboyant act, from her black clothes to the veil over her face that gave the staged illusion of hidden, solitary sorrow. A magician's game, meant to distract. You look here while something else happens over there.

Feel sorry for me. I've had such a hard life.

Had she killed her own children?

Maybe. Maybe not. All David knew was that she was a phony.

He knew grief. He understood grief. And you didn't carry it around with you like a fucking look-at-me flag.

Strata Luna stared at him, defiance in her face, tears long gone. Had they been part of her act too?

"I don't think anything is strange," she said coldly. "And there are no coincidences."

Something Flora had said to him. God. The girl had been brainwashed.

"You already admitted to having a fight," David said. "A lovers' quarrel—for lack of a better definition. Are you sure Enrique wasn't leaving you?" Such a thing would have really pissed off a woman like Strata Luna.

"Enrique would never leave me."

What ego. "There's only one way I can think of to be sure of that," David said.

Out of the corner of his eye, he could see Elise trying to get his attention, trying to get him to cool it. He ignored her.

"Are you saying I killed Enrique?" Strata Luna jumped to her feet, head tossed back, spine straight in indignation.

Acting?

She leaned close and for a minute David thought she was going to hit him. Instead, she swept her hand across his desk, sending papers, pens, files, and coffee flying.

Elise gasped.

"You are such a foolish man." Strata Luna's top lip curled in disgust and loathing. "But then, all men are foolish."

Remaining in his chair, lukewarm coffee soaking into his pants and shirt, David asked, "You don't like men, do you? You didn't really care for Enrique all that much, did you? He was just convenient."

"You should know about convenient."

Ah, Flora. So Strata Luna knew the details of their strange relationship. No surprise there.

Towering over him, the Gullah woman pulled in a deep breath. "Detective David Gould"—her next words were enunciated very clearly—"I curse you."

The keys stopped.

While the stenographer sat there, mouth agape, Strata Luna pulled the veil back down over her face and swept from the room.

After a moment, David reached out and shut off the recorder with a loud *click.*

Sitting behind the wheel of the Lincoln Continental, Flora blew her nose and threw the tissue on the floor with a deep pile of others. She hadn't wanted to come today, but Strata Luna had needed someone to drive her to the police station. Then she'd made her wait in the car, which was probably for the best because she couldn't quit crying. Every time she thought she was done for at least a few minutes, she would start all over again. Her head ached from it. Her face hurt. She couldn't breathe through her nose.

She reached up and checked her reflection in the rearview mirror and saw that her face was splotchy and swollen. Even though David had told her to quit coming around, she desperately needed to see him, but not when she looked so awful.

The passenger door flew open and Strata Luna slid inside.

Flora stretched across the seat and began raking in the wet, wadded-up tissues.

"Drive," Strata Luna demanded. "Just drive. To Bonaventure. I need to visit my children."

Leaving the tissues, Flora straightened and turned the key in the ignition. "Did you see David?" she asked, pulling away from the curb.

"I saw him," Strata Luna said.

"And?"

"I think it's time you found yourself a new boyfriend."

Shortly after Strata Luna stormed out of the building, Elise's phone rang.

"Got some news," Cassandra Vince, the GBI medical examiner, announced. "Using mass spectrometry, we were able to detect trace amounts of tetrodotoxin in Gary Turello's liver."

It was the information they needed to finally link the old deaths with the new ones. It meant someone had been killing people with tetrodotoxin for at least a year and a half.

Chapter 36

Even though David had never had a problem remembering the day his son had been born, most other birthdays and anniversaries eluded him. But that kind of memory lapse was history. He would never forget the day Christian died.

Now, alone in his apartment, he had to admit that subconsciously he'd known the anniversary was coming, even though he hadn't strung the words together in his head. He didn't have it marked on a mental calendar, where he would have crossed out each day as it drew near.

Maybe that would have been better. Maybe then he would have been able to deal with it when it came knocking. As it was, his avoidance of the approaching date had left him wide open.

It had been less than two days since Strata Luna had visited headquarters and put a curse on him. During that time, they'd scoured the city for Flora, hoping to get her statement, but she'd been elusive, always one step ahead of them.

And then there was Elise. So damn worried about

the curse. To David, her concern and preoccupation made about as much sense as fretting over an alien invasion. And if by some remote chance curses were real? Well, he'd been cursed years ago. What was one more?

By nine p.m. he was experiencing a strong sense of foreboding. A smothering claustrophobia that wasn't external, that had nothing to do with his apartment.

He was the cage. *He* was the dark pit.

By nine thirty he felt himself breaking.

Blond hair floating in the bathtub.

Blond boy. Blond baby.

Pull him out. Turn him over.

Blue lips.

Blue hands.

Little blue hands.

David's throat tightened. His eyes burned.

He'd been doing so well, but it had been a trick. He saw that now. He'd just buried it. Put it away because he couldn't bear to see it. His shrink had been right. And now he'd looked away for a minute, and when he looked back, there it was. Right there. Right in front of him.

Floating blond hair.

His life. His fucked, fucked life.

How could a human tolerate so much anguish? It didn't seem possible.

I should be dead.

He should explode, or his heart should just quit beating.

I have to get out of here.

He had to get out of his own head, had to somehow escape his thoughts, because if he didn't, he was afraid he might get stuck like this. And the pain would never stop.

Had to run. Run away.

His heart pounded. His hands trembled as he changed into navy blue shorts and a gray T-shirt.

The dark streets were welcoming.

Fragrant.

Humid.

Heat from the day clung to the asphalt.

This was familiar. This was something he could do.

Run.

Forget.

The rhythmic slap of his jogging shoes gradually lulled him. Relaxed him. Soothed him.

Put him in a trance.

How far could he go?

Into tomorrow. And the next day. And the next.

He imagined himself running on the surface of a giant globe. Running around the entire world. Never stopping. He wouldn't need food or water or sleep.

He was a machine.

And machines didn't think. Machines didn't feel.

His feet slapped the street.

May twelfth. May twelfth. May twelfth.

Don't think. Don't think. Don't think.

> *Goofer dust around the door*
> *Sprinkled in the bed*
> *Wake up in the morning*
> *Find yourself dead.*

May twelfth. May twelfth. May twelfth.

*   *   *

I watch him.

From my hiding place, I see him coming closer. Running down the middle of the street. Weaving.

Breathing hard.

His shirt is saturated with sweat, his hair dripping. He looks distraught, confused. A little out of his head, maybe. But that isn't a bad thing.

Poor David. Poor baby.

Let me make you better.

I can stop the pain.

I can make it all go away. . . .

David ran for two hours.

He didn't remember thinking about returning to his apartment, but suddenly he was there, on the front steps of Mary of the Angels.

Beside him, the bushes rustled. He caught a whiff of something that smelled faintly of piss, and looked up to see Flora standing there.

"David," she whispered in a small, trembly voice.

She looked sad. Full of pain and grief.

"We've been trying to find you," he said.

Her face lit up, then immediately dimmed. "For my statement. I can't talk about that now. And I don't know anything."

"Small, seemingly trivial things can sometimes help solve a case."

"I can't talk about Enrique. He was like a brother to me. We went to grade school together. I know you didn't want to see me, but . . . " She put a hand to her mouth, stifling a sob.

He held open the door. They stepped into the foyer and went up the stairs.

Inside his apartment, they clung to each other. Just stood there and hung on. Pretty soon clothes were dropping to the floor and they were moving toward the bedroom.

"Make me stop thinking," Flora begged.

Little blue lips.

Little blue hands.

"Just for a little while," she said. "I want to forget. I have to forget."

They tumbled across the bed and he plunged inside her.

Deep and dark.

Forget. Forget. Forget.

Each stroke took him closer to oblivion.

David was asleep and Flora didn't want to wake him. She followed her trail of clothes and quickly dressed in the living room while David's cat, Isobel, sat on the couch, eyeing her with suspicion. Since Enrique's murder, Flora had been staying at Strata Luna's. She'd promised she'd be home by midnight. It was past three o'clock.

Flora didn't like the way Strata Luna was suddenly acting as if she owned her. The woman had always treated her like a favorite, but Enrique was the one she'd lavished attention on.

Flora checked her cell phone.

Damn. Three calls from Strata Luna, one less than an hour ago.

She slipped out of the apartment, the door closing with a loud *click.* In the center of the hall, she passed through a cold spot and stopped.

"Enrique?"

She waited.

She listened.

The chill faded. What was that smell? A little herbal. A little earthy. A little like the cologne Enrique wore . . .

Flora had always wanted to see a ghost, and now that Enrique was dead she hoped he would come back to visit. But he wouldn't be hanging out in Mary of the Angels, she told herself as she continued down the hall. Not Enrique, who'd been scared to death of the place.

Outside, Savannah was quiet except for the sound of a street sweeper.

Flora got in her car, slamming the door.

The smell from the hallway was stronger now. Almost overpowering.

"Enrique?" Flora asked loudly. "Is that you?"

A shadow fell across her from the backseat. A gloved hand pressed to her mouth, something sharp against her throat.

Flora reached behind her with both hands, grabbing for eyes.

The sharp object sank into her flesh. One long slice, and she could no longer breathe, no longer make a sound. She felt a blanket of heat on her chest as blood soaked the cotton of her top. At the same time, her hands and fingers turned to ice.

She tried to see who had cut her throat, but she couldn't make her eyes work. And it really didn't matter anymore anyway. Nothing really mattered. Not Strata Luna, or Black Tupelo. Not even David Gould.

In movies, dying people always whispered the killer's name. That wasn't right, Flora now realized. Because in that last minute you've already moved on. You suddenly understand that the world is just a bunch of silly people doing silly things. . . .

Chapter 37

A phone conversation with someone named Sister Evangeline had given Elise the rough sketch of Loralie's present existence, along with an invitation to visit.

Although a cliché, it was understandable that a person who'd had a hard life might choose to hide from the world in a cloistered monastery. Elise's birth mother wouldn't be the first person to turn to such a sanctuary in a time of need. Elise herself had known a few people who'd lived in a monastery until they'd gotten their lives together, but she didn't know anybody who'd stayed indefinitely without joining the order.

The Savannah Carmelite Monastery was located in Coffee Bluff, on a dirt road that ran from Back Street all the way to the Forest River. As Elise bumped along the overgrown lane, she was reminded of her ill-fated visit to LaRue's home. The weather was similar, hot and humid, and she hadn't met another person since turning off Back Street.

She stopped at a pair of open iron gates, car idling,

air conditioner blasting. In the distance, down a straight and flat dirt road draped by trees and flanked by shrubs, stood a sprawling two-story brick colonial. It looked a little like an old hospital or school.

Should she be doing this?

Most of her life she'd wondered about her real mother, but after today there would be no more wondering. And sometimes the unknown was better than the known.

Elise stepped on the gas and eased the car forward through the pillars that marked the boundary where the real world ended and seclusion and counterculture began. She might end up regretting the visit, but it was something she had to do.

In earlier times, the Carmelites had no contact with the outside world. When the rare visitor came, he or she was forced to speak to the nuns through an iron grate that looked like a confessional screen. Times had changed. Now they could visit face-to-face.

An ancient nun in a brown habit met Elise in the entryway and introduced herself as Sister Evangeline.

"She's expecting you," the nun said, leading Elise through a chapel and out a side entrance. At the end of a short path stood a small log cabin with a red door. On either side of the door was a window with white panes and green planters overflowing with red petunias.

Elise's mother was inside that house.

Things were beginning to get surreal.

"The cabin had been empty for years when Loralie showed up here," the nun said. "The Carmelites' lives are all about prayer, and although we shun contact with the outside world, we took a vote and decided we couldn't send her away. Our numbers had dwindled, and the cabin was empty. . . . That was twenty years ago," she said with a conspiratorial expression.

Elise's heart was pounding, and it was hard for her to concentrate on what the woman was saying. She responded with a weak, distracted smile that was nothing but a lie of politeness.

"I'll let you go the rest of the way by yourself," Sister Evangeline said, coming to a halt, hands tucked under a layer of brown fabric. She turned and serenely followed the path back to the chapel.

Elise stared at the red door.

She wished Sister Evangeline hadn't left. She wished she herself hadn't come. She wished she'd talked to the woman inside first. On the phone. As an icebreaker.

Before her panicked thoughts took over completely, she stepped forward and knocked—a little too loudly.

A voice from deep inside the small building answered immediately, telling her to enter.

Elise opened the door, but remained with one foot on the threshold, the other on the flagstone step. The interior was dark, and Elise's eyes needed time to adjust.

One large room. Table in the far corner. Someone sitting there.

"Shut the door."

The voice was harsh, like somebody who had a sore throat, or someone who'd been born with a cigarette in her mouth.

Elise's breathing was weird and shallow; her palms were sweaty.

As a detective, she'd faced a lot of dangerous people in her years without a fluttering pulse or a rise in blood pressure, but this was the hardest thing she'd ever done.

As the room gradually lightened and objects became more distinct, she stepped inside. "Thanks for agreeing to see me." Her voice was tight, but nothing someone who didn't know her would notice.

The woman who was her mother lit a cigarette with a small butane lighter and tossed the lighter on the table. It had been too fast for Elise to get a good look at her. Shoulder-length hair. Possibly dark. That was all.

"When Strata Luna called," Loralie said, "I told her no. Told her I couldn't face you, couldn't see you, but when I thought about *not* seeing you . . . well, I would have regretted it. Plus I owe you this."

She sure as hell did.

Elise crossed the room, the soles of her shoes sounding hollow on the wooden floor.

There wasn't much furniture. No pictures on the walls. No rugs. Nothing to absorb the sound.

The table was small and narrow. Elise pulled out the only other chair—a fragile, brittle antique—and sat down, her legs shaking.

Loralie leaned back and crossed her arms, the cigarette held between two fingers. "She was right. You do look like him."

Now Elise could see that the woman's thin face was framed with frizzy gray hair, that her eyes were a faded hazel. She looked sixty, but couldn't have been over fifty.

Just your regular eyes, Elise noted. And a regular face. Hard, something Dust Bowl about it. That defeated-by-life kind of thing. No, it was beyond defeat. She was someone who'd moved on to total acceptance—which to Elise's mind was worse.

"Weird, isn't it?" Loralie took a long drag and blew the smoke at the ceiling with a twist of pale lips. "Seeing me. I've always known who you were, so I never had to wonder." She knocked the ashes into a glass tray overflowing with butts.

Had she been sitting there for hours, smoking one cigarette after the other while waiting for Elise?

"Strata Luna put a curse on me when I was pregnant with you. Did she tell you that?"

"No."

"Said it was because I was teasing and tempting her man."

"Jackson Sweet?"

"Yeah, except Jackson Sweet wasn't anybody's man. He was a free spirit. Wasn't my fault that he wanted me. And I sure as hell wasn't going to turn him down." She let out a single burst of laughter at the absurdity of the idea.

The shaking had stopped. A calm that Elise sometimes experienced under duress had come to her rescue, helping her through the moment. Things moved slower. She had time to think, analyze, react.

"Was Jackson Sweet my father?"

"At that time, I wasn't a prostitute. And I hadn't been with another man for almost a year. There is no way you could be anybody's kid but Jackson's."

Elise took a deep breath. Okay. So there it was. Her parentage laid out once and for all. "Was the curse the reason you left me in a cemetery?"

"I was scared the whole time I was pregnant. I was

just a kid. And when someone as powerful as Strata Luna puts a curse on you, it gets your attention. I went to Jackson and begged him to reverse it, but he just laughed. Said Strata Luna had no power over him or his child. But then he got sick, and I was afraid the curse had crossed some barrier and reached all the way to him. And when you were born and I saw your eyes, I went a little crazy and thought it had reached all the way to his child. I figured if I threw you away, offered you up as a sacrifice, then Jackson would get well."

"What were Jackson Sweet's eyes like?" They couldn't have been like Elise's; otherwise Loralie wouldn't have freaked out.

"Brown. Dark brown. I don't know where you got your eyes. Nobody in my family had eyes like that. Jackson had a granny who was a root doctor. People said she had square pupils. I saw a picture of her once, but her eyes were hidden by dark blue conjurer shades. The same shades she passed down to Jackson."

Elise's now. "What did you do after he died?"

"I wanted everything to stop, and got real sick because I wasn't taking care of myself. I did a lot of bad things, a lot of bad drugs. Lived on the street for several years and finally ended up in a hospital for loonies. There was a nun there who told me about this place. Thought maybe I could stay here awhile, because I didn't have any money or anywhere to go."

And she'd been there ever since. . . . . "Have you ever thought about leaving?"

"A couple of times, but it's nice here. Peaceful. Safe. I take care of the grounds for my room and board. It works out."

"Do you mind if I have one?" Elise indicated the cigarettes.

Loralie slid the pack and lighter across the table. "You shouldn't smoke."

"Someone else recently told me that." Elise tapped out a cigarette and lit it. Nonfilter. Loralie was serious about her smoking.

"Would you like something to drink?" Loralie asked, bracing her hands on the table, prepared to shove herself to her feet. "Water, maybe?"

Elise shook her head, picked a piece of tobacco off her tongue. The nicotine went straight to her bloodstream, making her heart pound.

"I want you to know I thought about you." Loralie settled back in her chair, pulled out a fresh cigarette, and lit it with the old one. The smoke was getting thick. "I knew you were okay. Knew you were with a good family, and that you had a better life than you would have had with me."

That was true. The family that took her in had never been mean to her. Elise had simply never fit, never adapted. Which was strange because humans were extremely adaptable. It was as if, like some endangered species, she'd stubbornly clung to an unknown heritage.

The conversation shifted and Elise talked a little about herself and Audrey. Then it was over. Loralie announced it was time for Elise to go.

Elise stubbed out her cigarette. It had been a strong one, and she felt light-headed. "Maybe I'll visit again." She would bring a few things from the outside world. A carton of cigarettes. Pralines and chocolate.

Loralie met her gaze without blinking. "It would be

better if you didn't," she said bluntly. "This has been hard for me."

Elise was disappointed but understood. Loralie was hiding from the world and her past. Closure was something they'd both needed, and now it was done. Now it was over.

"Could you send me a picture?" Loralie asked. "Of yourself and Audrey? And if you see Strata Luna, tell her I don't bear her any grudge. She's had a lot of heartache in her life. A curse can really backfire, can't it? Instead of chasing after me, she should have been painting her window- and doorframes blue and laying down a trick so evil wouldn't follow."

Elise let herself out.

As she drove back down the overgrown road, David called on her cell phone.

"A body's washed up on Tybee Island," he told her.

The good news just kept coming.

Chapter 38

Tybee Island wasn't in the Savannah Police Department's jurisdiction, but small municipalities often requested assistance in the case of a suspicious death.

Following the directions they'd been given, David drove the unmarked car along a flat, paved road.

"There." Elise pointed to a cluster of vehicles.

That part of the island was sandy, with very little vegetation. A few blades of cordgrass grew defiantly here and there, along with Spanish bayonet.

A Georgia Bureau of Investigation crime scene team was on location, a large area already taped off. Three canopies had been set up for shade and privacy.

"No media yet," David commented, shutting off the engine and slipping from the air-conditioned car. He'd parked the length of a football field away so that when the crowd showed up, he and Elise could get out.

"They've established a wide barrier," Elise said with appreciation. "That'll keep the morbid curiosity seekers under control."

They approached one of the officers standing guard.

"What's the story?" David asked. "Who found the body?"

"Local family, out for a walk on the beach."

"Male or female?" Elise asked.

"Female."

David looked at Elise. She could tell what he was thinking. Another victim that didn't fit the TTX killer's MO.

The sand was powder-fine and deep. She and Gould trudged through it, finally reaching a firm, packed area where the tide had gone out.

A bureau agent extracted himself from the crowd and eyed David and Elise with suspicion.

They flipped open jackets to display their badges, then let their clothing fall back into place. "Savannah Police Department."

"I'm Agent Spaulding of the Georgia Bureau of Investigation, Homicide Division." He passed a piece of paper to someone nearby. "The coroner's taking forever," he complained, jabbing a pen over his shoulder in the direction of the woman he was discussing. "Thinks she's Dr. Quincy or something."

Agent Spaulding spread his legs, rocking slightly in a typical military pose. With tablet in hand, he asked, "How do you spell your names?"

They gave him their names and badge numbers.

He took down the information, then appraised them both while chewing on the end of his pen. He finally narrowed his focus exclusively to David. "You're the Yankee, aren't you?"

"If I remember my history correctly," David said,

"there haven't been any Yankees in this country for well over a century."

"Yep," the agent said, giving Elise a look that was supposed to convey that they were on the same team. "He's the guy I've been hearing about."

"And what are people saying?" David asked.

"Let's go," Elise told her partner, before he said something he shouldn't and ended up with a complaint lodged against him. Spaulding obviously represented the small minority of investigators who'd gone into the business for status, and he saw David as a male invading his territory.

David refused to look in her direction. "I'll bet they've been saying I'm rude. That's it, isn't it?"

He didn't sound mad, only entertained. But he *was* mad. Elise could tell.

"That's right," the agent admitted.

"And that I'm not a team player."

"You said it, not me."

"And that I don't care about the cases I'm working on." David's voice was rising, his anger becoming more obvious, even to someone who didn't know him well. "And that I'm unstable. Was unstable on the list?"

"Get away from me," Spaulding told him. He looked at Elise. "Get your partner away from me."

"David." She hoped she wasn't going to have to haul him out of there by the shirt collar. "Come on."

He nodded. Without giving the agent another glance, they turned and walked toward the crime scene.

Elise thought they were home free when David

spun around. "Hey, buddy!" he shouted. "The fucking Civil War is over! It's *over!*"

Major Hoffman would be delighted when that complaint crossed her desk, Elise thought as they turned and continued on their way.

"Sorry," David said. "But I've had it with that bullshit."

It appeared that the body hadn't yet been moved. Nude. Face up. Bloated and discolored. Caked with sand.

Photos were being taken. Agents were diagramming the position.

The GBI had good crime scene investigators. She and David weren't there to process the scene, only to observe and offer suggestions and assistance where it might be warranted.

A young woman with a blond ponytail was dressed in khaki shorts and a white T-shirt that said CORONER across the back in black letters.

The victim had long dark hair. The face was grotesquely swollen and disfigured, the body mangled, most likely from the pounding of the surf. It would be hard to determine cause of death.

Everyone was engrossed in discussing elements of the situation, from tide flow to how long the body had been in the water.

"Ready for the other side," the coroner announced, a Polaroid camera in her hand. The body was rolled to its stomach.

Cameras clicked.

"What's that?" Someone pointed.

Elise and David leaned closer.

On the corpse's lower spine, half hidden by sand, was the Black Tupelo design.

Elise looked at David. He was staring at the body.

She pulled out her phone and put in a call to headquarters. "Hi, Eli. I need to know if anyone has been reported missing in the last few days. I'm particularly interested in any females."

She waited while he accessed the information.

It turned out there was one. She thanked him and slowly hung up.

David was still staring at the body, at the logo on the spine.

"Let's get out of here," she told him.

He didn't respond.

"David." She grabbed his arm.

He lifted his head, a dazed expression on his ashen face. Birds circled and cried overhead.

"We have to go," she told him firmly.

Her words finally sank in. He nodded numbly and stumbled toward her. Side by side, they trudged through the sand toward the car.

"It's Flora, isn't it?" he finally asked.

"Strata Luna reported her missing last night," Elise told him. "We didn't hear about it because not enough time has passed to make it an official missing-persons case."

"I knew it. I mean, I had a feeling right from the first. When I saw the dark hair I just had a feeling."

"Prostitutes live an untraditional lifestyle," Elise said, looking for words of reassurance. "They go missing all the time, only to turn up wondering what the fuss was all about."

"They should be able to ID the body fairly quickly," he said robotically.

She nodded. "Then we'll know."

"I was with her night before last." He glanced up to gauge Elise's reaction.

She must have appeared dismayed, because he repeated what he'd just said, this time with a twisted, self-defeated smile.

"I thought you were going to quit seeing her," Elise said. "I thought you *had* quit seeing her."

"She was waiting for me when I got home. It was just something that happened."

He looked in the direction of the crime scene. Toward a mangled corpse that may have been Flora. He closed his eyes and tipped back his head, as if trying to erase the image from his memory. "My life is so fucked," he whispered. "I don't know. . . . Sometimes it feels like I'm a magnet for bad things." He straightened and looked at her, as if she might have an answer. "Who's the 'Peanuts' kid? The one with the cloud of dirt around him?"

"Pig Pen?"

"Yeah. I'm that kid. But instead of dirt, it's bad stuff. Following me around."

She should have been formulating possibilities, mentally gathering a list of people to interview. She could have at least been trying to make him feel better, but the only thing she could think about was the curse Strata Luna had put on him.

She'd always surmised that curses only worked if the recipient believed. Kind of like a placebo. Now she wasn't sure, because David was right. His life was fucked.

Chapter 39

Starsky, of the Starsky and Hutch team, rapped on the open office door. "Got a positive ID on the Tybee Island body," he said, clinging to the doorframe.

David swiveled around in the chair so his back was to the detective.

"Flora Martinez," Starsky announced.

Something big and solid dropped in the pit of David's stomach. Even though he'd known it was going to be her, subconsciously he'd been holding out hope that it wasn't. "Thanks for the information," David said, staring at the fish screen saver in front of him.

Jesus. Flora.

Was her murder his fault? Was it somehow connected to the TTX case? Or was it the result of her dangerous lifestyle, completely unrelated to him or the investigation?

"That's not all," Starsky added. "The GBI's been looking into things, and it seems they want you brought downstairs for questioning."

David wasn't surprised. What was a surprise was how quickly they'd connected a few random dots.

He got to his feet, rolled down his sleeves, and slipped into his jacket. When he stepped into the hall, he saw that Hutch had been lurking a few feet away, practically rubbing his palms together.

The Yankee was going down.

It was a long way from his third-floor office to the interrogation room.

A regular gauntlet.

Curious workers filled doorways. People stood in clusters around drinking fountains and rest rooms. Familiar and unfamiliar faces jumped in and out of focus. In front of him, the hall was silent. But then, behind his back as he passed, whispers began.

David's personal history seemed to have taken on a life of its own, becoming an entity that filled the brick building. Everyone was talking about David Gould, discussing and debating the issue.

"I don't understand why they sent him here in the first place after being under psychiatric care."

"That doesn't mean anything," another voice argued. *"Half the force should be seeing a therapist."*

Ha-ha-ha.

"Did you hear about his kid?"

"He has a kid?"

A story like David's couldn't remain a secret forever. The truth had finally followed him to Savannah.

"Had. Dead. Killed by his wife. That's why he left the FBI. Had a breakdown. Snapped. They sent him back home to Cleveland. Cleveland didn't want him, so what do they do? Send him to us."

Don't listen, David told himself.

But he couldn't help it. They were all enjoying this too fucking much.

Don't think.

He couldn't help that either.

He was an outsider. The white horse in a black herd. The one the other horses killed for being different. It wasn't just that he was from the North. Some of his coworkers also took a twisted pleasure in seeing an FBI agent crash and burn.

In the interrogation room, Agent Spaulding, from the Georgia Bureau of Investigation, was waiting for him. Starsky and Hutch were also in on the event.

Great. His three favorite people were going to be involved in questioning him. A regular David Gould Fan Club.

The assholes should have felt uncomfortable, interviewing one of their own, but even though they weren't smiling, David got the idea they were struggling like hell to keep a lid on their excitement.

He took a seat. A camera and two tape recorders were turned on. After getting down the date and time, plus David's full legal name and date of birth, Spaulding moved to the real questions.

"Are you currently under psychiatric care?"

"I was until fairly recently." David leaned back. "I personally believe every police department should have a full-time shrink on staff."

"Are you taking medication?"

"No."

"No?" Spaulding pulled out a manila folder. "We were given access to your files, and it seems it was recommended you remain on a high dosage of Paxil, plus a tranquilizer, for an undetermined amount of time."

"I didn't feel I needed it anymore."

Spaulding nodded. "Interesting. And you have a degree in psychiatry?"

"Cut the crap."

Spaulding was using a standard interrogation technique of getting information. Bait and switch. You changed the subject, hit with something from left field, then went back to the real issue. David had used the method many times himself. Of course, he'd done a better job.

"Did you know Flora Martinez?" Spaulding asked.

"Yes."

"How well?" Spaulding sat across the table from David, Starsky at the opposite end, while Hutch held up the wall near the door.

"Fairly well."

"Weren't you a client of Ms. Martinez?"

"I wouldn't call myself a client. We were acquaintances."

"But you—a Savannah Police Department homicide detective—made use of her services. Isn't that correct?"

David was pleased to note that Spaulding was getting one of those pear-shaped bodies that often caught up with detectives who spent too much time behind the wheel eating fast food.

"Once."

"Only once?"

Spaulding placed a small open day planner on the table. "This date book belonged to the victim, Flora Martinez. Isn't that your name and address on page twenty-three?"

David leaned forward. "Yes."

"And your phone number?"

"Yes."

"Strange that a onetime—"

David was sure he would have said *fuck* if the interview weren't being recorded.

"—*exchange* . . . would gain you a permanent place in her address book."

"I called her once. After that, we became . . . friends." Not the right word. What had they been? Lovers? Not the right word either.

"Isn't it true that Flora Martinez was obsessed with you? That she often parked outside your apartment, waiting for you to come and go?"

"Obsessed? I wouldn't call it obsessed. She liked me because I'm a detective. Some women get off on that kind of thing. I'm sure you know what I'm talking about."

The GBI agent was the kind of guy who would have used his badge to get a woman in bed.

Spaulding placed a small plastic bag on the table. After snapping on a pair of latex gloves, he unzipped the bag and extracted a chunk of red flannel. The nose-stinging stench of old urine filled the small room, and everyone but Spaulding recoiled.

The flannel turned out to be a small drawstring pouch. Spaulding opened it and removed an object wrapped in wet grocery paper. "We found this with some of the victim's belongings." He unrolled the paper and spread it on the table.

David's full name was written over and over. Going in the other direction were the words *Love me or die*, also written numerous times.

Jeez. That was sick as hell. David thought about the way Flora had started coming around, as if he would welcome her as a girlfriend. The way she seemed surprised and shocked when he told her she was going to have to stay away. "This place is so fucked," he said, shaking his head.

"Have you ever seen this?" Spaulding asked, indicating the weird mess he'd dumped on the table.

"No."

"Do you know what it is?"

"I'll bet you'd like to tell me," David said, trying not to blink as ammonia fumes stung his eyes.

"It's called a mojo. It's supposed to cast a spell over the person whose name is written on the paper. Which would be you. I asked around. In order to keep the spell active, Flora would have urinated on it every day. I'd call that obsessed, wouldn't you?"

David would simply call it fucked-up.

Flora. Jesus. What had she been thinking?

"In fact, she was stalking you, wasn't she?"

"She wasn't a stalker. I was usually glad to see her, although I did eventually ask her to quit coming around."

"Did she?"

"For a while."

"Why didn't you report her to the police?"

David looked at him. "Totally unnecessary."

"If a prostitute was calling me, sometimes several times a day, plus hanging around my residence—I would have reported her."

"Of course you would have," David said sarcastically. Lying bastard.

"When did you last see Flora Martinez?"

"May eleventh." David thought a moment. "May

twelfth, actually." By the time they were finished having sex.

"So she was with you late on the eleventh, early on the twelfth? Is that correct?"

Spaulding stood and put a foot on the seat of his chair, an elbow on his knee, and leaned in closer. "Tell me about May twelfth."

There was no way David was going to tell him what led to his breakdown that day. "I went jogging. When I returned, Flora was waiting outside my apartment. End of story."

"Did she spend the night?"

"I don't know how long she stayed. I fell asleep. She was gone when I woke up."

The agent opened his briefcase, pulled out a piece of paper, and slid it across the table. The coroner's preliminary report. "You can skip down to the bottom," Spaulding said. "To where it says 'approximate date and time of death.'"

May 11, 2000 hours, to May 13, 0200. "That's a big spread," David said.

"Water does that. As I'm sure you know."

"Right."

"But as you can see, a significant portion of that time overlaps with Flora's visit to your apartment."

David slid the paper back across the table. "What are you saying, Spaulding?"

"I'm saying that you are a prime suspect in the murder of Flora Martinez."

"That's what I thought you were saying."

"Another thing you might take note of from the autopsy report—Flora Martinez's throat was cut, just like Enrique Xavier's. You know what I think? I think you mimicked the Xavier murder to throw us off. That's what I think. So, is there anything you'd like to tell us?"

David got to his feet. They had no evidence; they couldn't hold him. "Other than to ask if your mother picks out your clothes?"

Spaulding laughed and shook his head. David had to admit it was a pretty weak insult, but he was under stress.

"Major Hoffman wants to see you in her office." Spaulding looked at the two detectives. "Escort him, will you? We don't want him to get lost and end up in his car, heading for Florida."

"I'm going to have to ask you to turn in your badge," Major Hoffman said.

David already had it in his hand.

"I've had numerous complaints about you over the past three months." She lifted a small stack of papers. "Would you like to see them?"

"That's okay."

"These complaints, along with your unprofessional connection to Flora Martinez, reflect poorly on the police department. I have to let you go."

David placed his badge on Major Hoffman's desk. Then he pulled out his police department gun, unloaded it, and put it and the bullets beside the badge.

He didn't blame the major. She couldn't take a chance on him. And then there was the media. They were going to love this.

"This is a real shame," Major Hoffman said sadly. "I think you could have been one of my best detectives. Too bad you're hell-bent on self-destruction."

David thought about Strata Luna's curse and the cluster effect. All excuses. The major was right; he'd brought this on himself.

"Stay in town," she told him. "We may need to bring you in for more questioning."

He nodded and backed out the door, closing it firmly behind him.

In Elise's office, David shook the contents of his desk drawers into a cardboard box.

It was amazing how much shit a person could accumulate in a short time. It looked like he'd been there for years, not months.

He regarded his loot.

Pens. Pencils. Paper. Receipts. Notebooks. Notes.

Nothing. Just stuff taking up space.

He carried the box to the trash can and dumped it.

From the bulletin board, he removed the photo of him and Elise. He stared at it a moment before tucking it into his jacket pocket.

Footsteps sounded in the hall.

The door crashed open. "I just heard," Elise said.

She was out of breath. She was pissed. At him?

"They can't do this!" she said angrily.

"Forget it, Elise. Let it go," he told her softly.

He'd felt this kind of calm a few times in his life. It was a nice feeling. As if some gentle saint had taken up residence in his body. "It's okay."

"It's *not* okay."

"I wasn't going to last here. We both knew that. Everybody knew that. Didn't expect it to happen this way, but does it really matter?"

He was actually surprised to find that it *did* matter. To him.

All along, he'd been thinking he maybe needed to get out of law enforcement completely. But now that it was happening, it seemed wrong.

And then there was Elise.

She'd been a good partner. And they were really starting to click.

"Of course it matters!" Elise said. "I can't believe you're giving up so easily. That you allowed Mason and Avery to get to you."

"Who are Mason and Avery?"

She glared at him. "Starsky and Hutch."

"Oh. Them."

He let out a heavy sigh. "Elise, this has nothing to do with them. It has nothing to do with the fact that I keep losing popularity contests around here. I'm a murder suspect."

"That's bullshit if you think this has nothing to do with your status. Do you think Mason—Starsky— would be fired over this? No! They would cover it up until the real killer was found, and then all would be forgotten. He might get a little slap on the wrist for such a personal endorsement of prostitution."

"I'm sorry." He really was. He liked Elise.

"What were you *thinking?* Calling a prostitute to begin with? Getting mixed up with her?"

"That's rather self-explanatory."

His answer seemed to make her uncomfortable.

"David . . . did your ex-wife have long dark hair?"

"Yeah, but—"

"You know what people downstairs are saying? They're saying that the anniversary of your son's death was May twelfth, the same night Flora visited your apartment."

"That's right."

"And when Flora arrived that night with her long dark hair, you flipped out and killed her, thinking she was your wife."

He stared at her for a long time as she waited for an answer, a reaction. Not Elise . . . that hurt. That really hurt. "Thanks for the vote of confidence," he said.

He left the office.

As he passed a trash receptacle, he paused and pulled the photo from his jacket. He held it above the container for what seemed like minutes, but in real clock time was probably only a second or two.

He'd lived a lot of lives. Even though the photo now represented the end rather than the beginning, he couldn't make himself pitch it.

He stuck it back in his pocket and kept walking.

Outside, the media was waiting.

Bad news traveled fast.

Chapter 40

Someone was knocking.

David tried to ignore it while continuing to pack.

The knocking didn't stop.

Annoyed, he tossed a shirt in the suitcase on the foot of his bed, went to the door, and checked the peephole.

In the dim hallway stood a woman in a black veil and long black dress.

Lady in a black veil
Babies in the bed . . .

Strata Luna. Was *she* stalking him now?

He opened the door. "Come to remove your curse?"

She lifted a gloved hand and blew at her cupped palm.

He didn't see anything, but suddenly a bitter, metallic taste filled his mouth. Instantly, his tongue swelled and went numb.

Fuuuckkk.

He took two steps back and struggled to close the door.

She shoved it open, followed him into the apartment, and slammed the door.

Just the two of them.

Strata Luna. Who had probably killed her daughters. Had probably killed Enrique. Had probably killed Flora. Obsessed with death. Obsessed with killing. Playing God. It was just too easy . . . too obvious. . . .

He lurched and grabbed his cell phone from the kitchen counter.

How much time did he have before he was completely paralyzed? Two minutes? Three? At the most?

But he'd snorted the shit. That would be faster.

He stared at the phone in his hand.

He knew what he wanted to do, but his brain couldn't get the message to his fingers.

Where did he fit in? What did she want with him?

Woman in a black veil
Looking for something male
Fuck him till his eyes turn blue
Bury him when she's through.

He'd never claimed to be a poet.

The phone slipped from his numb fingers.

He began to float.

Up, up to the ceiling.

She caught him by the arms and pulled him earthward, holding him in front of her so he couldn't float away again.

His legs gave way and he crumpled to the floor and lay there, unable to move.

She swooped down and straddled him. She sank into him, the billowing folds of her gown swallowing him. Looming above, her veil fell over his eyes as she cupped his face in her hands.

She smelled like mold and mildew and damp rot. Plus something else. What? Something familiar . . .

Formaldehyde and rotten meat.

She pressed her lips to his, her breath filling him with poison. The air that came from her lungs tasted like rubbing alcohol.

He couldn't move. He couldn't close his mouth or turn his head away.

"Little boy," she crooned against his lips. "Sexy little boy."

Chapter 41

Elise was trying not to let the situation with David interfere with her investigation of the TTX case. And the best way to help David was to try to clear his name. With that in mind, she decided to drop by the Chatham County Jail for another visit with their buddy LaRue, to see if he might be in the mood to divulge any new information.

He seemed happy to see her.

She was company. A break from tedium.

She slid a photo of Flora across the table to him. "Ever seen her?" she asked.

"Once or twice. At Black Tupelo."

"Talk to her?"

"No." He passed the photo back. "I only noticed her, that's all."

She pulled out another photo, this one of Enrique. "How about him?"

Bingo. His reaction gave him away.

LaRue stared at the photo while obviously trying to formulate an answer, trying to figure out if he should tell the truth or lie. "I sold him TTX," he finally said with resignation, his shoulders drooping as he passed the photo back.

"Earlier, you said you never sold TTX."

He didn't answer.

"Which is it? Did you or didn't you sell TTX?"

"I did."

Elise leaned forward, elbows on the table. "Tell me about it."

"He would come in a big black car. A Lincoln, maybe. Somebody was in the backseat."

"Strata Luna?"

"Probably, but I couldn't see. The windows were dark."

"Why didn't you tell me this before?"

"I didn't want to get into any more trouble. But I'm no murderer. You know that, don't you?"

At least not a deliberate one, she thought. But he'd still poisoned her.

Elise got to her feet. "I'll see what I can do to get you out of here." She'd already decided to drop the charges, but she wasn't ready to tell him just yet.

He was a scientist. A screwed-up genius. Prison would be a terrible waste.

Heading for the parking lot, Elise mulled over the new information. If what LaRue said was true, then Enrique had been somehow involved in the TTX case, at least peripherally. A big black car with tinted windows. Pretty straightforward. Both Enrique's and Flora's throats had been cut. By Strata Luna? Because they'd known something?

Elise had grudgingly liked Strata Luna. She hadn't wanted to believe she was involved. Had she allowed

Strata Luna's connection to Jackson Sweet to cloud her judgment?

As Elise approached the car, her cell phone rang.

It was Seth West, Truman Harrison's coworker.

"You know how you said to call you if I thought of anything else?" he asked. "Well, I was on vacation in Disney World and we were on the Pirates of the Caribbean ride, and I remembered that Truman went into the tunnels under Savannah the day he died."

Elise perked up.

"We'd had a report of a possible sewer line break. Near the intersection of President and Bay. He had to go in through a grate in one of the old sealed cotton storerooms to check it out and write up a repair order if we needed it. I said no way was I going down there. I knew it would be nasty as hell, but Truman didn't seem to mind.

"He was gone a long time, and when he came back he said the place was full of cockroaches. They were crawling on him. In his hair. In his shirt."

"Did he tell you anything else?"

"Said it looked like homeless people had been living down there. Sleeping on filthy mattresses. Can you imagine?"

"Sounds horrid," she agreed.

"Does that help you at all? I kept thinking it was silly to bother you, but my wife said I should let you know."

"You were right to call."

After disconnecting, Elise immediately put in a call to Eddie, her favorite contact in the research department. He could find out anything, no matter how obscure.

"Remember that guy who was always in trouble for going into the Savannah tunnels?" Elise asked, heading for shade and a picnic table near her car. "What was his name?"

"Pascal. Adam Pascal," Eddie said. "For a while there, he was always in the paper and on the news."

She sat down at the wooden table and pulled out pen and paper. "Any idea where he is, or if he's still around?"

"Let me check." Elise heard the clicking of keys; then Eddie was back. "Lives on Isle of Hope. Was arrested about three weeks ago for his latest caper. Severely fractured a leg and is home recuperating."

Elise jotted down the number, thanked Eddie, and gave Pascal a call.

Like all obsessed people, the guy liked to talk about his obsession.

"Those tunnels go everywhere, man. Under houses. Businesses. Warehouses. Cemeteries. Hospitals. You should see the one under the old Candler Hospital. Creepy as hell, with gurneys and old wooden wheelchairs. The tunnels were used for all sorts of things, but mainly to transport bodies from the hospital to the morgue and cemetery."

"But aren't they sealed?"

"Long time ago. And not very well. You know how the city has always been about that kind of thing. Outta sight, outta mind. Been a lot of water through there over the years. They're crumbling. Dangerous as all get-out. People have died down there. *I* almost died down there. I'd offer to take you, but I'm laid up with a broken leg. A tunnel caved in on me, and it was three days before I dug my way out."

"You're lucky to be alive, Mr. Pascal."

"That's what I keep saying."

"What can you tell me about the tunnels and the Hartzell, Tate, and Hartzell Funeral Home?"

"Used to be a tunnel from the funeral home to a nearby morgue. It's not the morgue anymore. Now it's a residence."

"Description and location?" Elise asked, pen ready.

Before she'd finished taking it down, she knew the building he was talking about: Strata Luna's house.

"Black Tupelo?" she asked.

"Goes there too."

An alternate universe right under their feet.

"How about the Secret Garden Bed and Breakfast?"

"Yep. But don't you go down there in those tunnels, you hear me? I'm not exaggerating the danger."

"I won't."

"I'll fax you some maps. How's that sound?"

"Great." She gave him her fax number, then disconnected.

While Elise talked to Pascal, the manager of CD Underbelly had left a voice mail.

"You know that stuff you asked me to find?" the message said. "Well, I found it. The CDs were put on plastic. Charged to some dude named Enrique Xavier. The boss is cheap as hell and we still use the old imprint machines, so I was looking at the credit card imprint and noticed it was one of those business credit cards, and that it didn't belong to Xavier at all. Guess what other name was on it? Guess who owned the card?" He paused for effect. "That nutcase that rides through town dressed in black and wearing a veil over her face. Strata Luna."

Click.

Elise pushed number nine on her mobile phone, saving the message. Then she looked at her watch and realized it was almost time to pick up Audrey from softball practice.

Audrey heard tires squealing and looked up to see a familiar yellow car flying around the corner, her mother at the wheel.

Now what?

Elise jerked to a stop, leaned across the seat, and shoved open the door. "I hope you haven't been waiting long."

Audrey recognized her mother's hurry-up mode. She tossed her backpack and softball glove in the backseat, and jumped in the car. "Just a couple minutes."

"Good," Elise said with a distracted air. She checked over her left shoulder, then pulled from the curb. "You aren't anxious to get home, are you? I've got to make one or two quick stops."

"No problem."

Audrey changed her mind when, ten minutes later, they were turning into the parking lot of a funeral home. "Somebody die?"

Her mom opened the glove compartment and pulled out a flashlight. "People are always dying."

"I mean somebody you know."

"Oh, honey. I'm sorry," Elise said as if suddenly realizing she was acting a little weird. She looked at Audrey and smiled. "No. Nobody died. This involves a little investigative work. Something you might find interesting. It has nothing to do with dead people. I'm looking for a tunnel."

"Tunnel?" That might be okay.

"Come on. You don't need to wait in the car."

"Hey, isn't this the place that body was stolen from?" Audrey asked as they walked under the green canvas awning.

"Yes." Elise opened the ornately carved door.

"Cool."

They cornered the funeral director in the entry room.

The place had red carpet and a bunch of dark doors that probably had bodies behind them. Audrey hoped nobody opened a door.

If that happens, don't look. Just don't look.

"Well, sure, I've heard of the tunnels," the director said.

She stared at the man her mother was talking to.

He was creepy, with neck skin that hung over his tie. The place smelled too. Audrey had been to only two funerals in her life, both for great-grandparents. Both times she'd refused to look at the dead body, but she remembered that sickening sweet smell. Like something bad was being covered up.

"The tunnels have been sealed for years," the man said.

"I'd like to see the entrance anyway," Elise told him.

"We don't allow anybody down there."

"Mr. Simms, do I need to remind you that a crime was committed in your establishment?"

"It's just . . . that area of the home is kind of for overflow. . . ."

Audrey immediately imagined piles of dead bodies. The smell, along with the image, began to make her feel a little dizzy.

"I'm not an inspector," Elise reminded him.

"Okay, okay."

Annoyed, he led them to the elevator, which took them to the basement level.

What a switch, from all tidy and plush to damp and crumbling stone foundation that smelled like mildew and rotting wood.

The funeral director stayed in the elevator. "Keep to the right," he said, waving his hand. "The tunnel entrance is in the last small room. Low ceiling. You'll need to duck. I have to get back upstairs." He pushed a button. The elevator door closed. A motor kicked in, taking Mr. Mortician away.

The floor was tabby cement that had been poured over sloped, uneven ground. The light was bad, and there were a lot of deep shadows and dark corners.

Elise clicked on the flashlight.

It was one of those cool police flashlights that really lit up the room. The bright white beam darted around, then landed on a shelf full of small cardboard boxes. Each box had a name and date.

"Apparently relatives don't always pick up their loved ones," Elise commented.

Sweet kitty.

Audrey didn't like being down there with a bunch of dead people even if they were ashes. At the same time, she was thinking about how nobody was going to believe her at school tomorrow when she told her friends where she'd been. They were going to, like, think it was the coolest.

A lot of people thought cremated bodies burned down to a tiny little pile of ashes. But Audrey had seen a show on the Discovery Channel, and it told how after the thing they cooked them in was cool enough to open, bones and teeth were still there. Mixed with the ashes. They had a machine that looked like a little cement mixer they dumped everything into. The machine ground up what was left.

Gross.

She fell into step behind her mom.

"Watch your head."

Elise shone the flashlight at the low ceiling, then back to a floor that had turned to rock and dirt. They entered a second room lined with metal shelves crammed with supplies. Bottles of pink liquid claimed to be embalming fluid. Others were called cavity cleaner. Pore sealer. Jugular tubes. Body inserts. Expression formers. Casket Mate, whatever that was. On the floor were drums labeled *Drying Compound, Lightly Fragranced.*

Audrey was feeling dizzy again.

Just a tunnel.

Right.

Her mother had said they were looking for *just a tunnel.* Maybe, if it was a tunnel from *Night of the Living Dead.* Her parents—well, her dad and Vivian—wouldn't let her watch those kinds of movies, but some of her friends had seen them so many times that they laughed at the scary parts. Audrey had been initiated at a sleepover. She'd had bad dreams for two weeks.

Cavity cleaner.

Body inserts.

She felt like she was going to throw up. She took a few deep breaths, then hurried to catch up with her mother, who was peering into an even smaller room.

Audrey couldn't wait to see what was in there. Ha-ha.

They had to walk hunched over.

It was tiny. And thankfully empty.

One wall was brick instead of stone.

"Is that it?" Audrey asked.

She'd seen the sealed tunnel at the Pirates' House Restaurant, so she'd kind of known what to expect, but still it was a letdown. Just a wall. How boring was that?

"Look." Elise pointed the light along the left edge where the bricks stopped, then down to a pile of rubble. "Someone's been doing a little excavating."

Audrey hadn't known what she'd expected when she'd come along. She hadn't really thought about it. But now her heart began beating faster.

She'd heard about the body that had been stolen from the funeral home. It had been all over the news, but suddenly the story changed from things kids at school were joking about to an actual crime. And here was a clue! A real clue!

She'd never seen her mom in action, actually working on a case. Suddenly she felt kind of amazed by her, kind of *proud*.

Elise pulled some bricks free and shone the light through the jagged black gap.

"Should we go inside?" Audrey asked, excited and scared at the same time.

"No. I need to get a crime scene team down here before anybody disturbs anything."

"Can I at least look?"

"Here." Elise handed her the heavy flashlight.

Audrey stepped forward and pointed the beam through the hole.

A tunnel. Cut from rock and earth, with the ceiling curved and lined with brick. In the distance it appeared to end, but Audrey figured it really turned.

Something hit her arm with a *plop*.

A bug! A huge black cockroach!

She jumped back, shook her arm, and screamed, dropping the flashlight.

Elise let out a funny yelp and knocked the roach from Audrey's arm. The bug went scurrying away, hunting for darkness. Then Elise retrieved the dead flashlight. She shook it and it made a broken-glass kind of sound.

Audrey gave her a pained look. "Sorry. But did you see that thing? It was huge. Mutant or something. Like half cockroach, half dog." She shivered dramatically.

"Jesus," Elise said under her breath, her own shudder mirroring Audrey's. "I hate those things."

That made Audrey feel better. Mainly because she'd always thought her mom wasn't afraid of anything.

It was nice to know she was.

Chapter 42

I watched and listened, making sure the hallways of Mary of the Angels were quiet and no one was coming or going.

I didn't mind the wait. Detective Gould was with me.

I cuddled him. I tasted him in his state of simulated death.

Then I retrieved the gurney from the basement.

It was the perfect way to move deadweight. I only had to drag his limp body onto the stainless steel surface, then pop the release lever, raising him off the floor.

Before leaving, I laid down a confusion trick in the doorway so no one would be able to follow.

I double-checked the hall.

Empty.

My heart was beating madly as I silently wheeled him down the strip of carpet. I pushed the black button and hoped no one else summoned the elevator.

We made it to the basement with no trouble. I quickly pushed Detective Gould through a dimly lit room to the tunnel entrance. I lowered the gurney and removed him, dragging his body through the opening, then following with the collapsed gurney. In the weak glow of a small lantern, with Detective Gould lying near my feet, I replaced the bricks.

I'd become fascinated with the tunnels years ago while exploring my house, poking around in the secret rooms. Closed doors had always held a curiosity for me, and a sealed-up wall was an even bigger attraction. A few nights of digging and I'd made a hole big enough to crawl through. That had led to years of off-and-on exploration.

I put Detective Gould back on the gurney. *Time to be on our way.* I bent close and brushed my lips across his.

So still.

So silent.

Was he breathing?

I laid my cheek against his mouth, and was eventually rewarded with a soft stirring of air.

Why did I like my men so docile? I often asked myself. Helpless and at my mercy?

My answer was always the same. Why would anybody want them any other way? That and the fact that the state of death had always attracted me. A shrink might say it was all those years spent in a house that had once been a morgue. I don't think so. The fascination was something that came from deep inside, from my DNA.

The tunnel was darker than night, and the light cast by the lantern could illuminate only a few yards ahead.

I like the dark. It has always been my friend. Even

as a child, when others whimpered and cried for their mothers, I embraced the dark. At night, when I entered a room, I would never reach around the corner for the switch. Why have light when you can have dark?

"There was a waning moon the night I killed her," I told David Gould as I pushed him up an incline. "I coaxed her out of bed and out of the house. We were both wearing white nightgowns. What a pretty picture we must have made as I took her hand and walked with her to the fountain. At first we just sat on the edge with our feet dangling in the water. I said, 'Look at the reflection of the moon on the water.' Then I told her to pick up the image."

I was a little out of breath, my voice ragged.

The detective was heavier than he looked.

We'd reached a junction, which gave me the opportunity to pause. To the left was the cemetery, to the right the house.

"She slipped into the water," I said, continuing with my story. "And when she had the moon in her hand, I pushed her under and held her there until she was still."

In her office, Elise examined the first section of map that Adam Pascal had faxed. He'd been right about the tunnel system going to both Strata Luna's house and the Hartzell, Tate, and Hartzell Funeral Home.

Had Strata Luna drowned her own daughter? Had her other daughter really committed suicide, or had the woman killed her too? Did Strata Luna start her house of prostitution in order to have a handy place to feed, to satisfy, her strange death obsessions while at the same time perpetuating her own mystery?

They would never admit it, but half the cops in Savannah were afraid of her. That fear created a distance, gave her the ability to nurture her sickness.

Elise had enough evidence to justify a search warrant for Strata Luna's house. While Audrey sat at David's desk doing homework, Elise called the judge and put in a request for a warrant. While she was on the phone, the fax machine kicked in.

"Doesn't David live at Mary of the Angels?" Audrey asked when Elise hung up. She was holding another fax from Adam Pascal.

Elise removed her jacket and shoulder holster, checking the weapon. "Yes. Why?"

"I think one of the tunnels goes to his place."

Elise frowned and came closer. "Show me."

Audrey let her feet drop and sat forward, placing her finger on a small black square. "Here."

She was right.

Elise picked up the phone and dialed David's number. She got his voice mail. "Call me when you get this."

She hung up and shrugged into her Kevlar vest, attaching it snugly with Velcro fasteners. When it was secure, she replaced her holster and gun. That was followed by her jacket.

Audrey watched with vague unease. "Where are you going?"

"Serving a search warrant."

"Why are you wearing a bulletproof vest? Will it be dangerous?"

"It's routine, sweetie."

They were supposed to have gone out to eat together. Mother and daughter. "I'm sorry," Elise said, torn between her concern for David and the fact that she was once again putting Audrey last. "You'll have to wait here until I get back."

"That's okay."

Audrey didn't seem nearly as upset as Elise had thought she'd be.

"Here's David's number." Elise jotted it down and tore off the piece of paper. "Try calling him every few minutes. If he answers, tell him about the tunnels." She folded the maps and stuck them in her vest pocket, then retrieved a spare flashlight from the cupboard.

"What if he wants to talk to you?" Audrey asked.

"Tell him I'm bringing Strata Luna in for questioning."

Normally everybody jumped at the chance to conduct a search. But as soon as Elise mentioned Strata Luna's name, her request for assistance was met with mumbled excuses and downcast eyes.

Finally someone stepped forward. "I'll go."

Starsky. He probably realized in another second she would have pointed out who was in charge and ordered him to join her.

His partner flashed him a look of irritation before also agreeing to participate. Two uniformed police officers rounded out the team.

They would take separate vehicles and converge on the house at a predetermined time. The crime scene investigators would arrive later, once the building was secure.

Elise tried to call David again.

Still no answer.

She assigned Starsky and Hutch the task of picking up the warrant, which allowed her the time she needed to stop by David's.

Ten minutes later, she pulled up in front of Mary of the Angels, immediately spotting his black car in the parking lot.

At the door, she rang David's apartment—and wasn't surprised when she got no reply. She rang the apartment manager and introduced herself. He buzzed her in and met her on the third-floor landing, a set of keys in his hand.

"I need to see your ID." He was white, about seventy, with gray hair and gray stubble on his jaw.

Elise pulled out her leather case and flipped it open. He nodded and she tucked it back in her pocket.

Down the hall, to David's apartment.

"I told him he had to be out by tomorrow," the manager said. "Don't know if he killed that woman or not, but everybody in the building's scared. Nobody likes being scared."

Somebody was baking a cake. Elise could smell it.

A small dog was barking.

The manager unlocked the door and stepped back. "I'm not going in there. Last time I unlocked a door for a cop, I found a dead woman. I tell you, I'm tired of this country. I'm tired of living a life of fear." He turned away from the door, arms crossed.

Elise stepped inside and immediately smelled the rotten-egg scent of sulfur.

"David?"

On the floor, she spotted a dusting of something that looked like fine brown powder.

A trick. A spell.

She stepped around the powder to avoid getting it on the soles of her shoes.

A few feet away was David's cell phone.

"Is he dead?" the manager whispered loudly from the hall.

The living room and kitchen were empty.

Elise reached inside her jacket, unsnapped her holster, and pulled out her handgun.

She checked the bathroom. Then the bedroom.

On the foot of the bed was an open suitcase, as if David had been interrupted in the middle of packing. She slipped her weapon back in the leather case.

David's cat, Isobel, appeared from under the bed, meowing pitifully. Elise picked her up.

"Don't allow anyone in the apartment," she said, stepping into the hall and closing the door behind her. "It could be a crime scene."

The manager stared at Isobel.

"Cats and crime scenes don't mix," Elise explained.

He shook his head. "I should never have rented a room to that guy. I knew he looked shifty."

She ignored his complaints. "When did you last see David Gould?"

"Let me see. . . . This morning, I think. I came up and told him he wasn't going to get his deposit back."

Isobel was purring loudly.

"Early morning? Late?"

"Late. Around eleven as I recall. But don't hold me to that. My memory's bad."

"I need to see the basement."

"Basement?" The shift in conversation clearly puzzled him. "I'd better call the owner—"

"Now!"

"Okay, but I'm not taking responsibility."

Inside the elevator, Elise punched the basement button. From their earlier ride, she knew the elevator was slow; she would have run down the stairs if she hadn't needed a guide.

They hit bottom with a jolt. The door clanged open and they stepped into the basement.

"Where's the oldest part of the building?" Elise asked.

The manager led her through a catacomb maze of stone and damp, crumbling mortar. In the final room she discovered a wall where bricks had been removed, then replaced.

"Here—" She handed the cat to him and began digging at the loose bricks, dislodging several, causing them to tumble at her feet.

She straightened, pulled the two sections of map from her vest, and unfolded them.

It was a poor image, and the basement was dim, but she finally located Mary of the Angels.

She ran her finger along the line indicating the tunnel. From where she stood, she could get almost anywhere if the tunnels weren't blocked. To the Hartzell, Tate, and Hartzell Funeral Home, to Strata Luna's, and to Laurel Grove Cemetery.

She put in a call to dispatch and requested that they reroute the officers heading for Strata Luna's and send them to Mary of the Angels instead. Then she called Starsky and gave him the new location.

Officers at every possible exit would have been the ideal situation, but they didn't have that kind of manpower. And if David was unconscious, Strata Luna couldn't be moving very quickly. . . .

She checked her watch. "Wait upstairs for the patrol unit and the detectives," she told the manager. "When they arrive, show them down here."

"You think the person who killed that woman got in through there?" the manager asked, all of his earlier impatience gone, replaced by fear and a sudden reluctant respect.

Elise dislodged more bricks until the hole was large enough for her to pass through. She pulled out her flashlight and handgun.

In the broad beam of light, red dust particles curled toward the ceiling. She directed the beam to the ground inside the tunnel and immediately spotted parallel tracks and footprints.

Holding the gun and the light together with both hands, she paused. "Feed the cat," she said over her shoulder, then ducked through the opening.

Chapter 43

They always lost weight.

I touched his bare arm.

Cold as marble.

From somewhere behind us, cockroaches scuttled.

I have to admit they used to bother me. But then I started thinking of them as extensions of myself and pretty soon I began to actually like them.

I held the lantern to his face.

His closed eyes were cast in deep shadow. His lips were blue.

Skin like paste.

He looked dead.

I swung the gurney to the left, toward the cemetery.

I had a special place there. A secret place. A place where we could both play dead.

The tunnel smelled like mildew and sewage. Five minutes in and Elise's shoes were saturated, her pants soaked to the knees. Along with the odor of sewer was another smell. Something herbal and slightly medicinal, a mixture of ingredients a conjurer might use.

Elise had done a quick mental calculation, and she estimated it was a mile, maybe more, to Strata Luna's house. The indirect route of public streets would have been over two.

The powerful flashlight created extreme contrasts. There was the bleached area where the beam fell; outside that beam was absolute blackness.

Pascal had been right—the tunnel system was badly deteriorated, the curved brick of the ceiling having crumbled in numerous places, now lying in jagged piles.

As she walked, she kept her head bowed.

If David had been given a high dosage of TTX, it would be crucial for him to get medical attention as quickly as possible. And Elise doubted Strata Luna would mess around with the "recreational" amount LaRue and his buddies experimented with.

The other possibility was that David was already dead, his throat cut in the MO used on Enrique and Flora. Which would make more sense. But Elise couldn't think about that. She had to believe he was still alive.

She reached a T and pulled out a map. To turn left would take her to the cemetery, to the right, Strata Luna's.

She directed the flashlight to the ground. Two to three inches of sludge over a pathway of cement. No tracks to follow.

It seemed to make sense that David would be taken to the house. It was a huge place, and would have secret rooms where he could be kept. But even if Strata Luna hadn't expected a search warrant, she would have to know that the police would be watching her house.

Elise turned in the direction of the cemetery.

David was forced to listen to her prattle as she pushed the gurney, her feet sloshing through water and sewage.

The floor of the tunnel wasn't smooth, and sometimes the wheels would catch, almost sending him flying. Whenever that happened, she would grab him with a "Whoops!" Then, after some maneuvering, they would be on their way until the next time.

He could now actually understand how some people found TTX addicting. It was almost an out-of-body experience, because you lost all sensation. The only thing functioning was the brain.

But then, maybe this was death. Maybe he was dead and this was hell. Maybe he was going to spend eternity being wheeled around through an underground tunnel by a crazy woman.

She found another pit in the floor.

They crashed to a halt.

David's body slid forward, and he heard a loud *smack*—his head hitting the stone wall.

She cooed over him, dabbing at his temple with the sleeve of her dress. "You're bleeding."

That meant his heart was still beating. A good sign.

Maybe.

They'd had no proof, but David had always surmised that the TTX victims had been sexually assaulted. He could admit that he had a history of having sex with strangers, but what she had in her agenda book was something he was fairly certain he didn't want anything to do with.

David knew he was going to die; he just wasn't sure how.

Best case scenario?

Tetrodotoxin.

It could eventually shut down his system and that would be that. Or she might grow tired of him and dump him someplace where he wouldn't be found.

Death, again.

Or, since the last two killings had been pretty bloody, she might go for the slit throat.

All nice choices.

Chapter 44

"Stop!"

A familiar voice, coming from the tunnel behind us. I swung around, lantern high.

"I knew you were back," she said. "I could feel you."

She was dressed in one of her long black gowns, a flashlight in her hand. "You always loved these tunnels. Especially this stretch. I couldn't keep you away from them."

It was true.

"What are you doing here?" she demanded. "You promised to never walk the streets—*or tunnels*—of Savannah again."

She sounded confused, speaking in that exaggerated accent I'd always hated. The woman had lived in the United States her entire life. Why did she try to sound like some hoodoo priestess?

Four years ago, she'd paid me to leave. She paid me to leave and never come back so she could pretend I was dead. So she could wear her black clothes and pray over my grave. So people would feel sorry for her.

"I missed Savannah," I told her. "I missed the tunnels."

"How long . . . ?"

"I returned almost two years ago."

Strata Luna let out a strangled sob, then pressed a hand to her mouth to smother the sound.

Oh, she always pretended to be so strong, but she was just as weak as the rest of them.

"Where did you stay?"

"Sometimes in the tunnels. Sometimes on the street."

A chameleon, dressing like a man or a woman. Whatever struck me. Of course I hadn't done it all on my own. Enrique had helped. He'd brought food and clothing. Money. Whatever I needed. Whatever I wanted. He'd even purchased the CDs I took to Gary Turello's funeral.

I'd always suspected Enrique had been a little in love with me. Either that or he simply felt sorry for someone whose own mother had turned her back on her.

"I knew it was you, but didn't want to believe it," Strata Luna wailed, suddenly transformed from regal priestess to whimpering, frightened old lady. "Tell me I'm wrong! Tell me you aren't the one doing all this killing."

She stretched out an imploring hand, the movement graceful even in her overwrought state. "Enrique! Poor Enrique! He *loved* you. He would have done anything for you."

"He did. He died for me."

"Why?"

I thought of one of her favorite lines, *Evil doesn't need a reason to exist,* but I didn't want to quote her. I didn't want to honor her. "He meant too much to you."

"You were *jealous?*" she asked, still trying to understand.

I laughed. She was so far off. "I wanted to hurt you. I wanted you to be a lonely old woman. I wanted to take away everybody you cared about."

Her gaze fell to the gurney. "Who is that?" She stepped closer.

"David Gould."

"The detective? If what you say is true, what does he have to do with any of this? He means nothing to me."

"I just like him."

She nodded, remembering. "Even when you were little, you had a strong curiosity about death. Something unhealthy. Something compelling and twisted and sick."

"Go back home, old woman." I'd forgotten how she could annoy me so quickly. "I've had enough of you already."

"I should have destroyed you when you were young," she said. "When I realized you were evil. But I couldn't kill my own child. My own baby girl."

"I'm not your daughter! You conjured me!" Sudden tears stung my eyes. I impatiently wiped them away with the back of my hand. "You conjured me from twigs and cat intestines soaked in blood!"

"No!"

She pretended to be shocked by my words. What an actress.

"Who told you such a lie?" she asked.

How could I possibly recall the origins of something I'd always known?

"You are my daughter. A part of me. Just as Deliliah was my daughter. You pretended that you tried to
save her, but I could see through you. I could always
see through you. But you were never conjured. I wish
I could say you were. I wish I could say you didn't
come from me, but that would be a lie."

I pulled out the knife I'd used to kill Enrique
and Flora. It was very sharp, and I was filled with
hatred and rage. This woman had ruined my life.
She had showered attention on Deliliah, then Enrique and Flora, while ignoring me. While pushing
me away.

"You were evil," she said, trying to explain away
her failings.

"You should love all of your children equally," I
told her. "That's a mother's job. To love without
blame, without question."

"Even murderers?"

"Even murderers."

I lifted the knife high.

She should have zigzagged. She should have made
a crooked path out of there. Instead, she remained immobile, watching me. She placed a splayed hand to
her breast, where she must have had a *wanga* hidden.
Her mouth began to move, and she muttered words
meant to bring me down:

If I hang from a single thread
In a place no one shall see
It will bring fear into the heart of her who shall harm me
It will bring fear into the heart of her who shall harm me
She will be binded by fear from harming me
She will be binded by fear from harming me.

I came from the earth and dead things; I was stronger than any spell she could cast.

"Evil travels in a straight line," I told her. I brought the blade down, plunging it into the heart of my mother, the heart of Strata Luna.

Chapter 45

Elise listened to the crackling and scurrying of a million cockroaches, and the sound of dripping water.

Where was her backup? She pulled out her cell phone.

No signal.

She checked her watch. Starsky and Hutch should have reached Mary of the Angels by now.

Never go in without backup.

Every rookie knew that.

She returned the phone to her pocket and continued in the direction of the cemetery.

As she walked, her subterranean view never seemed to change. The tunnel stretched out before her, going on and on until reaching a vanishing point like some artistic lesson in perspective.

Suddenly her flashlight beam picked up a dark shape in the distance.

Elise shut off the light and jumped from one side of the tunnel to the other, quickly changing her position. Crouched, she pulled out her handgun and listened.

Poets and writers always tried to describe complete

and total darkness, but it couldn't be done. It wasn't just being unable to see the smallest flicker of anything. It was that weird and false sensation of having something solid right in front of your face.

Something all around you.

Closing in.

Audrey tried David Gould's number again. Still no answer. She hung up and slipped on her panda bear backpack. Maybe he was home. Maybe he just wasn't answering his phone. Some people did that. Audrey didn't know why, but they did.

Mary of the Angels wasn't that far from the police station. Probably eight blocks. She would just walk there. See if she could find David.

Her dad always told her to be careful in the Historic and Victorian Districts, not to walk around by herself, but it wasn't night, and there were lots of people out, especially tourists taking pictures and staring at buildings and talking about how hot it was.

It didn't take Audrey long to get to Mary of the Angels.

A spooky place, really old with lots of ivy. Up high, on top of the building, were weird iron silhouettes, the gray roof reminding her of a place where chimney sweeps would dance and sing and get dirty.

She spotted a police car in front of the building. And a lot of people standing outside. Two of them were detectives she recognized from the police station.

She went up to one of them and asked what they were doing.

"Aren't you Elise Sandburg's kid?" the detective asked. He had a red face and freckles.

Audrey clung to her backpack straps. "She told me to call David Gould, but he isn't answering his phone. Is something wrong with him?" She hoped not. That gave her a weird feeling in her stomach.

"We don't know."

"Where's my mom? Wasn't she meeting you at Strata Luna's?" Audrey was feeling more nervous by the second. "She told me you were serving a search warrant."

"Something came up here," the detective said, glancing nervously at his partner.

They were keeping secrets. Audrey could tell.

"Is my mom okay?" she asked, her voice rising.

He put out his hands as if she were a dog he was trying to keep from jumping on him. "She's in a little tunnel under Mary of the Angels, that's all. No big deal. She should be showing up here soon."

"In the tunnel? By herself? She wouldn't do that. I know she wouldn't do that."

"She's in the tunnel," the partner said, beginning to sound annoyed.

"Then why are you out here?" Audrey glanced around.

Two police officers were just standing by the apartment building, talking to a gray-haired guy holding a cat.

"Why aren't you in the tunnel too?"

The detectives looked at each other, and Audrey could see shame in their faces. "They're too dangerous," the freckled man told her. "Nobody is supposed to go in them. Not even the police."

"You have to go in there!" Audrey said, looking from one to the other. "You have to!"

She knew about public ridicule. After all, she was thirteen.

"Are you *afraid* to go in the tunnel?" she taunted. "Are you afraid of a few little bugs?"

Elise's heart was hammering in her head.

Her breathing was choppy.

She couldn't hear anything but the beat of her own fear.

Should have waited for backup.

No time!

She straightened to a half crouch. Slowly, her eyes open wide and straining at nothing, she moved forward.

She tried to retrieve the image. Tried to recall exactly how it had looked.

Dark. Misshapen. Maybe the size of a person, but it could also have been something else. Some artifact left over from the time the tunnels had been secretly used to cart plague victims to the cemetery.

She paused and straightened.

With feet spread and legs braced, she held her gun against the flashlight, aiming in the direction she thought the shape should be. But like someone driving in heavy fog, she found it impossible to gauge how far she'd come since turning off the light, and how far away the shape had been to begin with.

She pressed the switch, turning on the light.

Where?

She shifted the beam.

There.

And held it.

The shape was exactly as she'd remembered, but with more detail.

Dark fabric. The approximate size of a person.

She moved forward one slow step at a time, never taking her eyes off the object.

A dress.

Black lace.

The curve of a person's back under crumpled fabric.

A gloved hand.

For all appearances, a dead body.

Strata Luna's dead body.

But since dead bodies had a way of not being dead, Elise approached with caution.

She hooked a foot against the shoulder.

The body unrolled limply from its huddled, protective position, falling with an echoing thud against the floor.

Strata Luna.

Eyes open.

Mouth open.

A pool of blood.

Dead.

Where was David?

What was going on?

Who'd killed Strata Luna?

Where was David?

The dead body suddenly heaved, sucking in air.

Elise jumped, almost dropping the flashlight.

"*Go,*" the black, bloody heap rasped, pointing down the length of the tunnel, her monumental struggle to communicate conveying the utmost urgency.

Elise scrambled to her feet, turned, and raced toward the cemetery, keeping her head low.

No time to think, no time to try to figure out what was going on beyond the obvious.

The killer wasn't Strata Luna.

David Gould was in danger.

Those were the two things she knew. The only things she knew.

Chapter 46

She forced his eyelids open with her thumbs.

Broken light from a lantern near David's head radiated upward to disappear into a darkness of stone and marble.

They were in some kind of mausoleum, he realized. The woman was leaning over him, veil gone, face streaked with blood.

Not Strata Luna.

This was the daughter. The daughter who'd supposedly hung herself. Marie Luna. She'd killed her own sister—a case of sibling rivalry taken to the extreme. She'd killed Enrique and Flora for the same reason. And now she'd killed her own mother.

Elise had been right about her death obsession, her necrophilia.

Marie Luna let go of his eyelids and knelt next to him. Earlier, she'd removed him from the gurney and laid him out on some kind of platform. He felt like a sacrifice.

"If you eat the heart of your enemy, it makes you stronger," she told him.

He flinched—an actual movement, even though it was minuscule.

Was she saying what he thought she was? Had she feasted on Strata Luna's heart? Or was she going to eat *his* heart? Both ideas were too horrible, and his mind ran away. He felt himself sinking. . . .

She gathered up the black folds of her gown and straddled him.

He tried to close his eyes, but couldn't now that she'd opened them. All he could do was watch from a front-row seat.

She produced a knife. A wicked-looking weapon, made of forged steel. He watched it move south, finally disappearing below his line of vision.

Was she going to gut him like a fish?

Was she going to castrate him?

That wasn't her style, but something had slipped and she'd moved beyond her standard MO.

He'd met a lot of weird, fucked-up people in his life, but even the most horrendous had a line they wouldn't cross. There was always something they held as sacred in their own screwed-up heads. For some, it was children. Others, old ladies. Still others, animals.

The bitch in front of him seemed capable of anything.

David had spent the past two years wishing he were dead. Now, when that state of nothingness seemed imminent, he was surprised to find he had mixed feelings about dying.

How would he know how Audrey's pitching was progressing?

How would he know what kind of car Elise got when hers finally broke down for good?

Would she ever finish her house?

And what about Isobel? Who would take care of Isobel?

Would Starsky and Hutch wish they'd treated him with more respect? Would they feel like shit once he was gone?

He hoped so.

To die now would be like leaving the theater in the middle of a good movie. Or accidentally leaving a book in an airport.

But death was like that. An interruption of a work in progress. Maybe that's what LaRue found so intriguing about dipping his toe into the pool and being able to pull it back with only minor damage.

David heard the sound of tearing fabric as she ripped open his shirt.

Something cold—the knife blade—touched his stomach, above the navel.

Cold steel.

Sensation was returning.

Perfect timing. Now he would be able to feel the slice of the blade.

Instead of plunging it into his gut, she put it aside, and began unbuttoning his pants.

Oh yeah. Rape. In all the excitement, he'd forgotten about that part. She was going to rape him first.

The tunnel veered to the left and rose sharply. At the top was a metal door.

Laurel Grove Cemetery.

Elise paused and listened.

No sound of backup.

So it wouldn't prematurely announce her arrival, she pointed the flashlight toward her feet, then moved quietly forward, up the incline.

The door was ajar.

She gripped her gun. Bracing it against the flashlight, heart hammering, she stepped rapidly through the opening and swung to face the center of the room.

A mausoleum.

Marble walls lined with compartments that held bodies and ashes. In the middle of the floor was a sarcophagus. On top of it was a woman in a long black dress straddling a man. Straddling David Gould.

Who was she?

Elise struggled to put it together. Now that Strata Luna was out of the picture, she was having trouble making sense of anything.

Was this one of Strata Luna's prostitutes?

"Get away from him." Elise's voice was level, even though her heart raced.

The woman fell forward, sprawling across David, all the while watching Elise.

She was beautiful, with copper skin and strange eyes.

She stroked David's arm. Without speaking, staring at Elise, she nuzzled him, shifting his head around. She pressed against him so they were cheek to cheek, both facing Elise.

David's eyes were wide open.

Jesus.

A tremor ran through her gun arm.

Was he dead?

Jesus.

"Get off him," she said.

Kill her.

With the woman turned sideways, there was only one vulnerable spot. The middle of her forehead, which was only inches from David's.

Elise was a decent shot, but no sharpshooter. And in these conditions . . . low light. Lots of shadows . . . her gun arm shaking.

"Put up both hands and move away," Elise commanded.

Where was her fucking backup? Where were Starsky and Hutch?

"Or I'll blow your head off."

The woman's smile broadened. She lifted her hands high. Then, as if being pulled by a string, she sat upright, still straddling David. She swung her leg over his body, one of her arms dropping.

"Up!"

She raised her arm, then awkwardly slipped from the platform until she stood beside it.

"Move away from him."

Hands in the air, the woman shuffled sideways, skirting the foot of the burial vault.

Then she began moving toward Elise.

"Stop! Right there!"

She stopped.

Kill her.

"Who are you?" the woman asked.

Elise had the feeling she already knew the answer. "Detective Sandburg."

"Elise," the woman said slowly, with syrup in her voice. That sly smile again.

It was giving Elise the creeps.

Kill her now!

"Elise Sandburg. I know all about you. About how you were left in a cemetery as a baby. The daughter of a conjurer."

She stared at Elise a long moment, then began to chant:

> *Blue glasses of a conjurer*
> *Cast a fatal spell*
> *Get ready for the funeral*
> *Ring the coffin bell.*

Elise held her flashlight in one hand, revolver in the other. The next step would be to handcuff the woman, but that would take some cooperation—something that seemed highly unlikely.

"My name's Marie. Marie Luna."

Elise felt a thud deep in her belly.

This was Strata Luna's daughter. The one who was supposedly dead and buried. The one who was supposed to have hung herself.

She recalled Strata Luna's sadness when they were discussing daughters. Elise had thought she'd been sad because her children were both dead. Instead, she'd been sad because at least one of her offspring was twisted and evil.

What do you do with an evil child?

What Strata Luna had done? Pretend she was dead?

"We're sisters," Marie Luna said.

At first Elise thought she meant "sisters" as in all women were sisters.

"Jackson Sweet was your father," Marie Luna continued. "He was my father too."

The floor shifted.

All her life, Elise had wanted to know her roots, know where she'd come from, but this was a sick joke—that's what it was. Her father—a root doctor. Her mother a prostitute turned permanent monastery guest. Her sister a murdering psychopath? Didn't get much funnier than that.

Marie Luna was just playing with her head. Trying to trip her up.

"That makes us half sisters." Marie Luna took a step closer, then another, the fabric of her heavy skirt *shushing* across the stone floor.

She's lying, Elise told herself, her stomach churning.

Marie Luna stopped. "Look at me. Our skin isn't the same color because your mother was white—mine was black. But look at my eyes."

Oh, God. Those eyes. They were Elise's eyes. She could even see a resemblance to Audrey in the woman's face.

Marie Luna nodded and kept smiling that horrid smile, pleased that Elise was now convinced of their familial bond.

Kill her.

She laughed. "I'm your sister. You wouldn't hurt your own sister, would you?"

Emotions rose in Elise's throat and she let out a choke of denial. *This is a nightmare. This isn't real. It can't be real.*

Elise risked a glance at David.

Staring at her. Life in his eyes. Trying to tell her something.

*   *   *

She has a knife, David tried to say, but no words came out. *Hidden in her skirt.*

He could see the horror in Elise's face, see her struggling with what Marie Luna had told her.

Marie Luna would be able to see it too. She would be ready for the second Elise wavered.

Things were changing. David's body was waking up. He could feel sparks of electricity shooting along nerve pathways, zapping him.

He forced himself to let go of his thoughts of Elise and focus on the physical. *Don't think about anything but getting your ass off this slab.*

Move, his brain commanded.

Move!

Suddenly he lurched sideways, rolling off the marble vault, the lantern going with him.

He tried to catch himself. His arms didn't respond. He smacked into the floor, the lantern shattering.

Marie Luna lunged for Elise, screaming, the knife appearing seemingly out of nowhere.

Raised.

Plunging.

A gun discharged.

Marie Luna tugged the blade free, then brought it down again.

Elise's flashlight hit the floor, the lens shattering.

Absolute darkness.

Strata Luna's daughter continued to shriek, stringing words together that made no sense.

Elise was silent.

Silent.

Blond hair floating in the tub.

Little blue fingers.

NO!

This couldn't be happening.

Not again.

Another gunshot.

Deafening.

Followed by another, and another.

David's ears hummed hollowly as he dragged himself across the floor, digging his fingers into the cracks between stones, pulling his own deadweight.

From the tunnel entrance came the sound of running feet. High-powered flashlights blinded him.

"Jesus fucking Christ." Starsky. Hutch.

Too late, you assholes. Too damn late.

David followed their gaze to where Elise lay in a pool of blood. Sprawled across her was Marie Luna.

Tears burned his eyes.

Fuck, fuck, fuck.

Elise. Dead.

Marie Luna shifted.

The detectives jumped forward, guns and flashlights braced and ready.

A voice—Elise's voice—came from beneath the bloody pile. "Can someone get this evil bitch off me?"

Chapter 47

"What's that look about?" David asked with concern, eyeing Elise closely.

They were on the balcony outside her bedroom, Elise in a wicker rocker, David lounging against the railing. He was barefoot, dressed in faded jeans and gray Savannah Police Department T-shirt. Elise wore a pair of loose black pants and a top in various shades of red that Audrey had dug from the closet and convinced her to wear.

"Does evil move through bloodlines?" Elise asked fearfully. Would it resurface in future generations? In Audrey's children or grandchildren?

"You know what?" David pushed himself away from the railing with his hip and reached to pluck a magnolia from a nearby tree. "I'm just glad you're alive." He tucked the white blossom in her hair, above her ear. "And I'm glad I'm alive. I don't want to think about that other stuff."

He was right. It served no purpose to obsess about something that couldn't be controlled and would probably never happen.

Major Hoffman had offered David his job back, and he'd accepted, along with a year's probation. His criminal profile had been fairly accurate other than the sex and education of the perpetrator. And except for a bit of short-term memory loss that LaRue, who was out of jail and also on probation, assured them would go away soon, David didn't seem to be suffering any ill effects from the TTX.

After forty-eight hours in the hospital, two pints of blood, and eighty-some stitches to four defensive wounds, Elise had been sent home. The all-purpose vest had saved her from any fatal injuries.

Strata Luna herself was alive and in stable condition, the knife blade having missed her heart by a hair.

"When I get outta here, I'm gonna teach you some good root doctoring," Strata Luna had said from her hospital bed when Elise had stopped to visit.

The lights had been draped with blue scarves to chase away evil spirits, and Strata Luna had gotten into trouble several times for burning heal-me-now incense.

"I gotta have somebody to pass the mantle to, and who better than Jackson Sweet's daughter? And later, when the time is right, you can pass it on to your girl."

"I don't know . . . ," Elise had said noncommittally, while at the same time experiencing a sense of excitement at the thought of embracing her past so openly. But she was a cop. A detective. She shouldn't be messing around with root work. And yet . . .

"You can't let it all just stop. One more generation gone by and nobody will even know what root doctorin' is. Don't waste your heritage, girl," Strata Luna had told her. "You could be using it to be a better detective."

An intriguing notion . . .

Then the conversation turned to Marie Luna.

"I always suspected she killed her own sister," Strata Luna confided. "But as a mother, I couldn't believe it." She shook her head. "Thought I had to be mistaken. Just in case, I decided to keep her away from school and teach her at home. Maybe that's where I went wrong. Maybe she shouldn't have been denied the company of kids her own age."

"I think you made a wise choice," Elise said. History had proved that someone with Marie Luna's tendencies only got worse when forced into the public education system.

"There were the usual things," Strata Luna continued. "She was mean to animals. I learned real fast that she couldn't have any pets, but she still caught baby birds and tortured them till they died. I tried all kinds of spells, but they seemed to make her worse. For a while, I even tried to keep her sedated."

"With tetrodotoxin?"

"Not a zombie potion, but a relative of it. Meant to take the edge off her energy. Instead of knocking her out it made her so she couldn't sleep. She started prowling those damn tunnels all night long."

"I've heard of sedatives having that kind of negative reaction sometimes," Elise said. If only Strata Luna had asked for help. But there was no use telling her what she already knew.

"Then I caught her with a body she dug up from Laurel Grove Cemetery. She dragged it through the tunnel and brought it home like a dog would a bone.

That's when I'd had enough. I couldn't take no more. I told her she had to leave. I didn't just kick her out with nothing. I gave her money. Enough to last a long time, but she musta spent it in a whirl."

"How did you fake her death?"

"People don't ask me a lot of questions. An old coroner from St. Helena Island signed the death certificate in trade for two fifths of whiskey and a bring-me-wealth spell. And I already had a body to put in a sealed coffin."

"The one Marie dug up."

"Always felt bad about that. But he was a John Doe from a potter's field. Still, it's not right for him to be buried under Marie Luna's headstone. And now I need a place to put her. . . ."

"I can help get him moved."

"First I wasn't sure I wanted her next to Deliliah, but I sent Marie away once. Can't do that again. . . . And it was my fault. I cursed your mother when she was pregnant with you. She musta held up a mirror, cause it came right back on me. . . ."

Elise had subconsciously believed in the power of the root even during the years she'd turned her back on such things. But Strata Luna's statement was a little hard to swallow. If she believed her own curse had come back on her, could the strength of that belief have caused her to give birth to an evil child? Was it possible?

Now, days later, Elise was still puzzling over the question.

"Did I tell you they found Gary Turello?" David asked.

Elise looked up to see him extending his hand. She

took it, his grasp firm as he helped her from the chair. "He was in one of the tunnels, tucked into a cozy mattress."

"Turello and about a million cockroaches," she said.

"And the footprints in the cemetery where Jordan Kemp was found," David said, "matched the boots Marie Luna was wearing."

They were going for a short walk. Elise needed to get out of the house. See the neighborhood. "What's your theory on Harrison?"

"Victim of circumstance. Probably unknowingly came into contact with TTX when he was in the tunnel. Maybe got it on his clothes. Later that night, when he changed for bed, he inhaled the substance or absorbed it transdermally."

Elise nodded. "I wouldn't be at all surprised if Marie Luna didn't deliberately leave dustings of TTX near her lair."

"In the way of King Tut's tomb?"

"Seems highly likely."

The French doors were open, and they could hear music coming from Audrey's room. She'd insisted upon staying for the next two weeks so she could keep an eye out and help with the cooking and cleaning. Elise didn't think it was necessary to mention that she didn't cook and rarely cleaned. It was just nice having Audrey there.

While they waited downstairs for Audrey, David put on his running shoes and toured the front of the house, hands in his pockets, pausing in the foyer to admire the horrendous seventies wallpaper. It was shiny, with streaks of silver and pink.

The music above them stopped. A moment later, Audrey came bouncing down the stairs. "These are the coolest glasses."

She was wearing the blue conjurer shades Strata Luna had given Elise.

"I can get a steamer and help you strip this paper," David said. "There's also a product called Strip-Ease that works like a charm."

Audrey adjusted the blue-lensed glasses.

They looked cute. Very retro.

"I can help too," Audrey said. "And paint. I love to paint." She touched the flower in Elise's hair. "Nice."

Elise had finally told her everything about Jackson Sweet and Loralie. She'd taken it well. In fact, she'd been fascinated and intrigued. But Elise was holding back telling her that Marie Luna was Elise's half sister. Audrey was young and had enough to absorb right now.

"I'm thinking maybe a traditional color," David said, still contemplating the wall. "Say, taupe?"

Mother and daughter gave him a look of horror.

He shrugged, unconcerned. "Just an idea."

"Moss green," from Elise.

"Purple," from Audrey.

"Where are we going?" David asked. "I forgot."

"For a walk," mother and daughter answered in unison.

Outside, Elise waved to her neighbor, Mrs. Bell, who was sitting on the porch.

The temperature was seventy-two degrees Fahrenheit, with high humidity that wrapped around them like a blanket. The tabby shell sidewalk was wide, allowing them to walk three abreast.

Two years earlier, Elise had taken Mrs. Bell in for

cataract surgery. Afterward, when the older woman stepped outside, she kept saying, "Oh, the colors! The colors!" as if she'd never seen the world before.

Elise felt like that.

The grass was so vivid; the magnolia leaves were such a deep, dark green. The sky, with the setting sun, was so many beautiful shades of pink and orange. And the smells!

The odor of the pulp mill seemed to have taken a detour around the Historic District, leaving room for a true appreciation of the azaleas and grapelike clusters of crape myrtle, and the fragrant honeysuckle.

A few blocks into their stroll, they passed a group of girls jumping rope, the slap of shoes against cement pounding out a rhythm.

Elise and Audrey paused to wait for David as he picked another magnolia blossom—this one for Audrey's hair. While they stood under the fragrant branches, a chant came drifting in their direction:

A nod to the grim reaper
Kiss on shrouded bed
Faint whisper through marble lips
Only playing dead.

Elise's Follow-Me-Boy Mojo

Queen Elizabeth root (leave whole)
Rosebuds
Lavender
Lodestone
Spikenard
Name paper: Write the subject's name seven times
  in black ink. Rotate one quarter turn, write seven
  times in red.
One hair from subject's head

Put all the above in a red flannel bag. Dress the bag in
Follow Me Boy oil and carry it close to your heart.

Turn the page
for an excerpt from SLEEP TIGHT,
another blockbuster novel
of suspense from Anne Frasier

He hovered over the prone, unmoving girl, deftly drawing a thick black line on her eyelids, curving it upward at the corners. That was followed by a smidgen of rouge to her colorless cheeks. Next came the lipstick. Bloodred in a gold metal tube.

He could hear his own rasping breath as he carefully applied it to lips that had been soft and full but were now chapped and cracked. As carefully as a mortician he worked, and as he did he could feel his heart beating in his head.

He had the desire to kiss her, and leaned closer.

Wake up, my princess. My little princess . . .

Like a baby bird, her cracked lips opened under his. He felt her deep inhalation sucking the air from his lungs—a cat, trying to steal his breath. He pulled back to see her staring silently at him, her pupils dilated and glassy from drugs and the dark, windowless basement where she'd spent the last two weeks. Had she learned her lesson? Would she finally act like a lady now? Would she ask him how his day had been? Would she ask him what he'd like for supper? And later, would she sit on the living room floor near his feet while he listened to Kurt Weil records? Would she rub his temples until his headache stopped, saying in the most soothing of voices, "There, there"?

Her throat rattled.

Splat—something wet hit his cheek. It took him a moment to realize it was spit.

The thankless bitch! The thankless little bitch!

Heat roared through his veins until he thought his skin would split, until he thought his eyeballs might pop from his head. Enraged, he grabbed her by both arms and jerked her to her feet. "I've been working my ass off every day, out punching the clock, and this is the thanks I get?" He wrapped his hands around her neck. "I slave over you, trying to teach you basic etiquette! You bitch!" He shook her. "You spoiled, spoiled bitch!"

He squeezed and he squeezed, and when she went limp he kept on squeezing until he was certain she would never insult him again.

She continued to stare at him with accusation in her eyes long after she was dead.

Carnival Elation

7 Day Exotic Western Caribbean Itinerary

DAY	PORT	ARRIVE	DEPART
Sun	Galveston		4:00 P.M.
Mon	"Fun Day" at Sea		
Tue	Progreso/Merida	8:00 A.M.	4:00 P.M.
Wed	Cozumel	9:00 A.M.	5:00 P.M.
Thu	Belize	8:00 A.M.	6:00 P.M.
Fri	"Fun Day" at Sea		
Sat	"Fun Day" at Sea		
Sun	Galveston	8:00 A.M.	

TERMS AND CONDITIONS

PAYMENT SCHEDULE:
50% due upon booking
Full and final payment due by July 26, 2004

Acceptable forms of payment are Visa, MasterCard, American Express, Discover and checks. The cardholder must be one of the passengers traveling. A fee of $25 will apply for all returned checks. Check payments must be made payable to **Advantage International, LLC and sent to: Advantage International, LLC, 195 North Harbor Drive, Suite 4206, Chicago, IL 60601**

CHANGE/CANCELLATION:
Notice of change/cancellation must be made in writing to Advantage International, LLC.

Change:
Changes in cabin category may be requested and can result in increased rate and penalties. A name change is permitted 60 days or more prior to departure and will incur a penalty of $50 per name change. Deviation from the group schedule and package is a cancellation.

Cancellation:

181 days or more prior to departure	$250 per person
121 - 180 days or more prior to departure	50% of the package price
120 - 61 days prior to departure	75% of the package price
60 days or less prior to departure	100% of the package price (nonrefundable)

US and Canadian citizens are required to present a valid passport or the original birth certificate and state issued photo ID (drivers license). All other nationalities must contact the consulate of the various ports that are visited for verification of documentation.

We strongly recommend trip cancellation insurance!

For further details call 1-877-ADV-NTGE or visit www.GetCaughtReadingatSea.com

- -

For booking form and complete information
go to **www.getcaughtreadingatsea.com** or call **1-877-ADV-NTGE**

Complete coupon and booking form and mail both to:
**Advantage International, LLC,
195 North Harbor Drive, Suite 4206, Chicago, IL 60601**